Love can lead you out of the wilderness...

1851, Overland Trail to California. As a baby, Callie was left on the doorstep of an isolated farmhouse in Tennessee. The Whitaker family took her in, but have always considered her more a servant than a daughter. Scorned by her two stepsisters, Callie is forced to work long hours and denied an education. But a new world opens to her when the Whitakers join a wagon train to California—guided by rugged trapper, Luke McGraw...

A loner, haunted by a painful past, Luke plans to return to the wilderness once his work is done. But he can't help noticing how poorly Callie is treated—or how unaware she is of her beauty and intelligence. As the two become closer over the long trek west, Callie's confidence grows. And when disaster strikes, Callie emerges as the strong one—and the woman Luke may find the courage to love at last...

Visit us at www.kensingtonbooks.com

Books by Shirley Kennedy

Wagon Train Cinderella

Published by Kensington Publishing Corporation

Wagon Train Cinderella

Shirley Kennedy

LYRICAL PRESS
Kensington Publishing Corp.
www.kensingtonbooks.com

Lyrical Press books are published by
Kensington Publishing Corp. 119 West 40th Street New York, NY 10018

All Kensington titles, imprints, and distributed lines are available at special quantity discounts for bulk purchases for sales promotion, premiums, fund-raising, and educational or institutional use.

Special book excerpts or customized printings can also be created to fit specific needs. For details, write or phone the office of the Kensington Special Sales Manager:
Kensington Publishing Corp.
119 West 40th Street
New York, NY 10018
Attn. Special Sales Department. Phone: 1-800-221-2647.

Kensington and the K logo Reg. U.S. Pat. & TM Off.
Lyrical Press and the L logo are trademarks of Kensington Publishing Corp.

First Electronic Edition: February 2015
eISBN-13: 978-1-61650-701-5
eISBN-10: 1-61650-701-2

First Print Edition: February 2015
ISBN-13: 978-1-61650-702-2
ISBN-10: 1-61650-702-0

Printed in the United States of America

Dedicated to Dianne and Lindy, my two loyal, loving daughters. Without their help and support, this book wouldn't have been possible.

Chapter 1

Along the Overland Trail, 1851

Walking through the woods, Callie Whitaker was drawn to the sound of a waterfall. When a snake slithered across her path, she dropped her bucket and stopped in her tracks. It disappeared into the dense undergrowth. *What brought me here? I cannot believe this is happening to me.* Only a month ago, she was leading a dull but safe existence in the Tennessee farmhouse where she'd lived her entire life and rarely left. Now here she was in the middle of a wilderness she never knew existed, heading to California, a place she'd never heard of. Bone-tired from the endless work, she was sleeping on the ground under a wagon instead of her tiny bed under the eaves. The farm wasn't much, but she'd give anything if she could return to Tennessee where she didn't have to worry about Indians, snakes, and who-knew-what-would-happen-next?

A lump formed in her throat. *Silly girl, you have no time for feeling sorry for yourself.* Darkness was about to fall. She must get to the stream, scoop a bucketful of water, and hurry back to the wagon where everyone expected their supper. She picked up her bucket and trudged on. Through tall trees, the flowing water came into view. Ah, there it was. She drew close. How beautiful. Cascading water falling over moss-covered boulders, gorgeous ferns in every shade of green, clumps of tiny violets growing around the pool beneath and standing in the pool, the water up to his knees… *Oh, my stars.* She froze in her tracks, backed a few steps away, and peered over the top of a red hawthorn bush. It was a man—tall, lean, sinewy, with long, dark hair—and completely naked. He appeared to be bathing, bending to scoop water into his palms, then bringing it up over his head with a giant splash. The water cascaded over a powerful set of shoulders, down over the rippling muscles of his stomach to his sturdy thighs, to his…

Why was she gawking like a schoolgirl? Shameful. She'd seen her little stepbrother's thing many a time. She'd never forget when crazy Grandpa Pearson from the next farm escaped and ran naked down the road. So, of course, she knew what a man looked like, but still...*oh, my*. Neither her brother's tiny thing, nor that of Grandpa Pearson's, all shriveled, looked anything like this...so big, so very, very...

He looked up. She ought to run before he spied her, but she couldn't move a muscle. His gaze caught hers and his eyebrows lifted ever so slightly. He'd spied her! Oh, she should run, but her feet refused to move, and her eyes refused to turn away from the fascinating sight before her. Taking his time, he casually looked to the left, then the right, as if he might find some kind of cover, which, of course, he could not. He shrugged, as if admitting defeat. With a mischievous smile, he spread his arms wide and bowed toward her. "Good afternoon, madam. Taking in the sights?"

Oh, Lord. His laughter brought her back to her senses. Her cheeks heating, she clutched her pail and started to back away from the hawthorn bush, intent on running off as fast as she could. But wait a minute. Why should she make a fool of herself and bolt and skitter off like a panicky calf? *He* was the one at fault, the one who should have done his bathing farther upstream. She didn't back off. Instead, gripping her faded skirt, she held it out and dipped a deep curtsey, boldly returning his grin as she did. Only after she'd risen, forcing herself to take her time, did she turn and head downstream at a dignified pace.

She hadn't recognized him. He must be from the large wagon train that had camped close by. In the morning, it would be gone, thank goodness, and she need never lay eyes on him again.

* * * *

"Callie!" Hester Whitaker glared at her stepdaughter. "It's about time you got back. Where were you? Did you expect me to fix supper by myself?"

"Sorry, ma'am." Callie stepped to the campfire and set down the heavy pail of water. She didn't attempt any excuses. Ma wouldn't listen anyway. Nor would it do any good to point out that never in Callie's memory had her stepmother fixed supper by herself. "I boiled a mess of beans this morning and baked some bread. It'll be ready in no time."

Lydia, Callie's older stepsister, tossed her blond curls and pouted. "I'm getting awfully tired of beans."

"So am I." Nellie, her other stepsister, loved to complain.

"Sorry, girls. We'll just have to bear it until we reach California." Ma settled herself on a log next to their wagon and frowned at her stepdaughter. "Did you bake a pie today, or anything?" "No, ma'am, I did not." Long ago Callie had given up making excuses that always fell on deaf ears. Nor did she question why Nellie and Lydia, both older than she, were required to do only the lightest of chores. According to Ma, they were both much too frail and delicate for heavy work. Ma often said so, whereas she, the lowly stepsister, was as strong as an ox and should labor to pay for her keep and be grateful she had a roof over her head. That was the way of it, all she could remember since she was born. Not that she minded, or ever questioned her fate. Ma often pointed out how lucky she was the Whitakers had found her abandoned on their doorstep all those many years ago and, out of the kindness of their hearts, taken her in.

A ripple of laughter floated across their campsite. Pa, who'd been working on one of the wagon wheels, rose up and cast a look of disgust at the source of the sound, a large company of wagons, at least fifty, that had camped in a circle on the other side of the meadow. "We were here first," he muttered. "The damn fools should find their own place." He addressed his wife and daughters. "You're to stay away from them. Is that understood?"

"Yes, Pa," came quick answers. Caleb Whitaker ruled with an iron hand.

Ma gazed across the meadow. "Do you think I'd have anything to do with that trash? A while ago I saw one of the women wearing the most outlandish outfits I ever saw."

Lydia giggled. "Those are bloomers, Ma. They're like a man's pants only baggier and gathered on the bottom."

"Disgraceful." Ma's face took on its usual look of disapproval. "It'll be a cold day in hell before I, or any of my family, are caught in such an outfit." She addressed Callie. "Are you going to just stand there?"

"No, ma'am."

Callie went about fixing hot biscuits with fresh butter, salted meat, beans, and green peas gathered from vines along the trail. When supper was ready, she banged the bottom of a pan with a spoon. Tommy, the baby of the family at seven, came running. He was the only young'un left. Ma had birthed eight children altogether. The two older boys were grown and gone on their own. On the day the family left for California, Callie had paid her last sorrowful visit to the three tiny graves under the big oak tree. Far as Callie knew, Ma never went there. She had never mentioned the babies she'd lost at birth or soon after. As it was, she paid little attention to Tommy, whom she considered, "not right in the head." No one knew exactly what was the matter with the boy, except he seemed to live in a world of his own, never played with other children, and didn't like to be touched or held. Sometimes Callie wondered what would happen to Tommy if she weren't around to take care of him. The rest of the family had long since given up and considered him nothing but a burden.

Their two hired men joined them for supper around the cook fire. Andy and Len, both in their early twenties, helped drive the family's two wagons and cared for the hundred head of cattle they'd brought along. They were working their way west so they could get to the gold fields and make their fortune. Callie didn't much like Len, who had a sly way about him. She didn't trust him, either. Andy, the tall, awkward one, was "dumb as a stump," she'd heard Pa say, but at least he was always pleasant and did his work well. Lately, he'd been casting longing glances at Lydia. It was clear he was smitten. Sensing his feelings, Lydia had begun to make fun of him behind his back, calling him her little puppy dog, laughing at his "moonstruck gazes."

Callie felt sorry for Andy. He might not be very bright, but at least he gave Callie a sincere "thank you" after every meal, which was more than anyone else did. Tonight was no exception.

"Those beans was mighty good, Miss Callie," he remarked in his shy way.

"Why, thank you, Andy."

He was just being kind. They had been on the road for two weeks, eating beans every day. There was nothing special about them.

After supper, when Ma and her two stepsisters sat around the cook fire, and Callie had just finished washing up the dishes, someone approached from the wagon train across the meadow. Lydia pointed. "Looks like we've got company."

Ma looked toward the lone figure and frowned. "I do believe it's one of those women wearing pants."

"Bloomers, Ma," said Lydia.

Ma's lips tightened. "I don't want to talk to such a woman. I'm going in the wagon."

She half rose, but before she could retreat, the woman waved and cried a friendly, "Woo-hoo, everyone!" from halfway across the field. "Are you going or coming?"

"Too late now," said Lydia. "We're going to California," she yelled back.

"Now you've done it." Ma sat back down, brow furrowed in a frown.

The visitor approached. She appeared to be in her thirties, a big, full-bosomed woman with a round, smiling face, wearing a small white cap. Two young children clung to her short, full skirt that fell to her knees. Below the skirt, a pair of bloomers extended to her ankles. How strange. Never had Callie seen such an outfit.

The woman reached their campfire. "We're going to California too. Hello, I'm Florida Sawyer, and these here are two of my young'uns, Augie and Isaac. There's more where they came from." Without waiting for an invitation, she seated herself on a log by the campfire and thrust her pantalooned legs before her. "Lordy me, it feels good to get the load off." She turned to Ma. "And who might you be?"

Ma's lips pursed, as if she'd bit into a persimmon. Would she be nice? Callie held her breath. Ma could be the soul of politeness when she wanted. She could also get downright nasty with someone she even faintly disliked.

"We are the Whitaker family, Mrs. Sawyer. As my daughter said, we're traveling west to California."

Callie let out her breath. Ma's reply was decidedly cool but at least civil.

If Florida Sawyer noticed Ma's less-than-friendly attitude, she didn't let on. Seeing Ma's gaze travel to her bloomers, she laughed. "I know they look strange, but they're the perfect thing for a woman to wear when she's got to walk clear across the country. You'd be surprised how comfortable they are compared to a long, heavy skirt. You ought to try them sometime."

"That's not likely to happen, Mrs. Sawyer."

Undaunted, Florida continued. "I'm a widow traveling with my brother, two hired hands, and my seven children. My husband, God rest his soul, passed on a short time ago—mind you, after we'd already sold the farm and bought the wagons. He was dead set on moving to Oregon. Then, all of a sudden, he was gone. His heart. One minute we were nearly ready to leave, and the next, there was Henry slumped over the milk pail, stone cold dead. Can you imagine? Left me and the young'uns to fend for ourselves. I didn't know what I was going to do until Luke, that's my brother, stepped in and saved the day. He's a trapper and mountain man, the perfect guide for our wagon train. I don't know what we would have done without him, bless his heart."

"How fortunate for you."

Callie inwardly winced over Ma's abrupt answer to their friendly visitor. How could she be so rude? To cause a distraction, she got to her feet and indicated a pot of coffee next to the campfire. "I believe the coffee's still hot, Mrs. Sawyer. Would you like a cup?"

"Well, I don't mind if I do."

Callie had scarcely picked up the pot when a horseman approached. A man on a horse was one of the most common sights imaginable, yet the graceful, easy manner in which he sat in the saddle held her spellbound. He drew close. He was casually dressed in buckskin. Closer still, he was somewhere in his early thirties with long, dark hair and... *Oh, no, the naked man in the river. It's him.*

He reined to a stop.

"Here's my brother now." Florida's voice filled with pride. "Luke McGraw. Ain't he something? Luke, say hello to the Whitaker family. They're traveling by themselves."

In acknowledgement, Luke briefly touched a finger to the brim of his hat and returned the briefest of smiles. He addressed his sister, "Better come along. Hetty needs you."

Florida threw back her head and laughed. "Hetty always needs me. Luke, you come down here and be nice to these people. Hetty can wait."

Luke gave her a reluctant nod and swung from his horse, performing a graceful dismount that revealed his lean and sinewy body, muscular legs, and broad shoulders.

Lydia stepped forward, cocked her head, fluttered her eyelashes, and thrust out her ample bosom. "So, you're going west, Mister McGraw? Are you going to hunt for gold or go into farming?"

"Don't I wish!" Florida gave her brother a rueful glance. "Luke's a trapper. His idea of a wonderful winter is to live in a lonely log cabin high in the mountains by himself. Can you imagine? Nobody to talk to for months and months, which I'll never understand. Now, out of the kindness of his heart, he's guiding the Ferguson wagon train west. I keep hoping when we get there he'll decide to stay, but he says no, he'd rather be fighting Indians and chasing grizzly bears."

Luke flashed a wry glance at Florida and seated himself beside her. "My sister exaggerates. She's right, though. I've got wandering feet. I wasn't meant to be a farmer or a gold seeker either." One corner of his mouth pulled into a faint smile. "I do better when I'm off by myself."

Lydia came up with her best, most flirty giggle. "Perhaps you should try it. Don't you want to settle down someday and raise a family?"

Don't be so obvious, Lydia. Callie hid her amusement with her stepsister, a silly girl to begin with, vain and rather shallow. Actually, she had every reason to be conceited, with her curly blond locks, blue eyes with long, fringed lashes, and tiny waist.

Luke, apparently realizing he couldn't make a quick getaway, turned his attention to Lydia. "The day I settle down is the day I'm dead."

The arrival of a handsome young man had dispelled Ma's hostile mood. She gave Luke a friendly smile. "This is my oldest daughter, Lydia, Mister McGraw." She nodded toward her second oldest. "This is my second daughter, Nellie."

Nellie remained seated and managed a barely acceptable greeting. A sullen girl, she contrasted with her flighty sister in temperament as well as looks. She tended to sulk a lot when she didn't get her way.

Luke gave the barest of nods to the sisters. His gaze shifted to Callie as she stood by the fire, coffeepot still in hand. She froze. If he said anything about their meeting by the stream, she'd die of embarrassment.

He didn't. Instead, with an interested nod of his head, he asked, "And you are...?"

Callie opened her mouth to speak, but before she could, Ma replied in an offhand way, "That's Callie. She's my stepdaughter."

If Luke noticed the contrast in introductions, he didn't let on. Solemn-faced, with only the slightest hint of a twinkle in his eyes, he looked at Callie. "Haven't we met before?"

"I don't believe so." Warmth crept over her cheeks and she wanted nothing more than to run and hide.

"Callie, if you're going to pour the coffee, then pour it. And offer Mister McGraw a cup."

Grateful for the diversion, Callie busied herself serving coffee to their guests. She hardly noticed Ma's pointed reference to her being a stepdaughter, not a daughter. Long ago she'd learned her place in the Whitaker household, which was somewhere between unwanted stepchild and lowly servant. She should be grateful just to have a roof over her head and three meals a day. Grateful forever, she supposed, although every once in a while she gave some thought to the fact she was now twenty-two, old enough to have a family of her own. Not often, though. Working from dawn to dusk on the Whitaker farm hadn't left much time for contemplation.

Night had fallen. Florida pointed across the meadow where the glow from a large campfire cut through the darkness. "See our campfire? We have one every night when the day has gone well and the weather's good.

We sing, dance, play games, tell jokes and stories. Oh, we have grand time! One of the reasons I came over here was to invite you over to join us."

Lydia clapped her hands. "We'd love to come!"

Callie was about to echo her words when Pa, quiet until now, stepped forward.

A tall man with big square hands and massive shoulders, he gave the appearance of strength and rigidity, a man not likely to change his opinion. Like most older men in the train, he wore a bushy beard, which he seldom trimmed, wool pants held up by suspenders, a cotton shirt, and a wide-brimmed, round-crowned hat. The stiff way he held himself said it all. "This family doesn't hold with such frivolities, Mrs. Sawyer."

Ma nodded. "My husband's absolutely right. We keep to ourselves, so thank you, but we can't accept your invitation."

Callie wasn't surprised Lydia made no attempt to appeal her father's decision. She knew better. In the Whitaker family, Pa's word was law. None of them would dare disobey, although Callie was tempted to speak up. For once, it would have been nice to sit with people who were laughing and having a good time. The farmhouse where they'd lived in Tennessee had been isolated with only a few neighbors, none of them close by. She suspected Pa had wanted it that way. Aside from a monthly shopping trip, they had gone into town only on Sunday to attend church. Afterward, they had returned straight home, never joining any of the social activities. No picnics or parties, and certainly not the dances.

Another ripple of laughter filtered from across the field, causing Callie an odd twinge of disappointment. Yes, it would have been very nice indeed.

Soon after, Florida and her brother Luke bid them good-bye. The jovial woman left with a friendly wave of her hand. "If you folks change your minds, come on over."

Luke mounted his horse and followed, touching his hand to the brim of his hat. His eyes didn't seek Callie's. Why should they when Lydia was around? She was the beauty of the family. Nellie's dark looks weren't nearly as attractive, marred by a figure like Ma's, short-waisted and on the heavy side. Callie had no way to compare herself to her stepsisters. Pa didn't believe in the vanity of a full-length mirror, so she'd never seen her whole self reflected. Judging from Lydia's tiny, hidden scrap of a mirror, she had brown hair, maybe with a touch of red, which she pulled straight back into a bun and paid little attention to. Her face didn't seem remarkable in any way with its straight little nose and brown, wide-set eyes. Maybe not so bad—a face neither startlingly beautiful nor horribly ugly. *I wish Luke had at least glanced at me again.* She pictured how he had looked, standing in the creek in the altogether, an image that sent an unfamiliar tingle down her spine. *Am I crazy?* No man would look at her once, let alone twice. She wasn't much better than a servant girl and should be grateful for her keep. It wouldn't be fitting for her to forget her place and start getting grand ideas.

Chapter 2

Sleeping arrangements in the Whitaker family were tight at best. Ma, Pa, and Tommy slept in one wagon. Len and Andy slept in the other. Lydia and Nellie occupied the tent Pa erected nightly. The first week of their trek, Callie had slept underneath Ma and Pa's wagon. She hadn't minded because the weather was warm. In fact, she'd preferred it to listening to her stepsisters' constant chatter. When the nights had turned nippy, she'd begun sleeping in the tent. Lydia and Nellie weren't happy about sharing but had no choice.

That night, when Callie entered the tent, the glow from their neighbors' campfire still lit the sky. The merry sounds of a fiddle and occasional bursts of laughter wafted from across the meadow. She expected Nellie and Lydia would be sound asleep, as they sometimes were by the time she got to bed, but not tonight. To her surprise, both were wide awake, sitting atop their blankets, changed into fresh dresses, and in a state of suppressed excitement.

"Shh!" Nellie put her finger to her lips. "Don't you say a word, Callie Whitaker. Are they still awake?"

Callie sat on her blankets. "What are you doing?"

"Just tell me if Ma and Pa are asleep yet."

"They climbed in the wagon a long time ago, so, yes, I guess they're asleep." *Florida's invitation to the campfire.* "Didn't Pa tell you not to go over there?"

In the near darkness, Nellie gave a disdainful sniff. "He won't find out unless you tell him."

"I would never." She wasn't a tattletale.

"We won't be gone long," said Nellie. "Just you keep your mouth shut."

"Maybe we should take her with us," whispered Lydia. "Then if we're caught, Pa will most likely blame her."

"Good idea. You're coming with us."

Callie opened her mouth to protest but closed it before she could get the words out. Why shouldn't she go? She'd love to visit Florida, who seemed so jolly and friendly, compared to Ma, who could see nothing good in anything. Pa would be furious if he found out, but he was a heavy sleeper. The chances he'd wake up and discover them missing were slim. Besides, if he did find out, what would he do? As a child, she had lived in fear of the sting of a switch on her legs for the least wrongdoing. So had all the children of Calvin Whitaker, the two older boys receiving the most severe beatings. The switchings had stopped when she'd reached adulthood, but she still feared him. His thundering threats of eternal damnation still struck terror in her heart. She'd risk it, though. The more she thought, the more she wanted to join the laughter and excitement across the meadow. Would Luke McGraw be there? Not that he'd pay her the slightest attention, but still, she liked the idea of seeing him again.

"All right. I'll go with you." She'd worry about eternal damnation later.

Unlike her stepsisters, she owned only two dresses. The one she wore, a limp, worn hand-me-down of Nellie's, was far too big. She'd just washed the other, which was just as shabby, so she had no choice but to wear what she had on.

Hardly breathing, the three crept from the tent and crossed the field. When they reached the Ferguson train, they cut between two of the wagons in the circle and headed for the large campfire that blazed in the middle. A lively scene awaited. Around the fire, people sat on crates, boxes, and camp chairs, chatting and laughing. Two men with scraggly beards passed a jug back and forth. A sprightly fiddler danced as he played a polka, while several couples bounced and bounded around the bonfire to the lively tune.

Florida Sawyer gestured to them to come sit next to her on a long log by the fire. "Hello, girls. Come on over! Glad you could come. Where's your Ma? Did she change her mind?"

Lydia snickered. "Not exactly."

Nellie added, "We sneaked out. Don't tell Pa."

Florida grinned. "I reckon you girls are old enough to know what you're doing." She glanced around the campfire. "Luke?" When he didn't appear, she shook her head. "That brother of mine isn't much for dancing. Keeps to himself too much." She looked toward a tall man standing nearby who'd been listening. "Thank heaven, here's someone I'd wager will be glad to dance with you. This is the leader of our wagon train, Magnus Ferguson. We call him The Colonel."

Magnus stepped forward and gave them a warm greeting. Callie was struck with how handsome he was. Tall and powerfully built, he had a thick head of blond, curly hair and a strong-featured, clean-shaven face, an appearance she much preferred to men who wore wild, unkempt beards. Even had she not been told, she would have guessed Magnus was a leader by the way he carried himself with a commanding air of self-confidence.

Beyond his initial polite greeting, Magnus paid her no attention. He offered his hand to Lydia. "Care to dance, Miss Whitaker?"

"I surely do!" Eyelashes fluttering, Lydia instantly stepped forward. "I do love the polka, Mister Ferguson."

Callie laughed to herself. Not to her knowledge had Lydia ever danced the polka or anything else.

Magnus took Lydia's hand and assumed the correct position for a polka. How could her stepsister possibly manage? She needn't have worried. When they started out, Lydia hesitated, nearly stumbled, but then caught on to the step. The couple bounced away, Lydia looking as if she'd danced the polka all her life. How pretty she looked, her blue eyes bright, her long, blond hair swinging about her rosy-cheeked face.

"She sure is a pretty girl." Florida regarded Nellie and Callie, who sat beside her. "You need dance partners, too. Let's see…" Her gaze scanned the crowd. A young man spied them and headed in their direction. Florida made a face. "Oh, no, not him."

The young man strutted up. In his early twenties, he was tall, dark, and clean-shaven with slick good looks. His gaze focused on Nellie. "Don't believe I've seen you before. Introduce us, Florida."

"Nellie, this here is Coy Barnett. He's one of Jack Gowdy's hired hands." Florida's voice lacked her usual warm enthusiasm. Callie sensed she didn't much care for the young man who stood before them. Nellie seemed not to notice. When Coy asked her to dance, she eagerly said yes.

Watching the couple join in a cotillion, Florida frowned. "You'd best keep an eye on your stepsister."

"Why?"

"I don't trust the man. Don't ask me why, I just…there's something about him I don't like." She brightened and got her smile back. "Now we need to find you a dancing partner."

"Goodness, no." Callie hadn't given the slightest thought that she, too, might enjoy a dance. "Don't worry about me. I'm content to sit here and watch."

"Fiddlesticks."

Despite Florida's protest, no one asked Callie to dance. Not that she minded. She knew no man would want to dance with a straggled-haired girl in a ragged old dress. It was just a treat to be with people who were laughing and enjoying themselves.

After a time, another partner whisked Lydia away. Magnus Ferguson soon returned, all congenial, with a big smile on his face. "You haven't danced yet, Miss Whitaker? Would you like to—?"

"I don't care to dance." She wasn't a charity case.

He didn't pursue the subject but sat down beside her. They chatted. He'd been a merchant back in Pennsylvania where he came from. Successful, she gathered, although he didn't say. He was a widower, his wife having died in childbirth two years ago, and the baby, too. Wanting to start a new life and escape old memories, he had formed this wagon train and had been elected leader. Unlike other companies headed west, peace and harmony prevailed in the Ferguson wagon train, thanks to himself and his five-man council, called captains. So far, not a single dispute. "Your family ought to join us."

She reluctantly shook her head. "I doubt Pa would want to do that."

Magnus said no more on the subject. They talked a while longer before someone came with a problem and drew him away. What a nice man. She was grateful he'd taken the time to sit and talk to her. He seemed anxious to marry again. He wouldn't have a problem. A well-to-do widower like Magnus could easily find a wife, especially since he wasn't half bad-looking.

The music still played. Tired of sitting, she left the bonfire and dancers and went for a short stroll around the camp. Passing one of the wagons, she spied Luke McGraw occupying the wagon seat. In the bright moonlight, he was dressed no differently than the other men in a plain shirt, dark trousers, and sturdy boots. He appeared to be cleaning a rifle.

He looked up. "Good evening."

She nodded and kept on walking.

He gazed down at her. "So it's you. Not dancing?"

She stopped. "I don't know how to dance."

"Sorry I asked."

"Why aren't *you* dancing?"

"I've got better things to do with my time."

"Is this your wagon?"

"It's my sister's. A bedroll's good enough for me." He rested the rifle against the seat. "Florida won't give up and leave me alone. If it was up to her, I'd spend every evening charming the ladies."

She couldn't resist. "From what I've seen, there's not much danger of that."

He chuckled, climbed down from the wagon seat and stood before her, hands resting casually on his hips. "Why are you traveling by yourselves?"

Because Pa won't listen to reason. "Because my stepfather feels we can make the journey alone without any help. He doesn't get along well with other people."

"I can understand why he feels that way. When you throw people from all walks of life together in a wagon train, there's bound to be trouble of one sort or another."

She remembered her conversation with Magnus. "According to Colonel Ferguson, there's peace and harmony in this wagon train, no disputes."

Luke broke into laughter. "Magnus Ferguson is a fool. Even so, with all the dangers of the trail, it's not a good idea to travel alone."

"Tell that to my pa, not me. We do what he says, and that's that."

"Maybe so, but people change on these journeys. No one ends up exactly the same."

"He's not likely to change his mind."

He remained silent. She must be boring him to death. She wished she could think of something bubbly and amusing to say like Lydia would do, but nothing came to mind. He'd leave at any moment.

The fiddler in the distance ceased his playing and announced, "That's all for tonight, folks."

"I'd better go." She started away. "Good night, Mister McGraw."

"I'll walk you back."

In silence, they returned to the gathering where Florida was sitting. Lydia and Nellie returned, breathless from dancing. "I'm so glad I came," said Lydia. Seeing Luke, she gave him a dazzling smile. "Mister McGraw, they tell me you're acting as guide for this wagon train. I do so wish we could join you. Do you think you could speak to my pa?"

"Your pa made it clear—"

"You could try, couldn't you? Please? We had so much fun tonight."

"Please?" Nellie echoed.

Callie listened with disgust. She hated it when her stepsisters got that whiney tone in their voices.

Florida said, "I hate to say it, girls, but your father strikes me as a man who doesn't often change his mind."

Lydia pouted. "It's not safe to travel alone. Mister McGraw said so."

Magnus appeared. "Luke's right." He gazed at Lydia with admiring eyes. "Tell you what I'll do. I'll talk to your father in the morning."

Lydia clasped her hands together. "Wonderful! I'm sure you can persuade him." Her face clouded. "You won't tell him we were here tonight?"

"Your secret's safe with us, honey." Florida looked toward her brother. "You'd better go along with Magnus tomorrow. If anyone can describe the dangers of the trail, it's you."

Luke shook his head. "Magnus can manage just fine."

A pang of disappointment shot through Callie's heart. Magnus could never persuade her stubborn stepfather to join this wagon train. How wonderful it would be if he could. She'd make friends with all these nice people, have fun at the campfires, not feel so alone all the time. No use thinking about it, though. Pa would never change his mind.

Lydia was still fawning over Magnus. "It's been a delightful evening, Mr. Ferguson. We'll expect you in the morning." She looked toward Nellie. "Time to go. Are you coming?"

Callie watched her stepsisters start away. Lydia finally remembered and looked back. "Callie, I hardly noticed you sitting there, quiet as a mouse. Well, you'd better come along right now. You know how early you've got to get up tomorrow to start breakfast."

* * * *

Luke watched the three young women head back across the meadow. *Lydia*—pretty but not a brain in her head. *Nellie*—passably pretty if she smiled more and lost that permanent pout. *Callie*—poor creature, so obviously beaten down and made to feel inferior by the entire Whitaker family. She wasn't pretty…well, maybe she could be if she didn't have that work-worn look about her, like she lived in fear of not getting her chores done. Her figure wasn't bad. Despite that poorly fitting dress, he could tell that like Lydia, she had a good-sized bosom, tiny waist and slender hips. Nice face if it wasn't so pale and strained all the time. She should laugh more. Even her hair wouldn't look so bad if she didn't have it all pulled back in a scraggly bun, like she couldn't bother to spend more than a couple of seconds fixing it each morning.

Something about her intrigued him. What it was, he didn't know. It didn't matter because Caleb Whitaker had chosen to take the long journey alone. Beyond tomorrow, he'd never see any of them again. What a fool Caleb was, but that was his choice.

Maybe I will go along with Magnus in the morning even though it won't do any good.

Chapter 3

Caleb Whitaker was a man of stern convictions who never shilly-shallied and never, with rare exceptions, changed his mind. He'd grown up with ten brothers and sisters in a mirthless home where his parents waged a constant battle against wickedness, sloth, and sacrilege. Because his father never spared the rod, Caleb, who was a rather stubborn boy, trod the well-worn path to the woodshed many a time before the importance of obedience and discipline became deeply ingrained in his nature. It was no surprise he had followed in his father's footsteps, raising his children as he had been raised. Spare the rod, spoil the child.

Although Caleb was in many ways a fair man, God-fearing and hardworking, his children had learned in early childhood he could be a tyrant if anyone even thought of disobeying him. Both his two oldest sons had left home at an early age, grateful to escape their parents' tyranny. Only the girls were left, and the youngest son, Tommy, who hardly said a word and acted strange. Caleb ignored him. The boy was nothing but an embarrassment.

Hester Whitaker's unforgiving nature resembled her husband's. In fact, she was, in her own way, every bit a despot as he was. Raised in a home as strict as Caleb's, she saw nothing wrong with stern discipline. Her way was the only way—a belief that went hand-in-hand with her unyielding temperament. Lydia and Nellie were the only exceptions to her stringent rules. She doted on her two girls, constantly defending them against their father, never subjecting them to the firm punishment she meted out to her other children. Nobody knew why she favored her two daughters over all the others. She never explained, perhaps because she had no explanation.

Now, at dawn's first light, Callie and her stepfather were the first ones up, Callie making the coffee, Caleb yoking the oxen. At the sound of approaching horses, he uttered a curse and looked across the meadow. "What do those damn fools want?"

Callie followed his gaze. Magnus Ferguson and Luke McGraw headed their way on horseback. Her pulse quickened, but she wasn't sure why. It couldn't be Luke. He was rude and none too friendly. It had to be Magnus. Such a handsome man. Available, too, although he'd never look at her twice.

They rode up, Magnus in the lead. While Luke briefly touched his fingers to the brim of his hat, Magnus, in a grand gesture, swept his hat off and nodded to Callie. Smiling broadly, he introduced himself to Pa. "I take it you're Mister Whitaker?"

Caleb kept his usual stern-faced expression. "If you're here to persuade me to join your wagon train, don't waste your time."

"Are you sure, Mister Whitaker?"

"Positive."

A shadow of annoyance crossed Magnus Ferguson's face. "Then I won't bother you further. I'm a busy man with a wagon train to lead." He cut a sharp glance at Luke. "Let's go. Looks like we've wasted our time."

"Go ahead. I'll follow in a minute." As Magnus wheeled his horse around and left, Luke dismounted, looking not the least perturbed by Caleb's unfriendly words. "At least hear me out."

"Make it brief." Pa continued his task of yoking the oxen. "I'm listening."

"Coffee, Mister McGraw?" Callie would try to make up for Pa's rudeness.

Luke nodded. As if he'd been welcomed with open arms, he accepted the cup from Callie, took a leisurely sip, and addressed Pa again. "I've crossed the country several times and lived in the wilderness much of my life, so I know what I'm talking about. You don't want to make the crossing alone. There's safety in numbers, like when the Indians attack, or when crossing rivers, or when you get stuck in the mud. If you get injured or sick, we've got a doctor who's traveling with us. And there's also…"

By the time Luke had finished, Callie was more convinced than ever that crossing the country in a covered wagon by themselves was complete folly. They should not make the journey alone and would meet disaster unless they joined the Ferguson wagon train.

Pa listened with studied indifference, appearing engrossed in the proper yoking of his oxen. When Luke finished, Pa looked up. "Is that all?"

"Yep."

"We'll be going alone."

"If Indians, dangerous river crossings, snakes, and lack of medical care can't persuade you"— Luke shrugged—"then I wish you well on your journey, and may God be with you."

Pa shot Luke a piercing glance. "God is with me at all times, Mister McGraw. With His help, I will continue this journey alone, without the slightest doubt we shall arrive safely in the golden land. Now, if you'll excuse me, I have work to do." He turned his back and walked away.

Callie wanted to cringe at Pa's rudeness, even though Luke didn't seem to mind. He gave a wry grimace. "I hope he's right." He took a final sip of coffee and swung back on his horse. His gaze swept their campsite. "Where are your stepsisters?"

How disappointing. What he probably meant was, where is Lydia? No doubt he was smitten and wanted to see her again. "Lydia and Nellie like to sleep as late as possible. They won't come out until it's time to eat breakfast. Ma, too."

Luke frowned. His jaw tightened in a way that indicated he'd like to say something but thought better of it. "You're a hard worker."

"I like hard work."

"Really?" His expression held a touch of mockery. "Mind if I ask a personal question?"

"Go right ahead." Her life was a dull open book. She had nothing to hide.

"How long have you been with the Whitakers?"

"That's easy. From the day I was born, or soon after. They found me on their doorstep and were kind enough to take me in."

"You don't know who your parents are?"

"Ma suspects my mother was one of the fancy women who worked at the saloon in town. All I know is, they took me in and gave me a roof over my head. I'm forever grateful."

"I see that. You work very hard."

"Yes, of course I do—to repay them for their kindness."

"Hmm…"

He seemed to be fighting to keep his words back. "You have something to say, Mister McGraw?"

"Yes, I have something to say. From what little I've seen, you do more than your share. By now, isn't this debt you feel you owe paid in full?"

Nobody had ever asked her such a question before. No one had ever cared that much to ask. "It's a debt that will never be paid in full."

He frowned at her answer. "Do you want to spend the rest of your life being treated like a, like a…"

"Servant?"

"Yes, servant." He sounded annoyed. "That's not right."

"Perhaps not, but that's my lot in life."

His eyes rolled skyward. He swore something under his breath then remained silent.

She surprised herself by blurting, "Would you like to stay for breakfast?"

"I've got to get back." He touched a finger to his hat. "Good day then, Callie Whitaker. Have a safe journey, and for God's sake, put a little fun in your life."

He wheeled his horse around and headed back across the meadow. She would never see him again. She'd still be thinking about him, though. Never before had she met a man who saw her as a person, not just a servant girl. He said she was a hard worker. How strange to hear a man say something nice about her. If he'd told her she was the most beautiful woman in the world, she couldn't have been more flattered.

"Callie, have you got breakfast ready?" Lydia appeared, tousle-headed and still in her white flannel nightgown.

"Almost. You'd better hurry up." For once, Callie's usually agreeable voice held an edge. She'd clearly understood Luke's unspoken words. *You work too hard. Why aren't your stepsisters here to help?*

Why not indeed? Luke's comments had unleashed a vague feeling of resentment. Why did she have to do most of the work? According to Ma, both her stepsisters were too delicate and frail to make more than a token effort at doing chores. But were they really? Why couldn't they do more of the work? She always ended up doing all of it, and that wasn't right. Was she truly fated to be an unpaid servant all her life?

"Callie!" Ma called. "Soon as you finish breakfast and wash the dishes, see that Tommy is dressed and everything's packed."

"Yes, Ma." Reaching for the biscuits, Callie set her rebellious thoughts aside. Ahead lay another grueling day. There'd be no time for silly resentments. She'd need every bit of energy she possessed just to survive.

* * * *

Although she never had one of her own, Callie loved horses. They had brought along several: Pa's horse, a palomino named Duke, the mounts for Andy and Len, a reliable filly named Pearl, her buckskin yearling, Jaide. She especially loved Jaide and hoped she could train and ride him someday. In the meantime, riding Duke was one of the few pleasures of the journey. At home, she had taken care of the handsome gelding, although Pa had never let her ride him. Now, since Pa spent most of the day driving the wagon, he allowed Callie to saddle Duke and walk him alongside the train, a welcome break from having to trudge on foot. Thank goodness, Ma, Lydia, and Nellie didn't object. They'd never shown the slightest interest in horses. Lydia, in particular, tried to avoid "the scary things." Pa didn't trust Tommy with any of his animals, so, to Callie's delight, she had Duke to herself and rode as often as she could.

Today was no exception. After the two wagons started their daily trek and the handymen got the cattle moving, Callie swung into the saddle and urged Duke forward. She glanced across the meadow. The circle of wagons was gone. So they'd already left. *Ah, well.* The day was sunny, the heavily wooded scenery beautiful, and she shouldn't complain, even though she wished she could have talked to Florida again, and Luke, too.

Occasionally, one of the hired hands joined her when they weren't busy herding the hundred head of cattle. She enjoyed riding with them both. Andy, always smiling and friendly. Len, always arrogant and slightly condescending, but never boring. They both possessed a contagious enthusiasm that brightened her day, and no wonder. They were going to get rich! Soon as they got to California, they'd start gathering those gold nuggets that lay for the taking all over the ground.

Skinny, sharp-nosed Len pulled his horse alongside hers. "Little Mouse, how goes it today?"

Little Mouse. He'd picked that up from her family. She didn't like it but never thought to object. Not until now. "I wish you wouldn't call me that."

His mouth pulled into a mocking grin. "I call you that because you *are* a little mouse, a meek little mouse who always does what she's told."

"I could change."

"*You?*" Len snickered. "That'll be the day. Better stay like you are. You're safer that way."

She felt defeated and subdued, as she always did after any sort of confrontation and could think of nothing more to say. They rode in silence until Len remarked, "Guess your pa still wants to go it alone."

She nodded. "What do you think?"

"I think whatever gets me to California the fastest is the way to go, and that's traveling alone. Those big wagon trains are safer, but their pace is slower than molasses."

She remembered Luke's warning. "What about crossing the rivers? Won't it be more dangerous if we're alone?"

"Hell, no. Don't worry about it, Little Mouse. Your pa knows what he's doing." Len spurred his horse and took off to chase one of the cattle that had wandered away.

Toward the end of the day, they came to the Big Blue River. The wagons of the Ferguson wagon train were parked along its banks. Not one had crossed yet. Pa, still driving the wagon with Ma beside him, shaded his eyes for a closer look. "What in the Sam Hill are they doing?"

Callie, still astride Duke, reined up beside the wagon. "It looks like they're unloading everything."

"Look at those fools." Pa cast a look of disgust. "They'll lose at least two days trying to get across." He flicked his whip over the oxen and they started up again.

As they drew closer, Ma pointed. "Oh, look, there's that awful woman with the bloomers. Try to avoid her, Caleb."

Too late. Florida spotted them and waved. "Have you come to join us? Isn't this terrible?" She spoke in a cheery voice, gesturing toward the growing pile of possessions she and her children were unloading from the wagon. "Luke says we must take everything out of the wagons. Then, what scares me to death, is we've got to float them across. You should join us, Mister Whitaker. There's safety in numbers."

Pa gave her a thin-lipped smile. "We'll find our own place to cross farther upstream. Somewhere more shallow than this."

Luke rode up. "Not a good idea, sir. Those shallow crossings can be tricky. A lot of them are full of quicksand. Believe me, you don't want to get stuck."

"I'll take my chances." With a look of disdain, Pa flicked the reins. The wagon started to roll again on a trail by the riverbank, headed upstream.

"If you hit quicksand, whatever you do, don't stop!" Luke called after him.

Pa appeared not to hear and didn't slow his pace.

Callie, still atop her horse, paused to speak to Luke and Florida. "Wish us luck."

Florida glanced at the swift-flowing river. Her face filled with worry. "I'll say a special prayer for you."

Callie could tell she meant it from the bottom of her heart.

Luke, too, had a look of worry. "Be careful." He was smiling, yet serious.

She tilted her chin in an attempt to look a lot braver than she felt. "We'll be fine. Maybe I'll see you on the other side." She urged Duke into a trot and rode away. Acutely aware Luke's gaze must be fastened on her back, she sat straight in the saddle, tall as she could, and took care not to bounce like a beginner, like Lydia would do. At least he'd think she was a good rider, although why his opinion should matter in the least, she didn't know.

* * * *

Pa drove the first wagon, followed by Andy driving the second, nearly a mile upstream until they came to a stretch of the riverbank lined with a sparse fringe of trees. Len rode his horse partway into the stream. "This here spot is pretty shallow. I don't think we'll find one better."

Callie gazed in consternation at the place they'd chosen. This was the best the boys could find? Maybe the bank wasn't as steep, but the current still ran high and swift. She wasn't the only one concerned.

Lydia frowned with unease. "Are you sure, Len? That river looks way too dangerous to me."

Len laughed with scorn. "I'll show you how dangerous it is, Miss Lydia." Still laughing, he rode his chestnut gelding back into the river, only farther this time. "See how easy?" He held tight to the horse's mane.

Suddenly the horse sank almost from sight. It must have stepped into a hole. In a panic, it bucked, reared and threw its rider into the water. Len came to the surface only to find the panic-stricken animal lashing out in all directions. Everyone gasped when a fatal blow of the horse's hoof just missed his head. By some miracle, he managed to drag himself from the river and collapse exhausted on the bank. His horse scrambled out beside him. "Still think we can make it," he panted, struggling for breath.

Callie waited for Pa to disagree, to say they should find another place, but after a careful scanning of the river, he nodded his head. "We'll cross here, just a few feet farther upstream to avoid that hole. Andy, start driving the cattle across. We'll follow with the wagons."

Ma looked doubtful. "Caleb, are you sure? That water looks—"

"When I want your opinion, I'll ask for it. Go ahead, boys."

Ma shut her mouth. Callie dismounted and removed Duke's saddle. The women watched with growing concern as Len and Andy, whooping and waving their hats, drove the horses and cattle into the stream. Although an occasional errant cow balked, or swam in the wrong direction, they all made it across. When the last animal reached the opposite bank, Pa nodded with satisfaction and cast an I-told-you-so glance at his wife. "All that fuss for nothing. Get in the wagons. We'll cross right now and be way ahead of that idiot, Ferguson."

Andy made ready to drive the first wagon across with Ma on the seat beside him, Nelly and Lydia in the back.

Len, already on the far bank, called across. "Remember what they said, Andy. Once you get started, don't stop for nothing."

Andy drove the wagon down the bank and into the river. Callie caught her breath as she watched Ma gripping the seat, and Andy beside her cracking the whip above the oxen's heads. He was yelling like she'd never heard before, encouraging the animals into the swift stream. What if the wagon tipped and they were tossed into the icy water? Nobody knew how to swim. It would be a complete disaster.

No need to worry, they made it across. Callie's confidence soared as the wagon rolled to the top of the opposite bank and her family jumped down, all smiles. Now only she, Pa, and Tommy had yet to cross in the second wagon.

Pa grinned with satisfaction. "See how easy that was? Let's go."

Callie took her little brother's hand and started toward the wagon. He pulled back and started to cry. "No, scared! Don't want to go."

She stopped and knelt before him. "Don't be scared, Tommy. It's easy." The boy shook his head and continued to cry. She called to Pa. "We'd better wait. I need to get him calmed down."

Pa got down off the wagon seat and strode to where they were standing. "Why are you coddling the boy?" He pointed toward the wagon. "Get him on the seat right now or I swear I'll leave him behind."

Callie closed her eyes in frustration. This was the worst possible way to handle the frightened child. "Pa, give me a few minutes—"

"Into the wagon now, or I swear to God, I'll leave you both behind."

Before she could stop him, Pa jerked Tommy from her arms, carried him screaming to the wagon, and dumped him roughly on the wagon seat. He uttered a curse. "No son of mine is going to be a coward. Come on, Callie, let's go."

Callie climbed onto the seat, shifting Tommy so she sat in the middle and he didn't have to sit next to his father. She felt so powerless. All she could do was wrap an arm around the sobbing boy and hope for the best. "Hold tight, Tommy," she whispered. "Keep your eyes closed until we get across. Everything's going to be fine."

Tommy squeezed his eyes closed tight. With a sharp crack of the whip, Pa urged the oxen into the river. As they rolled ever deeper into the current, Callie wanted to close her own eyes and not open them until they'd safely reached the other side. She resisted the temptation. For Tommy's sake, she must look strong and confident, face the danger with her eyes wide open.

Why were they going so slow? Andy had raced his wagon across at top speed, cracking the whip the whole way. Not her stepfather. He seemed to be letting the oxen cross at their own measured pace. Long ago, she'd learned that questioning Pa's actions brought abuse piled upon her head, but she couldn't resist. "Why are we going so slow? Shouldn't we race across so we don't get stuck in the quicksand?"

"Hogwash." Pa's eyes narrowed. "I don't pay attention to fools who shoot their mouths off. Now shut up and let me drive."

She did as she was told, even though Len was waving his hat on the far bank, yelling, "Don't slow down!" They reached the middle of the river without incident. Maybe Pa was right. Maybe...

The wagon came to an abrupt halt. "Getup!" Pa yelled, cracking the whip again and again over the oxen's heads. Despite their struggles, the wagon didn't move. Pa continued to yell, but the animals were stuck where they were. Gripped by sheer fear, Callie clasped Tommy tight. The wagon tipped sharply. Next thing she knew, she wasn't on the seat anymore. She'd been thrown into the icy cold water, Tommy still clasped in her arms. She sank clear under and up again. Sputtering, gasping from the shock of the frigid water, she grabbed a large branch floating by. She held tight to Tommy with her other arm as the current caught them and swept them away.

Callie had no idea how far she traveled. What with her heavy boots, it was all she could do to keep her head above water, and Tommy's, too, but there was no way she could kick them off. They were drifting closer to the far shore. She kept reaching her feet down, trying to reach bottom. For a long time she couldn't, then all of a sudden her boot touched something hard. She could walk! She let go of the branch and staggered from the water, carrying Tommy in her arms. Thank God, she wasn't alone. Part of the Ferguson party must have already crossed over because people came running. Gently, she laid Tommy on his back in the grass at the water's edge where he lay unmoving, lips blue, skin deadly white. "Tommy, Tommy!" He couldn't be dead, not this dear little boy who so depended on her. What could she do? Never had she felt so helpless.

She had a vague impression of a horse riding up, someone leaping off. Luke knelt beside her. "He's swallowed a lot of water. Come on, we'll roll him over." With Callie's help, he rolled the boy over so Tommy lay on his stomach. "Got to get the water out." Luke grasped the boy around his middle and lifted him up. As he did, a gush of water flowed from Tommy's mouth. He lifted again and another gush of water followed the first. Finally Tommy coughed. It was an ugly, hacking cough, but the sound of it brought a cry of joy to Callie's lips.

"Ah, he's breathing."

Luke repeated the process until Tommy's eyelids fluttered open and he weakly gasped, "I fell in the water."

Callie stroked Tommy's forehead. "Yes, you fell in the water, sweetheart, but you're going to be fine."

Ma arrived, completely breathless. She must have run along the bank after them. When she caught her breath, she took a quick look at her son, then gazed at Luke. "Is he all right?"

"He's fine. Just a little cold and wet."

Ma glared at Callie. "You were supposed to watch him."

While Callie stared at her stepmother in amazement, unable to think what to answer, Luke spoke up. "You've got it wrong, ma'am. Callie saved the boy's life."

Ma appeared not to hear. "He shouldn't just lie there. Come on, Tommy." She yanked her son to his feet. He sagged, but she pulled him up straight.

Callie called, "He needs to rest. He—"

"Nonsense." Ma glared at Tommy. "You got your clothes wet." With a firm grip on his shoulder, she started to lead him away. He wobbled but managed to stay on his feet.

"What about Pa?" Callie called after them.

"He's fine." Ma threw the words casually over her shoulder. "So are the oxen and wagon. Andy and Len got them out. Come on, don't just sit there. We need you." She continued on her way, leaving Callie sitting cold and shivering on the ground.

Luke removed his buckskin jacket and placed it around her shoulders. "Are you all right?"

"I'm ju-ju-just fine." She pulled the jacket close as a wave of shivering engulfed her. She'd never been so cold in all her life, but even so, Ma's lack of sympathy and wounding words were all she could think of. Her teeth chattered. "How could she think such a thing?"

"We've got to get you dry. You can worry about your ma later." Luke lifted her effortlessly in his arms.

Florida waved from her wagon nearby. "Bring her over here!" When they arrived, she declared, "Put her in the back. She's got to get those wet clothes off or she'll freeze to death." Luke lifted Callie into the back of the wagon. Florida climbed in. With little help from Callie, who was too numb to move, she stripped off her boots and wet clothes, rubbed her vigorously with a towel, and wrapped her in a blessedly warm blanket. "You're a brave girl. You saved the little boy's life. Where did you learn to swim?"

Hugging the blanket close around her, Callie slowly stopped shivering. "I never learned to swim." It was hard to talk through lips still numb from the cold. "There was a branch I hung on to. I did what came naturally, I guess."

"That makes you all the braver. I'm going to get you something to wear."

Florida had barely climbed from the wagon when Luke stuck his head in. "How are you doing?"

Startled, Callie grabbed for the blanket and pulled it higher over her chest. "I'm fine." She wished she hadn't acted so flustered.

Luke laughed softly. "You're worried about modesty after you nearly drowned? Don't worry, I didn't see a thing."

Perhaps it was the amused arch of his eyebrow that made her see the humor of it all, or perhaps it was the easy smile that played at the corners of his mouth, but whatever it was, she forgot her embarrassment and laughed. "You're right. I should be thinking how lucky I am to be alive."

Luke climbed into the wagon and squatted beside her. "I talked to your folks."

"You did? What about?"

"Let's just say I wanted to correct any wrong notions they might have as to how Tommy ended up in the river. The blame lies solely with your stepfather. He should never have stopped in the middle of a patch of quicksand. Matter of fact, he was a fool to make that crossing in the first place."

"I hope you didn't tell him that."

"Only the part about you. I made it clear it was no fault of yours. Instead of being blamed, you should be praised and thanked for your bravery. If it hadn't been for you, Tommy would have drowned."

No one had ever stood up for her before. "You actually told them that?"

"I did."

"Did they believe you?"

"I got my point across." His gaze roamed over her. "You look like a drowned rat."

What a hurtful thing to say, although, of course, it must be true. But was it? Detecting a faint light twinkling in the depths of his dark eyes, she realized he meant his words in a playful, affectionate sort of way. "If I look so horrible, maybe you shouldn't look."

"Did I say you looked horrible?"

His eyes fell to her bosom, well-covered by the blanket. She grew acutely aware of her nakedness beneath and could hardly force herself to meet his gaze. No man had ever seen her this way before, with her arms bare and her hair hanging loose and tangled about her shoulders. Could he like her? Could he possibly think she was pretty?

"Don't underestimate yourself, Callie Whitaker." His voice held a trace of laughter. He parted the flaps and dropped from the wagon, leaving her gazing after him, both flattered and confused.

Florida soon appeared with Callie's spare dress, a blue calico that was every bit as faded and ill-fitting as the other one. She slipped it on, wishing she had something better to wear. She put on her boots, which Florida had set by the fire to dry, and laced them up. Luke was nowhere in sight. After thanking Florida for her help, she walked along the riverbank back to her family. The wagon that got stuck had been towed from the water and sat safely on the shore. By the time she reached it, her moment of revelation about her looks had faded from her mind. How could she possibly look anything but ugly in this horrible, ill-fitting dress? How could she possibly have thought a man as handsome and desirable as Luke McGraw could feel anything other than sympathy for a plain servant girl?

Everything was a mess. Pa was nowhere in sight. Various and sundry items from the wagon that had gotten wet were laid out haphazardly to dry. Her stepsisters were trying to build a campfire. They were choking and fanning themselves as billows of smoke blew in their faces.

"Callie! Where have you been?" Nellie cried.

Lydia stuck out her arm to show an angry red burn near her wrist. "Look here. I burnt myself trying to do *your* job."

Ma appeared. When she saw Callie, she jammed her fists to her hips. "Where have you been? Look at this mess. Where were you when we needed you? Now Lydia has burned herself, I'm exhausted and Nellie…"

She rambled on, piling everything that went wrong that day directly on Callie's head. "Now go fix supper and get caught up on your chores."

"Yes, ma'am." Callie listened humbly, head bowed. What trouble *she* had caused? She was truly sorry… *But wait a minute.* What, actually, had she done wrong? Why was she being blamed for anything? Hadn't Luke and Florida praised her for saving Tommy's life? She started to turn away then turned back again. "About Tommy—"

"Mister McGraw came by and told us what happened." Ma paused, like it was an effort to force the words out. "So I suppose you weren't

directly to blame, but that doesn't mean you should shirk your chores."
Ma gave her one more scathing glare and walked away.

Callie resumed her work, quiet as always, the little mouse grateful to
be working for her keep. Inside, though, an emotion totally foreign to her
began to brew. *How dare Ma say those things when all I did was save
Tommy from drowning? How dare she talk to me that way?*

Soon the habits of a lifetime took over. Being of an agreeable nature,
she couldn't stay angry for long. What good would it do her? Besides,
wasn't she grateful the Whitakers had taken her in? Given her a roof over
her head? Of course she was, so she shouldn't even think of complaining
and, most of all, she must remember her place.

Chapter 4

Pa was gone for a long time. When he returned, he gathered his family and hired hands together. "I've been meeting with Colonel Ferguson and his captains." He paused, appearing reluctant to continue. When he did, he seemed to be forcing each word from his mouth. "I have decided we will not make the journey alone. We will join the Ferguson wagon train."

Both Lydia and Nellie squealed with delight, prompting Pa to scowl. "No more outbursts. There's nothing to be pleased about. I made my decision with grave misgivings."

Ma looked genuinely puzzled. "Why did you change your mind, Caleb? You were so sure you wanted to travel alone."

"It's with good reason I didn't want to join. Before they set out, those wagon trains draw up constitutions. They elect officers. They've got all kinds of rules and regulations you've got to obey."

"You never were much on obeying the rules."

"Dang right I'm not. I don't care to answer to any man, but we'll join up with Ferguson because there's safety in numbers." He addressed his daughters. "You will avoid contact with the lowlifes in that train as much as possible. Do you understand?"

Ma looked doubtful. "Are you sure this is what you want to do?"

"It's done. We won't discuss it."

Judging from the firm clamp of her stepfather's jaw, Callie knew the conversation was over. No one dared say another word. Pa's way was the right way. When defied, his anger could be very ugly indeed.

In a somber mood, they traveled back down the riverbank and camped alongside the Ferguson wagon train. That night there was no community campfire, no merry fiddle and lively dancing. Everyone was exhausted from the demands of the difficult river crossing. Only when Callie crawled into the tent and heard her stepsisters' ecstatic chatter did she realize how happy they were they wouldn't be traveling alone.

Even Nellie, ordinarily so unexpressive, could hardly contain her excitement. "Just think, I shall be traveling all the way to California with that good-looking Coy Barnett. That's weeks and weeks! By the time we get there, he'll be madly in love with me."

"Don't be so sure, sister dear. Every girl in the company must be after him, the ones who aren't after Magnus Ferguson. He's a great catch. A widower, you know, and rich besides."

"Do you like him?"

Lydia's voice brightened. "Of course, I like him. He'll be eating out of my hand by the time we get there."

"What do you think of Luke McGraw?"

"He's rude and unfriendly. I don't like him."

"Ha! That's because he didn't dance with you."

Usually Callie wanted to close her ears to her stepsisters' silly conversation. Not tonight, though. She, too, thought of the long weeks ahead when she'd see Luke McGraw every day. But why Luke? Lydia said he was rude and unfriendly, and she was right. *But I'm not like Lydia. I don't dislike him.* She might even get to know him better. They'd talk. He'd treat her like an equal person, not like a servant, maybe even regard her with those dark, observant eyes as if he thought she was pretty, like he did today. But what was she thinking? If she was going to dream about a man, it ought to be Magnus Ferguson, not someone as remote and withdrawn as Luke. Did she honestly believe she'd have even the faintest chance to attract a man like Magnus? No, she wouldn't, not with beautiful Lydia casting her cornflower blue eyes in his direction.

I'll put it out of my mind. Callie snuggled into her blankets, dead tired from the grueling day. What a lovely day it had been, despite everything. Maybe she was an outsider who could never compete with her stepsisters, but her spirits soared. No more life of isolation. For the first time ever, she'd be with other people, not just her family, at least until they reached California, and who knew what would happen then? Back in Tennessee, when she'd first heard they were heading west, she had been overcome with dread, didn't want to go. How her thinking had changed! Who knew what the future held? Maybe she even had a future. What a wonderful thought. And yet…would there be any difference? When they reached California, Pa would buy another farm, so there she'd be, the same old drudge she'd been in Tennessee, only… No! *Don't underestimate yourself,* Luke had said, and he was right. From now on, she definitely would not underestimate herself. From now on, she wasn't sure how, but things would be different.

She fell asleep with a spark of hope glimmering deep in a corner of her mind.

In the morning, they became the forty-first and forty-second wagons in the Ferguson wagon train. Pa grumbled when they were assigned a place at the end of the line, the worst possible position. When the trail was dry, stirred-up dust choked the last wagons. When the trail was wet, the ruts in the road were deepest for those unfortunate enough to bring up the rear.

Callie hardly noticed, having discovered the best way to meet her new neighbors was to ride Duke alongside the train as it rolled along at its snail's pace, a good two miles an hour at best. She discovered what fun it was to go up and down the line of wagons, visiting families along the way. Why had they made such a drastic change in their lives, pulling up stakes and heading west? Each had a fascinating story to tell. Doc Wilson, the only doctor with the train, was from Virginia, traveling solo. The kindly Reverend Wilkins, his wife and son, Colton, were from Massachusetts, eager to start a new life in a new land. Jack and Gert Gowdy and their five children planned to farm in California. Jack was a burly, feisty man. His wife, Gert, claimed she was a medicine woman with a vast knowledge of herbs. She had a slovenly look about her, making Callie doubt she'd ever ask for the woman's advice.

Most families were large, their children scrambling about the wagons, poking their heads out or running freely alongside. Not everyone was headed to California. Some planned to split off at Fort Hall and head northwest on the Oregon Trail. All had cut their ties with home. Callie marveled at how brave the women were, leaving behind family, friends, and the only home they had ever known to traipse off into the wilderness and begin a new life.

Occasionally, she spotted Luke riding Rascal, his sorrel gelding. She wished he'd stop and talk, but he was always busy, and she never got a chance to speak to him. At mid-morning, the train stopped by a stream to rest both humans and animals. Callie was riding beside the Sawyer's wagon when Florida spotted her and called, "Come have a cup of coffee."

"Thanks, but I can't." Callie turned her horse around. Ma would need her. She'd better get back.

"Your stepmother can do without you for a few minutes. If she needs something done, she's got two healthy, strapping daughters to do it."

Florida's answer caught her by surprise. Lydia and Nellie weren't healthy and strapping. They were delicate and high-strung. Ma said so many a time. But were they really? Could Ma be exaggerating? They looked healthy enough in Florida's eyes.

Callie slipped from her horse. "I do believe I'll have that cup of coffee, Mrs. Sawyer."

"Call me Florida."

Soon, Callie was sitting comfortably with Florida beside the wagon, engaged in what amounted to a most ordinary conversation. They talked of the weather and if it might rain, how to bake a pie in the middle of nowhere, and the best way to wash clothes while standing knee-deep in a fast-running river. Yet despite their commonplace words, Callie couldn't remember when she'd enjoyed herself more. Here she was, having a conversation, not as servant to mistress, but woman to woman. A heady feeling indeed. Something she'd never experienced. Just as Florida was describing her recipe for johnnycakes, Luke rode up and joined them.

He scanned her critically. "I see you've recovered from yesterday."

She gave him a rueful smile. "I don't look like a drowned rat today, if that's what you mean."

"You certainly don't," Luke replied amidst their laughter.

A warm glow grew within her. She was so glad to be here, actually exchanging pleasantries with this puzzling man.

Florida continued with her johnnycake recipe. "You take one egg, half a cup of water, three-eighths of a cup of flour…oh dear, you'll never remember." She went to the wagon and returned with a notebook and pencil, which she offered to her guest. "Here, I'll recite the recipe and you can write it down."

In a twinkling, Callie's beautiful world fell apart. Her good feeling disappeared into overwhelming humiliation, and her face heated with embarrassment. She wished she could be anywhere, *anywhere* but here. Throwing up a hand, she waved off the pencil and notebook. "I cannot… You see, I… I…"

"You can't read or write," said Luke swiftly in the most matter-of-fact way imaginable. "Don't worry about it. Neither can a lot of people."

Florida caught her mistake at once. "Shame on me. I never thought… But, of course, Luke's right. There are lots of people in the world who cannot read or write and it doesn't…it doesn't mean a thing!"

If anything, Luke and Florida's efforts to smooth Callie's embarrassment made it even worse. She wanted to crawl in a hole and hide her face forever. She tried to find an answer but couldn't speak.

"You never went to school?" Florida's eyes brimmed with gentle sympathy.

Callie gulped over the lump that had formed in her throat. She must hold herself together, not let them see her burning shame. "Ma always needed help, what with the babies coming along and all."

"What about the other children? Did they go to school?" Florida's voice held an edge.

"Yes. They all went to school except me. I'm only a stepchild." She could stand no more. She had to get away or she'd burst out crying in front of everyone. She arose with haste and grabbed Duke's reins. "I'd best be going now." Without waiting for an answer, she swung to the saddle and headed back to her wagon, intent upon leaving the scene of her complete disgrace behind.

* * * *

As Callie rode away, Luke and his sister watched after her. "Oh, dear, I feel terrible," Florida remarked. "I humiliated the poor girl. It wasn't my intention. I had no idea she couldn't read or write."

Luke's gut wrenched. He'd learned to control his anger long ago, yet an overwhelming urge to confront the Whitakers took hold of him. He wanted to tell them Callie didn't deserve such treatment, not only this business about school, but it was plain to see they considered her a servant, not much better than a slave. Florida had called Callie "poor girl." Yes, she was all of that, yet there was something about her that stirred a puzzling emotion in his innards. It wasn't sympathy. Exactly what it was, he wasn't sure, except he'd been thinking about her a lot today, remembering how she looked wrapped in the blanket, naked underneath. He'd said she looked like a drowned rat. What he had failed to mention was she had looked like a very fetching drowned rat.

His sister kept shaking her head. "I feel *so* bad… Poor little thing. Do you remember the story of Cinderella? The mean stepmother, the two ugly stepsisters, the poor, mistreated stepdaughter who's forced to work from dawn to dusk. That's who Callie reminds me of."

"You're right. They've beat it into her head she's worthless." Luke frowned in thought. "Before this journey is over, she may surprise us."

"Everyone should know how to read and write." Florida's face lit. "I have an idea."

* * * *

As far back as she could remember, Callie had felt a deep shame she could neither read, write, nor had schooling of any kind. At one time or another, all the Whitaker children except her had attended the one-room schoolhouse three miles from the farm, a fact that made her shame even worse. The two older boys went clear through school. Even Lydia and Nellie had some education. Her flighty stepsisters were indifferent students at best, but at least they could read, write, and recite the multiplication tables. From an early age, Callie hid her deep envy of the stepbrothers and sisters who left each morning for that mystical place called school. She begged to go, but what with meals to cook, cows to milk, and babies to care for, she could never be spared for the luxury of acquiring an education.

"You don't need school," Ma had always said.

After a time, Callie had realized her stepmother would never change her mind. She stopped begging to go but never got over the embarrassment of being totally illiterate. Over the years, she had managed to hide her ignorance, but now, as she returned from her visit with Florida, her cheeks still burned from shame. It was bad enough Florida knew her secret, but far worse that Luke McGraw witnessed the disgraceful spectacle she'd made of herself.

That night, Callie cooked supper and did her chores in silence.

Later, when she joined her stepsisters in the tent, Nellie remarked to Lydia, "Here comes the little mouse. Did you notice how quiet she was tonight?"

"Callie, is something wrong?" Lydia asked.

"Just tired." Callie crawled into her blankets and turned her back. After a day like today, she had no desire to talk and hoped her gossipy stepsisters would soon go to asleep.

No such luck. Soon Nellie's excited chatter filled the darkness. "Oh, Lydia, he talked to me today. I knew he would!"

"Who do you mean?"

"You know who I mean. Coy Barnett, of course. You should have seen the way he looked at me. He likes me special. I know he does."

"You'd better watch out. They say he's a sly one."

"Don't be silly. I can take care of myself."

"Oh really? If he asks you to go for a walk in the woods, you'd better not go."

"If he asks me to go for a walk, I most certainly will go."

"Sister!" Lydia sounded truly shocked. "You wouldn't."

"I would."

"Then don't say I never warned you."

A long silence. *Good.* Callie hoped they were through chattering for the night. She was almost asleep when a soft whisper from Lydia broke the silence. "Nellie, are you still awake?"

"Yes."

"Magnus Ferguson likes me especially. I can tell because he's got that look in his eye, and he goes out of his way to talk to me."

"I thought you liked Luke McGraw."

"I do, but he pays no attention to me."

Nellie snickered. "You're not the only one. All the girls try to flirt with him, but he's not interested."

"I still think he likes me, but for some reason, doesn't care to show it. Why should I care? If I can't have Luke, I'll fall in love with Magnus."

"That's wonderful." Nellie's voice brimmed with elation. "I'm so glad we came on this journey. Pa can't keep us away from the boys anymore, much as he'd like to. I'll marry Coy, you marry Magnus, or maybe Luke, and Pa can't stop us."

Callie listened in silence. It would be nice if Nellie's little dream came true, but she doubted it. From what she'd heard, Coy Barnett was not to be trusted, no matter what Nellie thought. As for Magnus, she doubted a man so intelligent could have any real interest in empty-headed Lydia, no matter how pretty she was.

Soon the conversation drifted and finally stopped as both sisters fell asleep. Callie remained wide awake, even though she had to rise before daybreak. Far into the night, she lay staring into the darkness, her churning thoughts preventing her from slipping into blessed slumber. It had been a horrible day, made worse when Lydia's last words dragged her down to a new level of misery. *I still think he likes me but for some reason doesn't care to show it.* Maybe her beautiful sister was right, but it was more likely that her imagination affected her thinking. Lydia was so vain she figured every man in the company was after her.

But why should I care? I don't like him either. Like Lydia says, he's too blunt and unfriendly. As she tossed and turned, she resolved to save herself from future pain and embarrassment by eliminating Luke from her thoughts and speaking to him as little as possible.

Chapter 5

Hester Whitaker was never at her best in the morning, being inclined toward ill humor when she first arose. The day following Callie's visit with Luke and Florida, she was worse than usual. While Callie placed a pan of biscuits over the campfire, Ma addressed her in a strident voice that reeked with her discontent. "Where were you yesterday? You were gone much too long. What were you doing, having fun? And me here alone, trying to cope with the cooking and all the work besides."

"Yes, ma'am. I'm here now. You don't have to worry." Callie had a sudden notion to ask why Nellie and Lydia couldn't be of more help. She'd look ridiculous if she made a fuss at this late date so she kept her mouth shut.

"See you don't wander off today. There's work to do, and there's no time for you to be off somewhere enjoying yourself."

"Yes ma'am." Callie had long since grown accustomed to her stepmother's brusqueness. She couldn't remember a time when Ma gave her any love or, for that matter, showed affection to any of her sons. Perhaps that's why the two older boys had left home at an early age. The same couldn't be said for her daughters. Since the day each was born, Ma had lavished them with all her love and attention. They were the center of her life, her only joy. Callie suspected it wasn't always so. She recalled a faded painting of her stepparents that sat on the mantle in the parlor. It had long since disappeared, but she remembered how handsome Pa appeared in the picture, how pretty Ma looked, and how both were smiling. Callie used to wonder what had happened to make them change. Why was Ma so unhappy now? Hardly ever smiling and yelling all the time. Ma had never said. She'd always kept her feelings to herself, but after years of listening to her parents' bitter arguments, Callie figured she knew the reasons for her stepmother's unhappiness.

Hester Stinson Whitaker was born to a well-to-do family in Memphis. Growing up, Hester had lived a life of privilege and luxury. Although she was no great beauty, when she became of marriageable age, her family's prominence and social standing had made her one of the most popular belles in Memphis. She had her pick of suitors, but when Caleb Whitaker came to town, he'd swept her off her feet. Caleb had owned a cotton plantation not far from the city, a fact which made him one of the season's most eligible bachelors. Soon her family had discovered the truth. Caleb's so-called plantation was nothing more than a ramshackle farm that produced barely enough bales of cotton to eek out a living. Her parents had forbidden Hester to see him again, but the headstrong girl didn't listen. Having fallen head over heels in love, she had eloped with the then-dashing and handsome Caleb Whitaker.

Her family never forgave her.

Callie could only guess, but she suspected Hester soon realized she'd made a horrible mistake, but there was no going back. She'd made her bed and now she had to lie in it. Before long, the dashing young man she'd married changed into a tyrant who kept her isolated and controlled her every move. He didn't even look the same. The dark eyes Callie saw in the painting, which seemed so soft and soulful, had long since turned hard and passionless. The handsome features of the face that had so intrigued her stepmother were now covered by a bushy black beard, both ugly and threatening. Had her stepmother possessed a warmer heart and a greater desire to cope with life's challenges, Callie suspected she might have come to terms with her situation and made life easier for herself and those around her. As it was, she grew more bitter as the years went by, blaming the world, everyone but herself, for her troubles.

Callie planned to stay close to the wagon all day, just as Ma had instructed, but when her chores were done and the day's trek began, she couldn't resist taking Duke for a short ride. She decided she would pass right by Florida's wagon without speaking, but when her horse came parallel to the wagon seat, Florida called, "Stop and visit! I've been waiting for you to ride by."

More than once, Pa declared a woman was too weak, too incompetent, to ever manage a team of oxen, but there sat Florida on the wagon seat, the usual white cap on her head. Was she ever without it? Reins in her hand, skirt spread wide, pantaloons beneath, sturdy boots propped on the footboard. She snapped the reins smartly. "Don't look surprised. I can handle a team as well as any man. You could, too, if your pa would let you."

Callie pulled alongside and set Duke to the slow pace of the wagon. "That'll be the day. I'm just lucky he lets me ride."

"I wanted to talk to you."

"Go ahead."

"It strikes me you feel awfully bad you can't read and write."

Florida's bluntness caught Callie off guard. For a moment, she didn't know what to say. "Yes, I guess I do feel sort of bad." Pride kept her from revealing her devastation from yesterday.

"Sort of bad, my foot! You nearly cried you were so humiliated."

Duke walked several paces before she replied. "I guess I was. I've always wanted to learn how to read and write. I feel awful that I can't."

"Well, you can." Florida reached underneath the seat and brought up a book with tattered pages that was barely hanging together. "See this?"

"What is it?"

"McGuffey's Reader. When we get to California, I plan to open a school, so I brought a big box of books with me. This is the one I'll use to teach you how to read."

"Me?" What was Florida talking about?

"You're a smart girl. You shouldn't have any trouble. By the time this journey's over, you should be able to read and write, and I'll teach you some other things, too, like a bit of geography and simple arithmetic." Florida smiled. "How does that sound?"

At first Callie simply stared, so taken aback she could hardly comprehend what Florida was saying. Read and write? Up to now it had been the impossible dream, as hard to achieve as flying to the moon. "You mean I could actually…"

"Yes, yes!"

"But how——"

"Whichever way we can, honey. At the noon break, every time we stop, in the evening, whenever you have a spare moment, we'll have a lesson."

She, Callie Whitaker, was actually going to learn how to read! The whole idea of it was so new she could hardly comprehend. "I——I—don't think my stepmother will let me."

Luke had ridden up beside her and was listening. "Don't let anyone tell you what to do. You're not a slave. Nobody has the right to demand all your time."

The truth of his words sunk in. She was *not* a slave. She *would* learn to read, despite Ma, Pa, and anything else that might stand in her way. "When do we start?"

Both Florida and Luke smiled, just as the train came to a halt for the first break of the day.

"We start right now. Come join me in the wagon, Callie." Florida opened her tattered copy of McGuffey's Reader. "We start with page one. This here letter is the first in the alphabet. It's called 'A.' By the time we reach the Platte River, you'll know them all."

* * * *

The break ended just as Callie got back to her wagon. The train was underway again, and Ma, accompanied by Nellie and Lydia, was trudging alongside the plodding oxen. When she saw Callie, she burst, "Where have you been? Do you realize I've had no one to help me? Get down off that horse, Callie. I swear, I'll have Caleb forbid you to ride."

"Yes, ma'am." She slid from Duke, tucked the McGuffey's Reader under her arm, and tied the horse to the back of the wagon.

"What's that you've got?"

Callie held up the tattered copy. "Look, Ma, it's a primer. I'm going to learn to read. Mrs. Sawyer's going to teach me."

Nellie snickered. "Little Mouse learn to read? Can you imagine such a thing?"

"No, I cannot." Lydia cast a sneering glance at Callie. "What a silly notion. Why would you bother?"

Callie lowered the book. "Because I've always wanted to learn to read and write." Why explain further? They'd never understand. "Isn't that a good enough reason?"

"It's no reason at all." Ma scowled. "I've never heard of anything so pointless. A time waster if ever there was one. And when, pray, are you going to find time for all this?"

Pa, who'd been listening while driving the wagon, lashed his whip over the oxen. "You heard what your ma said."

"Don't worry. I'll get my chores done." Why couldn't they understand how important this was to her?

Ma's lips thinned with anger. "You most certainly will get your chores done. That's because you're going to take that book back to Mrs. Sawyer right now. Learn to read, indeed! You have no need of it. You know I count on your help. Why you would even consider anything so useless and unnecessary is simply beyond me."

"This means the world to me. It's not useless. It's not—"

"Not another word," Pa roared from the wagon seat. "You lived in this world for twenty-two years without knowing how to read. Got along fine.

Why the hell do you think you need to learn now?" He didn't wait for Callie to answer. "Soon as we stop, you take that book back."

"Yes, sir." Whatever had possessed her to think Ma and Pa would approve?

She should have known. She turned away and walked to the other side of the wagon, away from the others, where she trudged along, head bowed, disappointment weighing heavily on her shoulders. It hadn't occurred to her they would disapprove, but then, why wouldn't they? *Why do I need to learn how to read? Such foolishness.* She would not cry. Long ago, she'd learned tears got her nowhere. She must accept whatever fate life had in store and make the best of it.

She felt a tug at her skirt. Tommy was looking up at her. Usually, his expression was unreadable, as if he wasn't aware of his surroundings, but now he wore a worried frown.

She forced a smile. "I'm just a little tired, Tommy, but everything's fine."

She kept smiling, even though she had to return the McGuffey's Reader to Florida.

* * * *

The train stopped early when they encountered a clear, gently flowing stream, perfect for washing clothes, as well as a nearby meadow full of plush, sweet grass for the animals. When Callie finished her chores, she started toward Florida's wagon, book in hand. Before she got there, she passed Luke's campsite. He was there, building a fire. She would walk right by and hope he didn't see her.

"Hello, Callie, going for a lesson?"

She stopped in her tracks. He had spotted her and there was no way out. "I'm returning the book. I won't be taking any lessons."

"What?" He walked to where she stood. His eyebrows rose inquiringly as he faced her. "What do you mean?"

Being near him made her acutely aware of how overwhelmingly masculine he was. No man had ever made her knees go weak like they were doing now. No man had ever gotten her so disturbed her mind went blank and she had to grope for words. "I...I don't need to learn how to read and write. It's just...a waste of my time."

"The hell it is. You were dying to learn. Now all of a sudden it's a waste of time? I don't believe you."

His strong reaction surprised her. "Are you angry?"

He drew a deep breath, as if trying to quell some emotion welling within himself. "How old are you?"

"Twenty-two."

"You're a grown woman. Can't you make your own decisions?"

She wouldn't pretend she didn't understand his meaning. "Ma and Pa think I shouldn't be wasting my time with something I don't need. Maybe they're right. Maybe—"

"You know damn well they're not right. Why do you let them treat you that way?"

"Because I love them very much and owe them a lot."

"That's crazy. Why can't you stand up to them?"

It was hard to think straight when she was so close to such a powerful man, one so very sure of himself. For a moment, she couldn't speak. Even when she could, what would she say? She wished she could run away, but pride made her look him square in the eye. "You've asked a question I can't answer except that's the way it's always been."

"Then maybe you should think about—" The tenseness in his jaw relaxed. It was like he was trying to calm himself down. His mouth eased into a smile. "I have no right to tell you what to do, but I suggest you give some thought to what you want in this life. Maybe you should consider the possibility you want more than to be the Whitakers' slave for the rest of your days."

Before she could answer, a rider drew up. Luke was needed somewhere. "Got to go." He glanced down at the book in her hand. "Don't take it back yet. Think about what I said."

She was speechless.

Luke swing onto his horse and rode away.

Raising the book, she regarded the cover through eyes filled with tears. McGuffey's Reader. It might be old and tattered, but for the briefest of time, it held the key to her most heartfelt wish. And now... What did Luke say? *I suggest you give some thought to what you want in this life.* Maybe she should take his advice. Why shouldn't she learn to read if she wanted to? On the other hand...after all these years of obedience, how could she defy her stepparents? Imagining their wrath, her stomach tightened with anxiety. Ma was bad enough, but how could she face the bone-chilling anger Pa was sure to heap upon her head? On the other hand...

She so badly wanted to learn. Was it worth the risk?

What shall I do?

She made up her mind and headed back toward her wagon.

When Ma saw Callie, she inclined her head disapprovingly. "What's that in your hand? Didn't I tell you to return that book?"

Never in her life had she defied Ma. She swallowed with difficulty and finally found her voice. "I'm not going to return it."

A brittle silence followed, during which Ma simply stared at her, like she couldn't believe her ears. "You're disobeying me? Am I hearing you right?"

"I don't want to disobey you, but I do so want to learn to read. I promise I will in no way neglect my chores."

"What's this?" Pa came around the wagon. The sight of his angry face made her want to turn and run. "Did I hear you say you're disobeying your stepmother?"

Panic welled in her throat. She would admit she'd been foolish—beg forgiveness. Luke's words came back to her. *You might want more than to be the Whitakers' slave for the rest of your days.* No! She didn't want to be a slave. She wanted to learn to read and, by all that was holy, she would, despite God-only-knew-what might be the dreadful consequences. She pressed McGuffey's Reader to her heart and held on tight. "I don't mean to defy you, but this is important to me. I'm going to learn to read and write. I don't care what you say."

Ma gasped. Pa's mouth dropped open in disbelief. They looked at each other, signaling their astonishment that their up-to-now obedient stepdaughter dared rebel.

Callie took advantage of their shocked silence. "You don't have to worry. I'll get my chores done, like always."

"No you won't," Ma retorted. "You'll turn lazy. You'll be off to Mrs. Sawyer's every chance you get, having a high old time for yourself while the rest of us suffer because your work doesn't get done."

"That's not so." Despite Callie's fears, Ma's words sparked her anger. "How could you think such a thing? How could you even imply I'd turn lazy?" She had never complained about the tremendous amount of work she did, but now, like the force of a raging river, her resentment came tumbling out. "From dawn to dusk and beyond, I cook, I clean, and I mend. I wash the clothes for all of us because you can't do a thing and Lydia and Nellie are supposedly too fragile. When have I shirked my chores? When have I been lazy? Name one single time."

Now it was Ma's mouth that dropped open. "I'm not saying you've ever been lazy, Callie. What I'm saying is—"

"What you're saying is, you want to keep me ignorant." Callie clutched the book tighter to her bosom. "That's not going to happen. I *will* have my lessons from Mrs. Sawyer. I will also do my work, just as before, and that's the way it's going to be." Astounded at the words of defiance that had just left her mouth, she paused. She was in for it now. What would they do?

Pa's eyes grew hard. "I should throw you out for talking to your stepmother that way."

"Throw me out?" Callie could almost laugh if her situation weren't so dire. "Throw me out from where? From under the wagon? From out of the tent where I'm allowed a cramped little space in the corner?"

To Callie's amazement, Ma placed a restraining hand on her husband's arm. "We had best not throw her out, Caleb. She does work hard. To tell the truth, what with Lydia and Nellie being so sickly, I could hardly do without her."

"Suit yourself." Pa glared at Callie. "Take your lessons then, but be sure your work gets done." He walked away, obviously anxious to distance himself from all the unpleasantness.

"You heard him," Ma said. "As long as you keep up your chores—"

"You know I will."

"Then you have my permission." Ma turned on her heel and walked away. It was as if she, too, was anxious to escape a losing battle.

For a long moment, Callie stood where she was, stunned at her victory. Hard to believe all her fears were for nothing. All she'd had to do was stand up for herself, explain how she'd felt, and both her stepparents had eventually agreed with hardly a murmur. Unbelievable! Now, looking back, she couldn't imagine what she'd been so frightened about. She inhaled a deep breath and raised her chin. *I stood up for myself.* How shockingly bold. If she ever had another occasion to assert herself, she'd remember this small moment of triumph. She would also remember the man who gave her the courage to rebel. Now, more than ever, her heart did a flip-flop at the thought of him. *Thank you, Luke. How will I ever get you off my mind?*

* * * *

During the following week, the train made steady progress up the Little Blue Valley toward the Platte River. Callie began to see buffalo and other big game, including herds of Pronghorn antelope prized for their flesh, which tasted like the finest mutton. Andy and Len, who fancied themselves great hunters, had set out to shoot one but failed. The elusive animals, known for their beauty, grace, and speed, seemed to know the exact range of their guns. Much to the young men's frustration, they never got close enough for a decent shot. The company rejoiced when they reached the banks of the Platte River, knowing they'd safely put three hundred and sixteen miles behind them since Independence. That night, when Callie visited the Sawyers' campfire, she could have burst with pride when Florida exclaimed, "You've done it! In a week, you've learn the entire alphabet, A to Z. You should be very proud."

"I think I know Lesson One. Want to hear?"

"Of course."

Callie opened the primer. The page contained a picture of a dog at the top and words beneath. Pointing to each word with her finger, she read, "The...dog...ran."

"Perfect. See, you're reading already. Try Lesson Two."

Callie turned the page and again traced her finger over the words. "The...cat...is...on...the...mat."

Luke sat down beside her. "I knew you could do it. You've come a long way in just a week."

Callie's face warmed with pleasure. "They're not just funny-looking marks on a page anymore." Her family had pretty much ignored her efforts to read, so Luke's and Florida's praise made her feel doubly pleased. This was the first chance she'd had to talk to him since the day she defied Ma and Pa, all thanks to him. "I took your advice, you know."

A wry smile crossed his face. "How hard was it?"

"Not as hard as I thought." She described how, at first, she'd been worried, and then how surprised she'd been when Ma and Pa gave in with hardly a struggle. "I kept my word. I'm still doing all the work. They have nothing to complain about."

"So I've noticed."

Had she detected a touch of irony?

Apparently Florida had, too. "Don't mind Luke, honey. It's just he doesn't like to see you taken advantage of. Neither do I."

"I'm not. My family has been good to me. It's the least I can do. Maybe you can't see it, but they're really wonderful people."

She was surprised to see both Florida and Luke try to suppress their laughter.

"There are some of us who don't think so," Florida replied. "There are some who think you work far too hard while your stepmother and those two fancy princesses of hers don't work near hard enough." She bit her lip. "Uh-oh, I've said too much."

"Yes you have, Sis. It wouldn't be the first time." Luke cast an apologetic glance at Callie. "Don't mind us. We speak out of turn because we like you and don't like to see you taken for granted."

"I can take care of myself."

"Of course you can. You've got a lot of spunk, more than you realize. I'd like to see you use it more often."

Florida spoke up. "You're also a lot smarter than you realize, too. I'm amazed at how fast you're learning to read."

Callie didn't know how to answer. She wasn't accustomed to flattery of any kind. No one had ever called her smart before.

Florida went on, "Why haven't we seen you at the nightly campfires?"

Oh, no. They'd gone from one uncomfortable subject to another. Callie chose her words carefully. "I've wanted to come, but my chores keep me so busy there's never time."

"Humph!" Florida got an angry gleam in her eye. "Lydia and Nellie always find the time. Why can't you?"

If Florida only knew. Every night she heard the music and laughter from the campfire. She yearned to go, but Ma always found some last-minute chores for her to do, and by the time she finished, it was too late. And besides, she always had Tommy to feed and put to bed. Florida was right. Lydia and Nellie attended every gathering and always managed to have a wonderful time. Nellie, in particular, would crawl into the tent quivering with excitement. Coy danced with her! Coy said she had beautiful eyes! Coy was definitely in love with her, he just wasn't very talkative so he hadn't said so yet. Lydia was equally excited. She still flirted with Luke, but he ignored her. Now she had her eye on Magnus Ferguson. Each night, huddled under her blankets, Callie had to listen to her stepsister's ravings about how Magnus looked at her with fierce desire in his eyes. Without a doubt, he was madly in love with her, and it wouldn't be long before he told her so.

Callie gave Florida a rueful smile. "As you know, Lydia and Nellie are both in frail health. They—"

"Fiddlesticks! They're both as healthy as horses, far as I can see." Florida placed a firm hand on Callie's arm. "I want you to come to the campfire tonight. You deserve to come. If there's work to be done, let those two lazy stepsisters of yours do it."

"I'll try."

"Do more than try." Luke regarded her with sharp, assessing eyes. "People are thrown into an entirely different world when they go on these long treks clear across the country. Some change, mostly for the good, but there are a few who change for the worse. Either way, at the end of the journey, they're never the same as when they started out. That's especially true of you, Callie. You're changing. It's all for the best, but you don't realize it yet. It's time you did. It's time you valued yourself as highly as we do."

Florida clapped her hands. "Hear, hear! What Luke means is you deserve more than you think you do. You ought to be nicer to yourself. Am I making sense?"

"I suppose. Now you're making me wonder where I'd be if I hadn't gone on this trip."

"Where do you think you'd be?"

For several thoughtful seconds, Callie remained silent. "I suppose I'd be living as I've lived all my life, working dawn to dusk and doing as I was told."

Florida smiled with sympathy. "It's plain to see this journey is the best thing that could have happened to you. You've seen a bit of the world, and you must have noticed by now not everyone treats you like your family does."

"I suppose..." She would never say anything bad about her family, yet Luke's and Florida's words made a lot of sense. They had caught her unaware. She didn't know what to say but had a lot to think about. What she knew, for sure, was she very much wanted to join them at the campfire tonight, and she would be there, no matter what Ma said.

Chapter 6

Luke rode off. Callie finished her reading lesson with Florida. Soon they were joined by Florida's oldest daughter, Hetty. At sixteen, the tall, dark-eyed girl was pretty, vivacious and an indispensable help to her mother. When Callie rose to leave, clutching her reader, Hetty asked, "Will you be at the campfire tonight? There's going to be dancing and lots of single young men for partners."

"Yes, I'm going to be there." Callie looked down at her tattered dress. Who would dance with her, the way she looked? And her hair! "I won't be the belle of the ball, though, not in this dress, and my hair is such a mess."

"I've got an idea." Hetty arose and extended her hand to Callie. "You must come with me. I've been dying to do something with that hair of yours."

Florida nodded approval. At Callie's hesitation, she said, "Don't worry. Hetty has a knack for fixing hair."

Soon Callie was sitting in the Sawyers' large tent, a towel tossed around her shoulders. Hetty, armed with a pair of scissors, stood assessing her hair.

"What are you going to do?" Callie tried to conceal how nervous she felt. "It's never been cut. I just pull it back and tie it in a sort-of knot."

"That's the trouble. With your hair pulled back from your face like that, it looks awful. Sorry, but it does." Hetty untied the bit of fabric holding Callie's untidy bun in place and let her thick, auburn hair tumble down her back. "Look at that! You have beautiful hair, all long, thick, and curly. I never would have guessed."

"Do you have a mirror?" Callie wasn't sure what Hetty planned and wanted to keep an eye on her.

"No mirror. Not until I'm through."

"You won't cut it all off, will you? I like my long hair."

"Trust me."

If Hetty hadn't sounded so sure of herself, Callie might have fled. Instead, when she first heard the snip of the scissors, she resigned herself to the worst and hoped for the best. After all, she couldn't look much worse than she already did, so she didn't have much to lose.

After a lot of snipping, not only in the back but around Callie's face, Hetty announced, "I'm done. Want to see?"

"I'm dying to see."

Hetty handed her a small hand mirror. "You can't see the back, I'm afraid, but you'll see enough to give you an idea of what you look like." She grinned. "You're going to like it."

Fearing the worst, Callie gazed in the mirror. She hardly recognized the face that looked back. "Is this me?"

"Of course it's you." Hetty stood back to admire her work. "I never guessed, but your hair has a natural curl. See the little ringlets around your forehead and down around your ears? I cut it short in the front so that the curls soften your face. No more of that skinned-back look."

Florida pulled back the tent flap and stuck her head in. She took one look at Callie and whooped with delight. "Fantastic! Some women would die for that hair. I never realized. How lucky you are to have naturally curly hair, and such a rich auburn color. I swear, you must never pull it back tight again."

"Never." Hetty nodded emphatically. "I trimmed your hair in the back, too, so the ends look nice and smooth. Just one more thing…" She reached into a bag of clothes and pulled out a blue satin ribbon that she tied around Callie's hair, forming a pretty bow on top. "The finishing touch."

Callie stared into the mirror. "I don't look so bad."

Florida entered the tent. "Silly girl, you look beautiful. I just wish you had something decent to wear, like…" She turned to Hetty. "Do you remember those clothes we found by the side of the trail? Wasn't there a dress—?"

"A dress that was too tight for me, as I recall. It's in the wagon. Let's see if Callie can wear it."

While Hetty was gone to get the dress, Florida explained how they'd found the discarded clothing by the side of the trail, along with many household items. "Those poor people. I guess their animals got tired and they had to lighten the load, like so many others." She gave a sad sigh. "I can only hope it doesn't happen to us."

Hetty soon returned with a full-skirted dress and held it up for Callie to see. Made of cotton calico, it was patterned with tiny, light-colored clover leaves against a dark purple background. It had a fitted bodice, tiny buttons down the front, and simple, long, slim sleeves. "Isn't this adorable? You must try it on."

Callie loved it on sight. "It's beautiful. I couldn't possibly wear such a dress."

"Pray why not?" Florida inquired.

"Because..." She couldn't think what to answer.

"Because you think you're not good enough to wear it?"

"Not exactly." How could she explain she'd never had anything but worn-out hand-me-downs all her life? She'd never expected she'd ever wear anything so beautiful. This was all too new, too overwhelming.

Hetty looked puzzled. "I don't understand. Is it because you don't want to wear some woman's cast-off clothing?"

"Oh, no! That has nothing to do with it."

"Maybe you're feeling sorry for the poor woman who had to throw away her dress and you don't think you should take it."

"Yes, I do feel sorry for her, but it isn't that."

"Then what is it?"

After a long, thoughtful moment, Callie realized what her problem was. She'd been so deprived all her life she didn't know how to handle someone's generosity and kindness. *That's why I'm being so downright silly, and that's got to stop this instant.* She reached for the dress. "That poor woman is long gone, isn't she? We couldn't give it back even if we wanted to." She pulled her old dress over her head and slipped on the new one. Would it fit when she buttoned it? She'd die if it didn't. She fastened the row of tiny buttons that ran down the bodice. Perfect. Not too loose, not too tight.

"It was made for you," Hetty exclaimed.

Callie spread her arms and twirled around. "It does seem to fit. How do I look?"

Florida beamed her approval. "It's a marvelous fit and shows off that nice figure of yours. Land's sake! I didn't even know you had a figure in those two baggy old dresses you wear. I'm so glad we thought of it. I'd like to believe the woman who owned it wouldn't mind a bit."

"So do I."

"You must take it off now. Take it home. Do your chores. Then when you're done, you'll have the fun of getting all fixed up for the campfire tonight. I guarantee the boys will be after you, and you'll dance every dance."

Callie couldn't imagine such a thing, but she did as she was told and soon was back in her ragged gown, the new dress and ribbon securely bundled under her arm.

* * * *

When Luke returned, he found his sister alone by the cook fire. As he got off his horse, Florida remarked, "That was quite a speech you made to Callie, talking about how people change. I've never heard you put that many words together at one time."

"Just telling her the truth. She needed to hear it."

"That's true. I hate the way the Whitakers treat her. When she stood up for herself about learning to read, I thought that would be the end of them ordering her around, but now I don't know. That nasty stepmother of hers still heaps the work on her, and she allows it. All the while, those two lazy stepsisters act like they're Queen of the May."

"The Whitakers are the only family she's ever known. She doesn't see them as we do."

"She should." Florida gave a firm nod of her ample chin. "Speaking of the stepsisters, I've seen that Lydia Whitaker batting her big blue eyes at you."

"So?" Luke remained blank-faced.

"She's sweet on you, always trying to get your attention."

"I'll handle it."

"Oh, you are so exasperating. The girls fall all over themselves trying to get your attention. Why? I don't know. Is it because you never pay them any mind? You must have noticed. It's just so annoying you never tell me what you really feel."

"About what?"

"Damnation! About if you've ever been in love. Have you, Luke?"

"Come on, Sis, I haven't had the time."

"Bosh! You're thirty. You should be married with a dozen kids by now. Of course…" Her brow furrowed. "It all goes back to that horrible day, doesn't it? I so wish——"

"Don't."

She sighed. "Sorry. All the same, I hate to see you spend the rest of your life alone."

Luke shrugged. "I'm not a marrying man."

"That's what they all say. Out of all the women who've thrown themselves at your feet, there's not one you find attractive?"

"I didn't say that, did I?"

"Aha!" Florida's face took on a gleam of triumph. "Who is it? Someone here in the wagon train? Is it Lydia? If it is, I swear I'll try to like the little scatterbrain."

"My God, Florida, you're such a snoop." Luke gave his sister an affectionate pat on the arm and walked away.

* * * *

Callie had nearly reached her wagon when Coy Barnett fell in step beside her. She had never spoken with the young gold seeker, although sometimes when he passed by her campfire, she became aware of his probing gaze. She didn't know why he stared the way he did. With her ragged, poorly fitting dress and hastily combed hair, she wasn't anything a man would look at twice. Yet something about Coy's bold gaze signaled he liked what he saw. Not in a polite way, though. It was more in a slimy sort of way, like he'd do the same with anyone under the age of fifty and female. She always turned her head away when she saw him.

Coy walked along beside her, a cocky smile on his face. "You look nice today. Did you do something with your hair?"

Even his simple question made her mad. "Nothing much."

"Yeah? Well, it looks different. How come I don't see you at the campfires? Don't you like to dance?"

Funny how she resented Coy's asking. When talking about it to Luke, she hadn't minded. "I might be there tonight." She made her answer as curt as she could.

"Good." He raised a suggestive eyebrow. "You and me should get better acquainted."

Mercifully, they arrived at her wagon. "Got to go," she called over her shoulder as she darted away, grateful to escape the disgusting man. What did Nellie see in him? She could not imagine. She had to admit he was handsome with his dark good looks, but that bold, lustful look in his eyes annoyed her. Nellie could have him.

She plunged into preparations for supper, only half aware of what she was doing. Her head spun with all the things she had to think about. Should she or should she not insist on going to the campfire tonight? Luke had said they liked her. He was talking about him and his sister, but could he have meant he liked her in a special way? No, that wasn't possible and she'd be crazy to think he did. But still…

What would the family say about her hair? Would they make fun of her? She needn't have worried. No one noticed, or at least no one said anything. As she served supper and cleaned up afterward, more of Luke's words kept echoing in her head. *I want you to come to the campfire tonight.* His remark meant nothing, other than he was being polite. Even so, was it possible he might ask her to dance? The very thought caused a tug of excitement in the pit of her stomach. It also caused her to gather her courage. She stood up to Ma once. She would do it again.

When the last of the pots and pans were washed and stored away, Callie took a deep breath. "Ma, my work's done, so I'll be going to the campfire tonight."

"No you're not. You've got to stay here with Tommy."

It was the answer she had expected. "I'm taking Tommy with me. I'm sure he'd enjoy watching the fun and dancing."

Ma's eye widened with surprise. "You plan to keep the child up beyond his bedtime?"

She suppressed a smile. Ordinary routines fell apart on a wagon train. Parents had so much to cope with, they didn't have time for their children. Many were left to run wild. If not for Callie's efforts, so would Tommy. "It won't hurt him a bit. Lots of children attend the campfire and are none the worse for it."

Ma squinted in surprise. "Your hair! What have you done?"

"I had it cut a little. About the campfire, I'd like to go."

Ma shrugged with indifference. "I suppose just this once won't hurt. Mind you, keep an eye on Tommy."

"I won't stay real late." In her small triumph, Callie wished she'd said that "just this once" wasn't enough. Well, she'd fix that later. Her spirits soared. She was going to wear her new dress tonight. Wear that blue ribbon in her hair. She'd see Luke and, maybe, just maybe, he'd ask her to dance.

* * * *

A festive mood reigned that evening among the members of the Ferguson wagon train. As the moon rose over the pine trees, nearly everyone gathered around the big campfire in the middle of the clearing. By the time Callie and Tommy arrived, Jake, the fiddler, was playing, accompanied by Reverend Wilkins's son, Colton, on his banjo.

"Glad you could make it," Florida called with a friendly wave. "Come set yourselves over here." When Callie drew closer, she saw Florida's eyes light with approval. "You look as pretty as a picture in that dress."

Soon Callie had Tommy comfortably seated with a good view of the dancers. Wide-eyed, he watched the couples twirl and prance to a waltz, then a polka. He was fascinated, not the least bit frightened, as Ma predicted. Callie watched, too. Not far away, Ma and Pa sat observing the dancers. Nellie was dancing with Coy. Lydia was dancing with Magnus, looking mighty pleased with herself.

Florida patted her arm. "You should be dancing, too."

Callie made a rueful grimace. "Remember? I don't know how to dance."

"We'll soon fix that. Hetty, come here," Florida called to her daughter who was dancing with one of the hired hands. Hetty broke away from her partner and joined them. "Do you think we could teach Callie to dance?"

"Sure, Ma." Her young face flushed from dancing, Hetty clasped Callie's hands and pulled her to her feet. "There isn't much to it. In the cotillions, you just watch close and do what the other girls are doing. If you're dancing with a partner, you follow his lead."

"You make it sound so easy."

"Where's the fun if it isn't easy?" Florida said. "You worry too much. You should relax and enjoy yourself."

Florida's words worked their magic. With Hetty's help, Callie put aside her doubts and soon caught the rhythm of the music. Before she knew it, her feet were doing the steps without her having to think about it. "I'm dancing." Her heart lifted to the rousing version of "Goodnight, Irene" Jake was playing on his fiddle.

Just then Magnus walked up. He stood watching her with admiring eyes. "See, it's not so hard."

She felt so good, so pleased with herself, she laughed aloud. "I guess it's not."

He stepped forward and tapped Hetty's shoulder. "I'm cutting in." After Hetty backed away, he gave her a slight bow. "Would you care to dance, Miss Callie?"

Magnus Ferguson, the esteemed leader of the wagon train, was asking her to dance! How flattering. From what she'd heard, several of the single women in the company had, as Florida put it, "set their caps" for the handsome bachelor. Even so, sudden doubts assailed her. "I'm not sure—"

"Of course you can." Magnus gestured toward the uneven, rock-strewn ground. "If you trip, you can blame it on a rock or a weed. Besides, who cares?" He took her hand, circled his arm around her waist, and off they went to the lively tune of "My Home's in Montana," which Jake had just started on his fiddle. After a few faltering moments, Callie got the hang of the dance. Before long, she felt like she'd been dancing all her life. What fun this was. While she danced, she felt many eyes upon her. Ma and Pa, sitting on the sidelines, stared like they'd never seen such an astounding spectacle as Little Mouse dancing. Lydia watched, too, her expression changing from astonishment to disdain, to disapproval, to... Was that anger? Never mind. Nothing was going to spoil her good time.

When the fiddler took a break, Magnus walked her back to where her little brother was sitting. Tommy clapped his hands. "Callie...dance!" His eyes sparkled with interest.

"He's smiling." Callie looked toward Ma and Pa in hopes they'd be as delighted as she was to see their son looking happy and showing an interest in his surroundings.

They weren't. Their expressions hadn't changed except Ma now glared in her direction. "He should be in bed," Ma called, her lips set in a grim line.

"He's fine, Ma."

Lydia approached, batting her eyes and flashing a dazzling smile at Magnus. "You must dance this with me. You know how I love the waltz."

Magnus smiled pleasantly, excused himself to Callie and danced away. To Callie's surprise, she wasn't left alone for long. Soon one of the Gowdys' hired hands asked her to dance. After him, a steady stream of partners prevented her from sitting down for even a moment. The single young men of the train wondered where she'd been and why they'd never noticed her before.

Where was Luke? Florida must have been right. Luke never attended these gatherings.

She couldn't stop dancing. The older people began to leave, including Ma and Pa, who retired for the night, taking Tommy with them. Callie hardly noticed. She had so many partners, she never sat down. Late in the evening, Magnus Ferguson returned. While they stepped to a lively waltz, he peered at her intently. "You look very pretty tonight, Miss Whitaker."

His praise was the crowning touch to a wonderful evening. They danced every dance until Jake stopped playing and lowered his fiddle. "That's it, folks! Time to git to bed."

Magnus took her hand, his eyes warm and friendly. "Good night, Miss Whitaker. I trust I'll see you here more often."

Someone doused the campfire. As the last of the crowd drifted away, Callie started back to her wagon. Luke appeared out of the darkness and fell in step beside her.

"Luke, I'm surprised. I didn't see you at the bonfire."

He returned a cynical chuckle. "They don't pay me to dance with the ladies."

"Even so, you can't be working all the time. Isn't that what you accuse me of doing?"

He let a long moment pass. "So you danced with Magnus."

"You think he's a fool, but I don't. I'm honored he asked me." She waited for his reply, but other than a muttered oath under his breath, he remained silent. "You told me to put a little fun in my life, and that's what I'm doing."

"Having fun with Magnus Ferguson?" He moved his shoulders in a shrug of disgust. "Are you planning to join all the single girls in his train who are after him?"

She stiffened at his words. "That's none of your business."

They had almost reached her wagon. He stopped. She turned to face him. In the light of a half-moon, she could hardly see his face, yet she knew he was peering at her with an intensity that surprised her.

"You're right. It's not my business." His hands slid up her arms, bringing her closer. With a swift motion she didn't expect, he gave her a swift kiss on her forehead. "Good night, Callie." Abruptly he turned and disappeared into the darkness.

Why had he sought her out? Why had he kissed her? It was only on the forehead, yet it wasn't the way he'd kiss his sister. Hard to know what Luke was thinking. Could it be he liked her and was jealous because she danced with Magnus? There was something awfully strange about Luke, Florida, too. They didn't like to talk about themselves. It was like they had a secret, something terrible from their past. What was wrong? Maybe someday he'd tell her. She hoped so. Lately, she was finding it hard to keep Luke off her mind. And now, that kiss. It was only on the forehead, but she wasn't going to forget it.

Chapter 7

When Callie entered the tent, Lydia's irritated voice cut through the pitch-black darkness. "Where have you been?"

Callie could hardly think what to answer. "Nowhere."

"Were you with him?"

"Who?"

"Magnus," Lydia fairly screeched. "I saw you dancing with him."

"So? He danced with all the girls."

"Where's Nellie?" It was more an accusation than a question.

Callie peered in the direction of Nellie's blankets but in the darkness couldn't see a thing. "She's not here?"

"No."

"Then I don't know."

Lydia's voice filled with a combination of worry and disgust. "Then she's gone off with Coy."

"Are you sure? If she did, Pa will—"

"Pa will kill her. She'd better get back here, and soon."

Callie had fallen asleep when, in the small hours of the morning, she was awakened when Nellie stealthily entered the tent and crept into her bed.

Lydia woke up, too. "Nellie, is that you?"

"Of course it's me."

"Where have you been?"

"Coy and I took a walk." Excitement bubbled in Nellie's voice.

Lydia drew in a shocked breath. "What if Pa finds out? He'll skin you alive."

"He won't if you don't tell him." Nellie sounded not the least concerned. "Oh, Lydia, I'm so in love with Coy Barnett. I'll die if I can't have him."

An alarmed "Shhh" came from Lydia's direction. "Don't wake up Pa. Is Coy in love with you?"

"Yes."

"How do you know?"

"Because he said so."

"Did he ask you to marry him?"

"Not yet, but he will. I know because we've sealed our love. It was beautiful."

There was a long, shocked silence. "Sealed your love? Dear God, don't tell me you did it."

A soft, knowing trace of laughter said it all. "Isn't that what people do when they're in love? If you expect me to say I'm sorry, I won't."

Callie had listened in silence but could no longer hold her tongue. "Oh, Nellie, I'm afraid he's deceiving you. Coy Barnett is—"

"I knew you were listening," Nellie harshly whispered. "You'd better not say anything."

"What is there to say except you'd better be careful."

"Listen to Little Mouse! She actually has an opinion."

Lydia giggled. "She thinks she's smart now she knows how to read."

"She's not so smart when it comes to love. She's never even been kissed."

"And probably never will," Lydia added.

Callie turned her back and burrowed deep into her blankets. Nellie could be heading for a world of trouble. Maybe she should say more, but she was only Little Mouse and not worth listening to. *That's not true.* In the past, she'd always accepted her stepsisters' sneering remarks without question. Was she really so stupid her opinion didn't matter? Florida's words came back to her—*you're a lot smarter than you realize.* By God, she was! Not only that, she might be smarter than both Lydia and Nellie put together. Even after they'd been to school, they could barely read and could hardly put one intelligent thought next to another.

Lydia was mad at her because of Magnus. Not that she cared. In fact, she wouldn't waste another moment thinking about them. She wanted her last waking thought to be about Luke, not her stepsisters. She wanted to fall asleep thinking about that wondrous moment when he had kissed her on the forehead. Maybe he wanted to do more. He was such a mystery, she still wasn't sure.

* * * *

Next morning, after Callie fixed breakfast and finished her chores, she found she had a few spare minutes before the train began its trek for the day. She got out McGuffey's Reader and sat down with Tommy.

Thank goodness, the boy had completely recovered from his near drowning in the river. Only a few weeks had passed, but he seemed to have forgotten his terror. In many ways he'd improved since they left Tennessee. Back home, he had hardly seemed aware of the world around him. He'd hardly spoken, had only repeated a few words over and over again. He would sit on the floor in a corner for hours, rolling a ball, or rocking back and forth. The family had ignored him most of the time, all except Callie, but with her endless chores, even she had barely spared enough time to keep him clean and fed.

The weeks on the trail had done him good. Now he seemed more alert, spoke words that were meaningful, and didn't rock as much. Callie wasn't sure why he'd improved. Perhaps it was because there were no dark corners for him to sit in anymore. Of necessity, the family paid him more attention, Callie most of all. She was trying to teach him to read, a hopeless task thus far.

She opened the reader to Lesson Four which pictured a hen standing on a box. "The...fat...hen...is...on...the...box." She ran her finger over the page as she read. Tommy gave no reaction, but that was all right. She wasn't about to give up.

Nellie appeared. When she saw what Callie was doing, she shook her head and laughed with scorn. "What a waste of time."

"No, it's not." How many times had she said those words before? Why couldn't her family understand Tommy needed help and encouragement, not their constant ridicule? Nellie was the worst, always scoffing at the boy. "Can't you see how he's improved?"

Nellie peered down her nose. "I can't be bothered."

Just then Coy and a couple of friends came riding by. As he passed, he touched a finger to the brim of his hat and looked at Nellie in such a lecherous way it made Callie's skin crawl.

"You'd better watch out, Nellie." The words came out of her mouth before she could stop them. "Coy Barnett is nothing but trouble."

Nellie's expression turned dark as a thundercloud. "Mind your own business. I know what I'm doing." She strode away.

What was the use? Why had she bothered? From now on, she'd keep her mouth shut. Nellie wasn't going to listen no matter what she, or anyone else, said, and that was too bad, because Nellie's so-called romance wasn't going to end well. In fact, it could easily end in complete disaster.

Later in the morning, Callie, holding Tommy's hand, was walking alongside the wagon with her stepsisters when a group of Indians on horseback approached from behind. The wagon train halted. Apprehension grew as the single file of Indians passed by with hardly a glance in their direction. The company had encountered a few Indians along the way, but these looked the strangest of all with feathers in their hair, bare-chested, wearing nothing except buckskin breechcloths, leggings, and moccasins. At the sight of them, Tommy screamed and buried his face in Callie's skirt. Lydia and Nellie, both shrieking, ran to the rear of the wagon and clambered inside just as Luke rode up on Rascal and came to a dust-stirring stop. "Nothing to fear."

Ma and Pa sat frozen on the wagon seat.

"They're Pawnees passing through on their way to their hunting grounds. They're looking for buffalo, not white settlers to massacre."

Pa asked, "Will they attack us?"

Luke shook his head. "Those Pawnees are a lot more interested in saving themselves than attacking us. There's a party of Sioux in the neighborhood. There's bad blood between the Pawnees and Sioux. Like as not, they'll soon be battling each other."

"Are you sure?"

Fear filled her stepfather's eyes. It dwelt in his voice. So surprising. She'd grown up believing nothing in the world could frighten her strong, all-powerful stepfather. He could handle any situation that came along. Here was a side of him she'd never seen before.

Luke gave Pa a reassuring smile. "They won't attack us, Mister Whitaker. To be safe, we're going to circle the wagons and stop for the day. There might be trouble ahead, and we want to avoid it."

Despite Luke's reassurances, Lydia, wide-eyed with fear, parted the canvas flaps and stuck her head out. "Are they going to scalp us?"

"Just a precaution. Nothing to be alarmed about."

Ma pointed a trembling finger at the Indians, mounted on spotted horses, who still passed silently by. "Aren't they all savages who'd kill us rather than look at us? Look at how they're dressed, practically naked." Her voice bordered on hysteria.

"That's the way they dress, ma'am. They won't bother us."

"What do you suggest we do?" The tremor in Pa's voice gave his nervousness away.

"Do nothing. If we hear the sounds of battle, we stay alert. Otherwise, we ignore them. This is the Indians' business, not ours. The farther we stay away, the better." Luke was about to leave when he caught sight of Tommy peering at him with frightened eyes from the folds of Callie's skirt. He swung from his horse. "Don't be afraid, child." He knelt beside

Tommy and put a comforting hand on his shoulder. "The Indians aren't going to hurt you."

Tommy turned his head toward Luke. "Bad...Indians."

Luke, his dark eyes gentle and understanding, gazed straight into Tommy's gray ones. "I promise they won't hurt you. Do you believe me?"

After a moment, Tommy nodded his head ever so slightly.

Amazing! Hardly anyone ever got through to the child, and it was Luke, of all people, who did. Callie gave him a grateful smile. "Thank you, Mister McGraw. He believes you."

Luke got to his feet. "He should. We're going to be fine." After a final, confident pat on Tommy's shoulder, Luke mounted his horse and rode off to the next wagon in line.

Callie watched after him. There'd been nothing in his manner to indicate they'd had a special moment the night before, but why should there be? A kiss on the forehead didn't mean a thing.

The wagons formed a circle. Soon they spied another group of Indians in the distance. Word rapidly spread this was a party of Sioux Indians. They came closer. Judging from the guns and bows and arrows they carried, it was a war party. Along with everyone else, Callie watched warily as the Sioux passed silently by on their horses. They were dressed much like the Pawnees. Some wore heavy buffalo furs around their shoulders. All wore necklaces and armbands made of seashells, metal, and beads.

When the last of the Sioux passed by, disappearing over a ridge in the distance, the nervous members of the wagon train heaved a collective sigh of relief. But too soon. Callie was building a fire for supper when gunshots rang from the other side of the ridge, accompanied by wild shouts and horses neighing. Lydia and Nellie hid in their tent, loath to come out where, according to Lydia, they could be scalped and worse at any moment.

Ma panicked immediately. "We'll all be killed! We should never have left Tennessee."

"Shut your mouth, woman." Pa had retrieved his guns from the wagon and now sat ramming gunpowder into his rifle.

Callie continued fixing supper. If Luke said not to worry, then she wouldn't. Indians or no, her family and the hired hands would still expect to eat. By the time they finished an uneasy meal, the sounds of battle had faded. Everyone waited warily, but as time went by, and no wild savages burst into their camp to slaughter them all, tensions eased. Finally, just before dusk, some of the young men of the company, including Coy

Barnett, stopped by to announce they were riding to the top of the ridge to see what happened.

When Coy returned, he stopped by their campsite. "Good evening, ladies." Still on his horse, he swept off his hat in an exaggerated greeting, an annoying gesture because of its mockery and insincerity. Everything about him was deceitful. She didn't understand how Nellie could tolerate someone so despicable.

By now, both her stepsisters had gotten over their fright. They gave Coy a warm greeting, especially Nellie, who fell all over herself, so smitten was she by Coy's presence.

He looked down from atop his horse, a smirk on his face. "Want to see some dead Indians?"

A wave of giggles and feigned hysterics met Coy's question. Nellie slammed a hand to her chest. "Oh my stars, you mean the Indian battle?"

"Silly girl, what do you think I meant?"

"What if they're still there?"

"They're not. They're gone, at least the live ones."

"Then what—?"

"You'll have to come and see for yourself. Unless you're chicken." Coy gave a contemptuous lift of his lip. "Well, girls, are you too chicken to go?"

Lydia thrust her hands to her hips. "We are no such thing, Coy Barnett. How do you know there are dead Indians there?"

"We saw them from the top of the ridge. If you're too sissy to go, say so. I'm going. I want to get me some of that Indian jewelry. They wear silver, you know."

Ma and Pa were listening from the wagon seat. At the mention of silver, Ma's face lit up. "Maybe we should all go. Wait up, Coy." Tommy was playing quietly by the wagon. Ma climbed down and took his hand. "Come on, boy. We're going to see dead Indians."

"Oh, no!" Callie blurted the words before she even had time to think. "Ma, that's a horrible idea. Tommy's much too young to be looking at dead people."

Pa snorted with disgust. "That's foolishness," he shouted down. "Those Indians aren't people. They're animals. Take him, Hester. It'll do the boy good. Make a man of him."

Callie continued to argue until she could see Pa's mind was made up, and so was Ma's. She had no desire to see dead Indians. The very idea was disgusting, but in order to watch over Tommy, she'd have to go along whether she liked it or not.

Except for Pa, who declared he had better things to do, the entire Whitaker family soon was following Coy on foot, trudging through a heavy growth of cedar and pine trees. It was a merry group. If Callie hadn't known better, she'd have thought they were on their way to some sort of party. Nellie and Lydia, in particular, kept up their laughter, acting as if it were a cause for celebration. When they reached the top of the ridge, Callie looked down on a sight she'd never forget. A large meadow lay before her. At first glance, it appeared to be a pleasant spot, covered with green grass, dotted here and there by splotches of color provided by tulips, larkspurs, roses, and other flowers Callie had never dreamed grew wild. Several objects lay scattered about the meadow, dark shapes of some sort that, at first, Callie couldn't make out. Full of self-importance, Coy pointed. "There's your dead Indians, girls. Let's go take a look."

They all walked down to the meadow and started across, Lydia and Nellie chatting excitedly. Ma went right along, eager for a closer look. Callie followed with dragging steps. She dreaded going closer, but Ma still held on to Tommy, so she had no choice.

They drew close to the first body, that of a young Indian, not more than twenty or so. He lay on his back, empty eyes staring at the sky. The feathered shafts of several arrows protruded from his body. His scalp was gone, leaving his head bare, bloody, and so ghastly, Callie could hardly bear to look.

Coy nudged the body with the toe of his boot. "See? Nothing to fear, girls. He's as dead as they get."

Nellie made a face. "Eeew. How disgusting."

Coy nudged the corpse again. "You know what they say—a good Indian is a dead Indian." He gazed expectantly at Lydia and Nellie. "Anybody going to throw up?"

Lydia tilted her chin. "Not I."

Nellie answered, "I won't be throwing up over any Indian."

Coy prodded the Indian's head, causing blood to spurt from the young brave's scalp. Tommy gave an anguished cry and broke from his mother's grasp. He ran to Callie and threw his arms around her. Clasping him tight, Callie opened her mouth to yell at Ma, then clamped it shut again. *I mustn't.* Never had she raised her voice to her stepmother. How could she start now? She'd never do such a thing, regardless of the reason. "Tommy needs to go back, Ma." She managed to sound almost pleasant, the best she could do considering the rage growing inside her.

"Then take him back." Hester didn't seem at all concerned over her son's welfare. She pointed to the silver bands that circled the dead brave's arms. "Could those bands be of silver?"

Coy nodded.

"Then I'd like to have them. Can you cut them off?" She directed her attention to a necklace of what appeared to be grizzly bear claws that circled the Indian's neck. "How about that necklace he's wearing? It's pretty fancy, but maybe my girls can get some use out of it."

Nellie shook her head. "I don't want to wear some dirty old Indian necklace."

"We should take it," said Lydia. "Maybe I could use it for a decoration. After we get to California, I could hang it on my bedroom wall or something."

Ma nodded. "Go ahead, Coy, cut it off."

Callie watched Coy bend, knife in hand, to cut off the bear claw necklace. The words burst from deep within her. She had no way of stopping them. "Stop! Don't you dare cut that necklace off."

Coy looked up in surprise.

"You heard me, Coy Barnett. I don't care if he is an Indian. You should treat him with respect. He's not an animal."

Ma's mouth dropped open. "Callie! Apologize this instant."

Still pressed against Callie's skirt, Tommy let out a wail so pitiful it filled Callie with more fury. She directed a scathing gaze at her stepmother. "See what you've done? The child is terrified. You should never have brought him here. None of us should be here, laughing and making light of something so horrible." Her voice gained strength as she talked. It was like a dam had broken, releasing her pent-up anger in a horrendous gush of words impossible to contain.

Ma shook her head in amazement. "I don't know what's come over you."

Before Callie could answer, a voice came from behind her. "Put down that knife, Coy. You touch that necklace, and you're dead." *Luke*. He barely spoke above a whisper, yet no one could mistake the cold authority in his voice.

Coy slipped the knife in his pocket and backed away. "Golly, Mister McGraw, it's only a dead Indian. He won't care if I take his necklace."

Luke stepped forward. At first glance, he appeared calm and composed like always, but Callie sensed his anger from the way his jaw clenched, the way a vein throbbed above one eyebrow. "It's not an ordinary necklace.

Shirley Kennedy

Pawnee men must earn the right to wear a grizzly bear claw necklace. They earn it through an act of bravery."

"That so?" Coy struggled not to wither under Luke's stony gaze. "Still, he don't need it now. Why can't I take it? They're nothing but savages."

Luke cast a withering gaze at the little group gathered around the corpse. "Go home, all of you. There's nothing to see here. You don't want to be around when the Pawnees come back to bury their dead." He turned his attention to Coy. "They're not savages. They're people whose land we're stealing. They don't like it. Can you blame them? Don't condemn them because they're different. You only condemn yourself if you do. Now go, and go quietly. Remember, this isn't a meadow anymore. It's a sacred burial ground."

"Can't we take the jewelry?" Coy asked.

"It's a sacrilege to loot their bodies." Luke's words came out as cold and clear as ice water. "Go. Just go."

Shocked into silence, the group left without further protest. Starting back, Callie, Tommy in hand, walked behind Ma and her stepsisters.

"So Little Mouse found a voice." Nellie murmured, loud enough for Callie to hear.

Lydia shrugged and whispered, "Now she's in big trouble with Ma."

Callie's rage rose again. Maybe it had never gone away. "I am *not* Little Mouse. Don't call me that anymore."

"Well, listen to *her*." Nellie jested.

Ma glanced back to make sure they were out of Luke's hearing. "If you ask me, that man has lost his mind."

Nellie sniffed indignantly. "Imagine! Treating Indians like they are human."

Ma turned around and glared at Callie. "And what got into you, missy? How dare you talk to me like that! I've a mind to——"

"What, Ma?" Callie tossed her head. "Send me to bed without my supper? It's a little late for that, isn't it?" She hardly heeded the shock on her family's faces. At this point, nothing they said or did could possibly matter. She'd seen them for what they really were. Shocking! How could she not have realized after all these years? Disgusting! She must get away, go someplace where she could calm down, pull herself together. Below, through the trees, she spotted the slim blue line of a stream. "Lydia, take Tommy." She placed Tommy's hand in Lydia's, bolted from the group, and found her way down the wooded incline to the stream. Big boulders lined the banks. She found a flat one and sat down, grateful no one had followed.

For a time, she sat in a daze, waiting for her heart to stop hammering. "What are you doing here by yourself?" It was Luke, calling from atop the steep incline. Somehow he'd spotted her.

She called back, "I'm fine. I don't want to go back yet, that's all."

Luke swiftly descended the hill to where she sat. The flat space on the rock was big enough for two, so he settled himself beside her, his closeness knocking all rational thought from her head. The tough, lean look about him, the set of his broad shoulders in his buckskin jacket—oh, yes, everything about him was so disturbing. He frowned. "It's not a good idea to be out here by yourself. In case you haven't noticed, there are Indians around who are none too friendly."

"I don't care. I—" She swallowed hard. Biting back tears, she couldn't continue.

"It's that family of yours, isn't it?"

At first, loyalty prevented her from replying until she could no longer control the words of anger and resentment that were bursting to be said. "Ma—Nellie—Lydia—I'll never forget how they talked over the body of that poor dead Indian. How could they?" She balled her fists, making no effort to control her trembling. "How heartless! How disgusting! How—"

"They're your family, Callie."

Luke's calm voice brought her back from the depths of her blind rage. "I know they're my family. I love them all, but I think they acted horrible today. It's like…" She fought for the right words. "All these years I've always looked up to them, like I was nothing and they were so much better than me. Not after today. How could I have been so blind? Why did I never notice how selfish and shallow they are?"

"Remember when I told you how some people change on these long journeys?"

"I remember." How could she forget that night she first met Luke? She remembered every word he'd said.

"Your family has stayed pretty much the same, but you've changed. Now you see them through different eyes."

"I should never have left Tennessee."

"Leaving Tennessee was the best thing you ever did. If you'd stayed home, would you have learned how to read?"

"Probably not."

"If you'd stayed home, would you ever have stood up to your Ma like you did today?"

"Never." She bit her lip in thought. "I'm not sure how I feel about talking to her that way. I know I was right, but I feel guilty just the same."

"You shouldn't." Luke pressed his hand over hers. "The old days are gone. You can never go back to what you were."

"Ma was really mad. I doubt—"

"Don't worry. Soon as she realizes she can't push you around anymore, she'll come around. So will your pa and sisters." He scanned her critically and nodded approval. "You're tougher than you realize. I knew it the first time I saw you."

The first time I saw you. His words brought up the image she couldn't forget. Luke standing naked in the creek…every bit of his lean, hard body exposed. Bold words rushed to her lips. Why not say them? This appeared to be her day for honesty. "The first time you saw me, you were bare-ass naked."

Luke threw back his head and let out a great peal of laughter. "So you remember."

She'd become acutely aware of his hand over hers. Its warmth had spread, pushing all other thoughts from her mind. "Of course I remember. So do you." *What am I doing?* His overpowering presence caused a panic to rise within her. "I'd best get back." She rose to leave, but before she could take a step, strong fingers held her wrist like a vise.

"Not so fast." He rose and clasped her upper arms. "I find you…" After a brief pause, he pulled her roughly to him so she was wrapped tightly in his arms. He pressed his lips against hers, gently at first, but then more hungrily, caressing her mouth in a kiss so searing it made her senses reel. She slid her arms around his neck, pressed close, and returned his kiss with reckless abandon. Time stood still while blood pounded in her brain and her knees trembled until finally he broke away, clasped her shoulders, and shoved her away at arm's length. "No more."

She stood breathless. *Luke kissed me.* She had imagined kissing him many a time, but now that he had, she had no idea what to say.

Before she found words, he shook his head, as if to clear his mind. "Forget this happened." His breathing slowed. He backed a step away, appearing to have gained control over the passion that had gripped him.

But I don't want to forget. She swallowed her words. The purposeful look in his eyes told her not to argue.

The unbelievable moment of passion had passed. He took her arm. "Let's get back to the camp. I'll give you a ride."

Callie couldn't think straight on the ride back to camp. Perched behind Luke on Rascal, she was obliged to circle her arms around his waist, thus pressing herself tightly against his broad back, aware every minute of its warmth and strength. She had hoped to slip back quietly, seen by no one, but no such luck. Both Lydia and Nellie were standing outside their tent when Luke and Callie rode up to the wagon. They stared in astonishment when Callie, vowing to act as if nothing unusual had happened, slid off Rascal's back. "Thank you for the ride, Mr. McGraw." She could have been talking to a stranger.

"You're welcome, Miss Whitaker."

Lydia tilted her head to one side, her standard flirtatious pose. Her full lips formed an enticing smile. "I do hope you're not mad at us, Mr. McGraw."

"Of course not."

"Will you stay for supper?" She slanted a sharp glance at her stepsister. "It'll be ready soon, won't it, Callie?"

"Thanks. Another time." Luke quickly rode away.

When he was out of sight, Lydia spun around to face Callie. "So what was that about?"

"Why, I...I..."

"What were you doing with Luke?" Lydia tossed her head. "Looks to me like you're going after every man in this train."

Callie had to clamp her mouth shut to keep it from dropping open. "What are you talking about?"

"I'm talking about last night when you made a fool of yourself chasing after Magnus Ferguson. You know he belongs to me."

"Does he?"

Ma appeared. "He most certainly does. Callie, I'm shocked at your behavior. Yelling at me...trying to steal Lydia's gentleman friend away. Is this how you act after all we've done for you? What were you doing with Luke McGraw just now?"

"I...nothing." Faced with Ma's and Lydia's anger, Callie wanted to run away all over again, but this time there was no escape. She'd had enough upheaval for one day. At least it was suppertime. If she knew her family, their desire to be fed would far outweigh any other emotions they might have. She squared her shoulders and addressed them all. "If you have anything else to say, say it now because I'm going to start supper." She waited. No one said a word. Hiding her little smile of triumph, she went to light the campfire.

That night, one rumor after another swept through the camp. The Indians had left the area. No, the Indians were lurking close by, waiting for the dead of night so they could attack and kill them all. As a result, no one had the slightest interest in merriment around the campfire. They could hardly wait to depart as early as possible the next morning and leave this dangerous area behind.

Callie did her best to act her normal self for Tommy's sake. After his frightening experience with the dead Indian, he had crawled into the wagon and not come out. No one else seemed to notice the boy's distress until Callie, with her usual patience, persuaded him to come down from the wagon and sit by her side. "Shall we have another reading lesson?" She still shared her lessons with the boy, but no progress yet. He sat quietly by her side, seeming to pay attention, although she was never sure if she was getting through or not. She just kept trying.

"We're starting with Lesson Seven today." She opened the McGuffey's Reader to the proper page and pointed to the picture of a boy bending to feed a hen. "Ned...has...fed... the... hen. Do you understand, Tommy?" The boy sat motionless. She read the sentence again, moving her finger slowly from word to word.

Laughter from across the campfire reached her. Ma, Pa, and her stepsisters regarded her with great amusement. "Is something funny?"

This time it wasn't Nellie full of ridicule, it was Ma. "You're the funny one if you think you can teach the dummy to read."

"Told you it's a waste of time." Nellie's face carried its familiar smirk.

"He's not a dummy and this is not a waste of time." Callie knew her words would fall on deaf ears, but she had to say them anyway. "He might not talk, but that doesn't mean he can't learn to read. I believe he understands everything we say."

Pa made a scoffing sound and walked away.

Ma said, "Nellie's right. You're wasting your time."

She wanted to scream *he is not a dummy! You are the dummies because you don't understand. Can't you see he's hurt by what you say?* Instead, she returned her attention to Tommy and focused on the book in her lap. "She...is...a...black...hen. Just like it shows in the picture, Tommy. Now let's see if you can read it to me."

The boy stared silently at the page. Finally he placed a finger under the first word. In an unwavering voice, he read, "She...is...a...black... hen." He looked at her with a pleased smile, like he was saying, *See? I can so read!*

She wanted to shout with joy, clap her hands and do a little dance, but she hid her delight and acted as if nothing unusual had occurred. "That's very good, Tommy." She hoped to share this momentous occasion with her family, but they'd all wandered off. No one had heard. "That's all right, Tommy, you and I know this is just the beginning, don't we?" She continued the lesson. Not easy, considering her brain was bursting with so many things to think about. Tommy was learning to read! Wonderful news, but that was the good part. What if the Indians attacked? They could all be killed and it wouldn't matter in the least who could read and who couldn't. And what about Ma? Today, for the first time ever, Callie totally defied her. What would happen? What should she do?

What occupied her brain most was the amazing fact that only hours ago she'd been in Luke McGraw's arms. Why was she thinking of him? She should feel more excited that she, more than any girl in the company, had captured the attention of Magnus Ferguson. Strange how little she cared. Maybe Luke's low opinion of Magnus had something to do with it. Or maybe the overwhelming thrill when Luke kissed her knocked every sensible notion from her head. Callie cast a quick glance at her stepsister who'd just returned to the campfire. Lydia's withering glance in return spoke volumes. She was fit to be tied, and Callie hadn't the least notion what to do.

Chapter 8

By the third day after the Indian battle, the collective mood of the Ferguson company had changed from fear to cautious optimism. They were making good time, averaging over twenty miles a day along an easy trail. Food and water were plentiful, both for humans and animals. For the most part, Callie's life remained the same. With Florida's help, she finished the last lesson in McGuffey's Reader and progressed to Florida's tattered copy of *The New England Primer*. At last she could read! She hadn't realized how much her illiteracy made her feel like an inferior being, not worthy of respect. Now she could hold her head up, knowing she could read as well as Nellie and probably better than Lydia.

No one in her family had said another word concerning her rebellion at the Indian battlefield. For her part, each day's grueling trek left little time for dwelling upon her family's shortcomings and the shabby way she'd been treated. She'd hardly thought about it since. Ma treated her the same as before. Nellie, caught up in her romance with Coy Barnett, seemed off in a dreamy world of her own, barely aware of her surroundings. Lydia acted friendly enough, but every now and then Callie caught her casting a hateful glance her way. Did the glance say *stay away from Magnus* or *stay away from Luke?* Probably both. No problem there. Callie hadn't spoken to Luke since the day they'd kissed. The times they did see each other, he acknowledged her presence with a quick, impersonal nod, the same he would give every other woman in the train. It was like he was deliberately avoiding her. As for Magnus, he stopped by their wagons to chat at least once a day. Obviously he was interested in her, but as much as she tried, she couldn't feel anything but friendship for the leader of the wagon train.

One day the captains decided to stop early when they came across a beautiful spot for the wagons to camp, a wide clearing surrounded by dense green woods, bordered by a sparkling stream. As usual, Callie ventured out in search for fuel for the fire. At the beginning of the trek, she'd mostly gone alone. Ma and her sisters had always found excuses to beg off, but lately she'd formed the habit of joining Florida and her daughter, Hetty. She looked forward to these strolls, filled with woman talk and chatter about the events of the day.

Hetty stooped to pick up a round, brown object and placed it her gunnysack. "Just look at me. I never thought I'd be collecting Buffalo droppings and not think a thing of it."

Florida grinned. "Don't say droppings, honey, say chips. It's easier that way." She sighed and picked up a chip of her own. "Luke said we'll soon be grateful for the buffalo. It won't be long before the woods will be gone and these things will be our only fuel."

Hetty raised her eyebrows. "I don't see those high and mighty stepsisters of yours out here." She made no secret of her dislike for Nellie and Lydia.

Callie made a wry face. "They can't stand touching buffalo dung."

"Ha! Do they think they're better than us?"

Callie had no answer, aware nearly everyone in the train felt as Hetty did. Ma, Nellie, and Lydia had become known for their laziness and the lofty way they acted, as if their social standing was a cut above the rest.

"Looks like rain," Florida commented.

Callie looked up. The sun disappeared behind swirling dark clouds. She held out her hand and caught a raindrop. "We'd better get back."

Holding tight to their bags full of buffalo chips, the three turned and headed toward the campground. All of a sudden, the few drops of rain turned into a torrent. They'd wandered a long way from camp, farther than Callie had thought. "Let's run!" They started running. The wagons weren't even in sight yet when she felt a thud on her head, and then another.

"It's hail," Florida yelled.

A torrent of hailstones almost as big as Callie's fist began to pelt them from above, so hard the three had to stop in their tracks. They dropped their bags and threw their arms over their heads to protect themselves from the increasing force of the stones. Callie's heart thumped madly. She'd heard horror stories about people unlucky enough to be caught in a vicious hailstorm. They could be hurt, badly injured, or killed. No time to reach the wagons. She spotted a large oak tree with spreading branches and pointed. "Let's go there! It'll give us some sort of shelter."

As the heaviest deluge yet sent huge balls of ice hurling down upon them, they raced for the oak tree. When they reached the thick, sheltering branches, they found instant relief as they huddled underneath, soaking wet and shivering. Only a few hailstones crashed through, their progress slowed by thick branches that rendered them harmless by the time they reached the ground.

"Dear Lord, I have never seen hail stones this big." Florida spoke through chattering teeth. "Thank goodness for this tree. I think God put it here just for us."

Callie thought of the horses and cattle out in the fields with no shelter. "I feel sorry for the animals. I hope they're—"

A strange, low, thundering noise interrupted. She looked toward its source and gasped, "Oh no!" The animals were stampeding. Panicked cattle ran at top speed, not directly toward them, which was a blessing, but rushing wild-eyed by their tree, their nostrils flaring. The deluge of hailstones abruptly ceased, but still they kept running.

Several men on horseback, ropes at the ready, were soon behind them, making chase. Luke rode by, as did Pa, Andy, and Len. "Come on, Callie," Andy called as he rode by. "We need help."

Florida shook her head with disbelief. "There go some of my cattle. I hope we didn't drive them animals halfway across the country just to lose 'em now."

"Let's get back to camp. We need ropes." Callie picked up her skirt and ran, Florida and Hetty close behind.

When they reached camp, they separated, Callie hurrying to her family's wagon. When she arrived, no one was in sight except Lydia. Wet and bedraggled, she stood by Ma and Pa's wagon, panic on her face. "Callie, where have you been? That awful hail tore a big hole in the canvas. Ma sent me to find you so you can fix it."

Callie caught hold of one of the wagon wheels and leaned on it to catch her breath. "Can't right now," she managed between heavy heaves of her chest. "Got to get rope...round up the cattle."

"What if it hails again? All our clothes will get wet."

Callie opened the toolbox that hung on the side of the wagon and found a coil of rope. "I can't do everything." For once she made no effort to hide her annoyance. "Fix it yourself."

"With these?" Lydia held out her dainty hands. "They're too delicate for sewing canvas."

"You'd do better if you had a few calluses, like the other women in this wagon train." Callie slammed the toolbox cover, hoisted the coil of rope over her shoulder and started away. "I'm going to help round up our cattle. You and Ma at least try to patch the canvas while I'm gone. If you can't, then I'll do it when I get back."

She left camp satisfied she'd stuck up for herself. In the end, she'd softened and offered to help, but she'd wager Lydia would still be mad no matter what she did. She headed out, aware she had further angered her stepsister. Judging from those spiteful glances Lydia had been throwing her lately, she'd better not turn her back.

Pa came riding up on Duke, herding a dozen or so cattle. Passing Callie, he shouted, "There's more out there. I've got Pearl. Get Jaide. He's down by the river."

"Yes, Pa." She picked up her pace, horrified the colt might get lost in the wilderness, frightened and wanting his mother. She reached the river and scanned the shore. Where was he? What if she couldn't find him? Panic welled in her throat. A heart-breaking number of animals died on these long treks. Already, she'd seen the remains of countless oxen, burros, and horses strewn along the trail. Most died from the lack of food and water and from sheer exhaustion. Some got lost in the wilderness or were stolen by Indians. Whatever the cause, losing Jaide would be awful. She'd never get over it.

Out of the corner of her eye, she caught a movement on the other side the river. She looked across and there stood Jaide. In his panic, he must have run across the shallow stream. Now he was peacefully grazing on a few blades of grass, not panicked in the least. "Jaide, you come here!" At the sound of her voice, the yearling raised his head briefly then down again to nibble. She called again, several times, but he ignored her. Should she go back to camp for help? Go after the colt herself? At that point, the Platte River was wide, at least two hundred feet across, but it was quite shallow, and the flow of the river seemed hardly to move. Jaide got across without difficulty and so could she. Besides, if she left now, Jaide might wander off, never to be found again. No, she wouldn't take that chance.

She removed her boots and bundled them in her apron. Coil of rope resting on her shoulder, clutching the bundle, she hiked up her skirt and stepped into the muddy Platte. Wading across, she noted that compared to some of the deep, swiftly flowing streams they'd already crossed, the Platte provided an easy stroll. At its deepest, the water barely came to her knees.

She reached the other side. "Here, Jaide!" Taking his time, the horse raised his head, gave her a disinterested look and continued his grazing. She started toward him and called again. This time he returned a frightened whinny and backed away. "Don't be afraid. Look, it's me, Callie, your very best friend. I'm going to take you home to your ma."

She took another step forward. Wide-eyed, Jaide bolted and took off at top speed for a stand of woods beyond the riverbank.

"Jaide, for heaven's sake, it's me!" Good, Lord, now she'd have to follow him. Stopping to pull on her boots, she followed the horse's trail into thick growths of cedar, birch, alder, and cottonwood trees. Try as she might, she couldn't catch the high-strung animal. He seemed to be teasing her, letting her get close, then breaking away, heading deeper into the woods. Now she was angry. "All right, Jaide, just wait 'til I catch you!" At last, after what seemed like hours, Jaide came to a barrier he wouldn't cross, a raging, tumbling stream that made such a loud noise, he reversed course and headed back. Callie instantly grabbed his mane, slipped the rope around his neck and made a knot. "I've caught you at last, you silly horse." She almost cried with relief.

Leading Jaide, docile now, she started walking. Which way had they come? She wasn't sure but wasn't worried. She'd soon see something familiar that would put her on the right track. She kept going. Thorny bushes tore at her skirt. The thick branches overhead obscured her view of the sky. Why hadn't she paid more attention to where she was going? She had no idea of time, but it seemed like hours since she'd waded across the river. Better hurry. They'd be wanting dinner by now.

At sundown, a sudden fright came over her. Soon she and Jaide would be alone in the dark, lost in the wilderness.

What was that through the trees? *Thank God, the river.*

"Come on, Jaide. We're almost home." She led the colt across the sluggish water, arriving at an unfamiliar spot on the other side. Where was she? Instinct told her to head upstream. Sure enough, after a short walk along the sandy bank, she spied her footprints in the mud that marked the spot where she'd crossed. "We're almost home, Jaide." The colt picked his ears up, as if he knew he'd soon be back with his mother.

She could hardly wait. She didn't like being alone. It'd be good to see other people again. She hadn't eaten for hours and her stomach was sending up hunger pangs. It was getting dark. They must have eaten by this time. She had to laugh, picturing Lydia and Nellie trying to fix supper. Even if the beans were undercooked and the biscuits as hard as rocks, she'd give anything for a plateful right now.

She cut away from the river and headed toward the clump of trees where the company was camped. Exhausted though she was, she quickened her pace. Oh, it'd be so good to get back! Why had no one come after her? Someone must have wondered where she was, but then, everyone had been busy chasing cattle and cleaning up the mess left by the hailstorm.

The closer she got to camp, the more she realized something was wrong...

Something was very wrong...

The wagons were gone. The people were gone.

She knew she had the right place. The burnt-out remains of the campfires and the scattered piles of garbage and debris gave proof a group of wagons had recently camped here.

"Where have they gone, Jaide?" Still clutching the colt's tether, she stood in shocked bewilderment. "How could they have left me?" Had they deliberately gone off without her? Of course not. She must have been overlooked, although how that could happen, she couldn't imagine.

Surely someone would come back for her. Or would they? *Do they even know I'm gone?* "Oh, Jaide!" She wrapped her arms around the horse's neck and clung tight, trying for a panicked moment to block out the fear that engulfed her. She had nothing to eat. Her legs ached from fatigue. And nobody cared. They'd left her behind. Of all the low moments in her life, this was the lowest. Her tears ran into Jaide's soft mane, which she clutched tightly.

The colt's soft nicker brought her out of her despair. In the semidarkness, he'd turned his head to gaze at her, a questioning look in his eye, like he was asking, *are you going to stand there all night?* She must keep calm. Decide what to do. First, without question, she needed to look for food before total darkness set in. Maybe she could find something she could eat among the piles of garbage left behind. She tied Jaide to a tree and began to scour the campground, not a pleasant chore considering the ground was muddy and some of the garbage already smelled. She had no luck until finally, just as she was about to give up, she spied two biscuits, not on the muddy ground, thank goodness, but nestled amid some unburned twigs in the remains of a campfire. With a joyful cry, she scooped them up and popped one after another into her mouth. They tasted wonderful. Best biscuits she'd ever eaten.

Now what? Finding more food was impossible. Tired though she was, lying down was impossible, too. Not in this mud. She'd have to keep walking until she found the train. It shouldn't be too difficult. The skies had cleared and the moon was out. They'd be following the river for many miles to come, so all she had to do was stay close to the Platte, and sooner or later she'd find them. They couldn't have gone far.

"Come on Jaide. You must be tired, too, but we've got to keep going." Leading the colt, she started out, thankful for the bright moonlight that lit her path. As she walked, she concentrated on positive thoughts. She would *not* be scared, even though the wolves howled—or were they coyotes?—in the distance. Her legs were like lead, they were so tired, but she would keep on. *Lost in the wilderness. Left behind. Starving.* Those two small biscuits didn't begin to relieve the hunger pangs in her stomach. No one had noticed she was gone. That's what hurt the most. Never in her life had she felt so wretched, yet she'd keep up her spirits and keep walking.

She followed the moonlit trail for what seemed like hours. At last, when she couldn't go another step, she led Jaide to the river and let him drink to his heart's content. He'd found plenty of grass along the way, so his stomach was full. *Lucky horse. Whereas I...*

She tried to ignore her gnawing hunger. Thinking about the pains would only increase her misery. Maybe she could fool her stomach by filling up on water. She pulled off her dress and waded into the sluggish river. After taking a long drink with cupped hands, she plunged her whole self into the water, loving the feel of the gently flowing current as it washed away the day's miserable accumulation of dust, dirt, and sweat. When she was done, she led Jaide back toward the trail. Finding a tree with a patch of grass underneath that looked fairly soft, at least softer than the sand and gravel she'd been traveling on, she tethered the colt to a nearby sturdy bush. She sank exhausted to her makeshift grass bed and used her rolled-up dress as a pillow. For a few seconds, troubling thoughts swirled in her head. What if someone should find her dressed in her white cotton drawers and chemise? What a silly thought. Besides, modesty was far from her main concern right now. The constant howling bothered her the most. The unsettling sound hadn't ceased for a moment. She pictured a pack of snarling, ferocious animals attacking her, tearing her apart. What if they did? There was nothing she could do about it, awake or asleep. She was so tired she didn't care. Nothing else mattered...

"So, here you are." A deep voice startled her from sleep.

She shot to full wakefulness in less than a moment, opening her eyes. A dark figure stood above her. Sheer panic welled in her throat and she couldn't speak.

"It's me, Luke." He dropped down beside her. "Did you get lost in the woods?"

"It's you?" Heart pounding, she struggled to a sitting position, grabbed her dress, and held it in front of her.

"Are you all right?"

A vast relief swept through her. "Luke, it's really you?"

"Of course it's me."

"You scared me to death."

"Not quite. What happened?"

"They left me behind, that's what happened." She regarded his dim figure in the moonlight. "How could they have done such a thing?"

"Not long after the hailstorm, we decided to move on because of the muddy ground. It wasn't until hours later, when we stopped for the day, your ma came around looking for you. Said you were supposed to start supper and couldn't be found."

How hurtful they cared so little for her they hadn't bothered to check if she was there or not. "You'd think Pa would at least have missed Jaide."

"Your Pa was mighty busy rounding up his cattle, not that I'm making excuses for him. We'll get this straightened out when we get back. So you're all right?"

"Fine, thanks. Just very, very hungry."

"We'll soon take care of that." Luke arose and went to Rascal, tethered next to Jaide. He retrieved a canteen and something out of his saddlebag and sat beside her. "Biscuits and a chunk of roasted deer meat. Not much, but I'd wager you'll eat it."

She had to restrain herself from grabbing the food from his hand. As it was, she was hard put to keep from gulping it down like some hungry animal.

He watched in silence until she finished then handed her the canteen. "Take a good swig. It's from a clear stream, not the muddy Platte."

After a long drink of water, she exhaled a long sigh of contentment. "That was wonderful. Best meal I ever had. I feel so much better." A sudden shiver struck her.

"Are you cold?"

Nothing had mattered except her empty stomach. Now it was full, she needed to think more clearly, like how she was dressed in only her bloomers and chemise! "Turn around. I've got to finish dressing."

He took the dress from her hands and held it up. "Raise your arms. It's not all that warm tonight. You don't want to catch a chill. Don't worry, I've got my eyes closed." He sounded amused at her modesty.

She stood up, raised her arms, and let him slide the dress over her head. She started to button the buttons, but her fingers shook so badly she couldn't.

"Got a problem?" Laughing softly, he fastened the buttons up the front, his eyes opened this time, she noticed.

By now she was beyond modesty and didn't care. Besides, who was to see them here in the middle of nowhere?

It was a simple thing, his helping put her dress on, yet when his fingers lightly touched her skin, a quiver surged through her veins and she ached to touch him. She would not, of course. He was only being helpful. She would make a fool of herself if she revealed how she felt, yet, how astonishing someone actually cared she was cold, especially a man like Luke. He was tough as nails, but from the beginning, he'd shown her nothing but kindness. His hand brushed against her hair, causing a hungry throb deep in the center of her being.

He drew in his breath. Yes, he did care.

She would have willingly fallen into his arms, except he withdrew his hands and stood gazing at her. "When I realized you were gone... That jackass family of yours. What are they thinking to leave you like that?" He sounded angry now. "You're worth a dozen of any one of them."

His outburst caught her by surprise. She didn't know what to say.

"Don't mind me. If we leave now, we should reach the camp by dawn." After a long pause, he gave her a rueful smile. "You have no idea the power you have."

"Me? I guess I don't." His remark was truly bewildering. "I don't have any power. My whole life I've been a nobody, just grateful somebody took me in. I—"

"You, a nobody? That's not so, Callie." The anger in his voice told her how deeply he meant his words. "I sensed a strength in you from the time you caught me bare-assed in the creek and gave me that smart-alecky curtsy. When I saw how your family treated you, I couldn't believe it. It took me a while to realize why you were what you were, and how that family of yours tried to beat the spirit out of you. They nearly succeeded. What saved you was this journey."

"And you." She remembered their talk the day of the Indian battle, when he told her leaving Tennessee was the best thing she ever did. "Tennessee seems so far away now. I look back on the life I used to lead and wonder how I stood it. Cook breakfast, wash dishes, feed the chickens, scrub the clothes...go to bed, wake up, and start over again. I'm working just as hard now, but each day is different. It's all so exciting, even the bad things, like having to collect buffalo chips and seeing that dead Indian brave. So different from my life in Tennessee."

"I'm glad you see that." He drew in a deep breath, as if reaching deep for his willpower and backed away. "There's a lot you don't know about me, Callie."

"Then why don't you tell me?" She waited for his answer. In the distance a wolf howled, reminding her how completely alone they were.

Nothing but wilderness—no prying eyes. They could do anything they wanted and no one would know.

"We've got to get back."

"Why? They're camped for the night, so we don't have to rush." She wanted an answer. For once she wouldn't be her usual docile self and agree to whatever he said. "Why did you kiss me that time and then go out of your way to ignore me?"

He remained silent, the rigid lift of his shoulders showing she'd taken him by surprise.

She wouldn't give up now. "I thought you liked kissing me, but maybe I was wrong. Maybe—"

"Didn't like kissing you?" He stepped so close the heat of his body radiated off him. He seized her shoulders. "You can't begin to know..." His arms encircled her. His uneven breathing blew on her cheek as he pulled her to him and crushed his lips to hers. Her arms went around his neck. She quivered as his kiss continued, loving how their bodies locked together in an embrace so tight, every hard, lean inch of him pressed against her. He finally pulled his mouth away. "Don't ever think I don't want you." He bent his head to kiss the pulsing hollow at the base of her throat. It was as if he couldn't get enough of her.

Next thing she knew, they were on the ground. His mouth was crushing hers again, and his hands were making their warm presence known on her bodice. They caused a burning desire, an aching need she'd never felt before. "Oh, Luke..."

His breathing came hard, his voice a harsh whisper. "Looks like I put your dress on too soon." He fumbled for the buttons of her bodice and then stopped abruptly. "What am I doing?"

"You're kissing me."

She reached to caress the back of his neck, but he pulled away. "We can't do this."

"Why?" She wanted him back. Every throbbing part of her body wanted him back.

"Lots of reasons." He stood, took her hand, and pulled her to her feet. "I was hired to guide this wagon train, not paw the ladies."

"You weren't pawing me, and you know that." She smoothed the front of her dress. "You're not telling me the real reason."

"No, and I'm not going to. It won't happen again. Come on, let's go." He'd apparently made up his mind. Further protests would be useless.

There's a lot you don't know about me, he'd said. As she suspected, something in his past hung over him. She couldn't imagine what it was.

except it had to be something so dreadful he couldn't get past it and remained remote and unreachable. "What don't I know about you, Luke?"

"We'd better get started. Like I said, it'll take 'til dawn to get back."

She'd get no answer tonight. In silence, she followed him back to the horses. Maybe she'd never get an answer.

* * * *

The sun had barely peeked over the horizon when they caught up with the train. At her wagons, Callie slid from the back of Luke's horse, untied Jaide, and bid Luke good-bye. In a state of exhaustion, she could hardly wait to crawl into her bed and get a bit of sleep before the day's trek began. Pa climbed from the wagon just after Luke rode away. He frowned when he caught sight of her and said none too kindly, "So you're back."

"Yes, Pa."

"I see you got the colt."

"Yes, Pa. He crossed the river and ran into the woods. I had to—"

"You were out all night." His stern voice contained not a bit of sympathy or concern.

"I was, but you see—"

"I'll deal with you later." He turned his back and started away. "Get breakfast started," he called over his shoulder.

What! How could he? She would not turn the other cheek this time. She had a burning question on her mind, and by God, he would answer. "Why did you leave me behind?"

Pa slowed but didn't stop. "Ask your Ma."

"I want an answer from you."

Pa stopped and turned, just as Ma poked her head out of the wagon. She glared at Callie. "Don't talk to your Pa that way."

"How could you have gone off and left me?" If her anger showed, she didn't care.

Ma blinked as if she'd been taken unaware. "Don't blame us. When we left, Lydia said you were visiting over at the Sawyer wagon."

Callie swung her gaze to Pa. "You knew I'd gone after Jaide."

Pa shrugged. If he felt the slightest guilt, it didn't show. "We needed to leave, get out of the mud. Now I want no part of this. You women settle your differences among yourselves." He turned around and walked away fast.

Ma climbed down from the wagon. She looked as if she'd like to walk away, too, but before she could, Callie asked, "Why would Lydia say such a thing? I don't understand how you could have left me that way."

Her stepmother regarded her as if she'd lost her mind. "Why are you so upset? You caught up with us, didn't you? I'm sure Lydia didn't do it on purpose."

Callie clenched her fists and felt the blood rushing to her face. "That's right, Ma, rush to her defense. You always do. Lydia lied deliberately. I know she did. Do you realize you left me in the wilderness? I might have died out there if Luke hadn't found me."

Ma leveled a suspicious gaze. "What's going on between you two?"

"Don't change the subject!"

"You were out all night with a man who isn't your husband. What are you trying to do, disgrace the family?"

Callie gasped at Ma's remark. So outrageous. She should reply, but what was the use? Ma would never understand. Why waste her breath? She spun on her heel and started toward the tent.

"Where are you going?" Ma called.

"To bed. In case you've forgotten, I was up all night."

"Callie Whitaker, you come back here and start our breakfast."

"Not on your life, Ma." She didn't slow down. "If you want breakfast, fix it yourself."

Callie's overwhelming anger carried her out of her stepmother's sight and into the tent, where Nellie was still asleep and Lydia, sitting up, rubbed her eyes and stretched. "What was that noise?"

Callie rolled out her bedroll and practically dived under the blankets. "It's me. I've been up all night and now I'm going to get some sleep."

"Where have you been?"

She turned to look at Lydia. "Why did you say I was at the Sawyers when you knew I wasn't?"

"I thought you were." Lydia shifted her eyes away. "How am I supposed to know where you are every minute?" Her lips formed a pout. "You were with Luke, weren't you?"

"Thank God he found me."

Lydia glared at her with hate-filled eyes. "So, you were out all night, disgracing the family."

She'd been right. Out of malice, jealousy, whatever the reason, Lydia told a deliberate lie, knowing full well she was putting Callie's life in danger. Even worse, Callie could scream and complain all she wanted, but it wouldn't do her any good. She'd never get past her family's unconcern. Other than Tommy, nobody cared.

She went to sleep, remembering what Luke said. *Your family's the same, but you've changed. Now you see them through different eyes.* So very true. The old Callie would have apologized for taking up space on this earth. The new Callie was something else. Exactly what, she didn't know and, at the moment, was too tired to care.

Chapter 9

Aware her complaints would fall on deaf ears, Callie refrained from any further comment concerning Lydia's outrageous lie. Nobody said a word. Life went on as usual. Callie worked as hard as ever, only now, because of her protests, Ma and her stepsisters helped more than they had before. Still, the main burden fell on Callie's shoulders. For the sake of peace in the family, she did her chores without complaint, speaking when spoken to. On a day-to-day basis, she coped with her stepsisters as best she could. No problem with Nellie, who seemed wrapped up in her own little world, so in love with Coy she could talk of nothing else. Lydia continued her dark glances, not so much about Luke, who stayed away, but because Magnus Ferguson had begun to seek Callie out.

One day Lydia asked, "Do you think you'll marry Magnus?"

The question took Callie by surprise. "He's a fine man, but right now I'm not thinking of marrying anybody."

"You'd be a fool if you didn't." Lydia's shrewish voice revealed her annoyance.

Callie took special pains to stay away from Luke, which wasn't difficult since he made no effort to seek her out. She told herself he was deliberately staying away. It was for the best. Luke wasn't a marrying man. Soon as he could, he'd head for the wilderness again, content to live alone. She should be overjoyed Magnus Ferguson often sought her out, but she wasn't. Maybe she should try harder to like Magnus. Lydia was right. She'd be a fool not to marry a man so wealthy and attractive. The problem was, whenever she tried to picture herself as the wife of the esteemed Magnus Ferguson, the vision of herself in the arms of Luke McGraw blocked everything else from her mind.

As they traveled on, Callie came to realize how petty her problems were compared to the depressing sights beside the trail. Never a day went by that they didn't pass hastily dug graves. Some were unmarked or had a simple wooden cross with a name. Some had a more elaborate marker that gave the cause of death. Callie read every one, always distressed by the number of ways a person could die on the trail. Death by disease was the most common, mostly cholera, typhoid, or pneumonia. Children's deaths were the saddest, like the six-year-old boy riding on the yoke who fell off and got run over. The high number of accidental deaths continually reminded Callie of how dangerous this journey could be. Killed by a grizzly. Bitten by a rattlesnake. Drowned in the river. Shot accidentally.

One morning during breakfast, gunfire sounded from a nearby wagon, a sound so common they hardly noticed anymore. Magnus rode up soon after, a look of disgust on his face, and spoke to Pa. "One of Riley Gregg's boys just shot himself in the foot. Once again, I'm making the rounds with a warning, Mr. Whitaker. We've got to stop these accidental shootings."

Pa, who was an excellent shot and took good care of his guns, nodded in agreement. "Some of these dang fools never even saw a gun before. Now seems like every man in this train is armed. Guns all over the place, and they don't know what they're doing."

"There are far too many arms on this wagon train, and far too many accidents caused by careless handling." Magnus looked toward the campfire where Len sat finishing his breakfast. "You'd best pay attention, young man. How many guns do you have?"

Len broke into his customary cocky smirk. "Three. My colt revolver, my double barrel pistol, and my rifle." He stuck out his chest. "I'm not a fool like some. I know how to handle them."

"You don't need that many guns."

"That's my business, ain't it, Mr. Ferguson?"

Magnus frowned with displeasure. "You do *not* know how to handle them. I've seen you sticking your pistols in your pants with no regard to safety. That's dangerous. You're a menace to yourself and to others. Even the animals aren't safe around you."

Len's upper lip curled with contempt. "I don't need your advice." He threw down his plate and stalked off.

Callie expected Magnus would be offended by the young man's insolence. Instead, he shrugged and shook his head. "Arrogant young fool. If he gets to California without killing himself or some poor innocent soul, it'll be a miracle."

One day later, they had stopped for the noontime break when a shot rang out, followed by an agonized scream. Along with everyone else, Callie rushed to where Len lay on the ground clutching his stomach.

Andy, his face white with shock, knelt alongside. "Len shot himself. Had his gun in his pants and was pulling it out when the dang thing went off."

Doc Wilson was summoned. After he examined the ugly wound in Len's stomach, he shook his head. "Won't last the day." He dug into his bag for a bottle of laudanum. "Give him this to ease the pain."

They made a bed for Len. Pa and Andy pitched a tent over his head.

Andy choked back a sob. "Guess we can't do nothing except wait for him to die."

Wait for him to die. Callie had never thought much of Len, but hearing his screams, knowing he would soon be gone, caused a wrenching grief within her.

Magnus appeared. When he saw Len and heard what happened, a look of disgust crossed his face. "What a fool. I warned him and he didn't listen. Serves him right." He strode away.

How could he be so heartless? Maybe he cared and was just trying to hide his true feelings.

During the long afternoon, while the saddened company waited for Len to breathe his last, Callie, struggling with her anguished thoughts, had to get away. She saddled Duke and rode him out on the wide stretch of prairie.

Luke, on Rascal, soon rode up alongside. "Are you all right?" His voice held an infinitely compassionate tone.

Tears rolled down her cheeks. She wiped them away with the back of her hand. "It's not fair! He's only twenty and full of life. He was going to California and get rich finding gold. But now… Oh, I can't bear it."

For a time they rode in silence, broken only by the muted sounds of hooves clopping on the hard-packed earth.

Finally, Luke leaned to one side and caught Duke's bridal. "Stop a minute." The horses halted. "Look around you, Callie."

She wasn't sure what he was getting at, but she took a long look at the scene around her. A bird, likely a hawk, soared in the sky. The branches of a nearby cottonwood tree stirred in the slight breeze. A prairie dog popped its head from a hole in the ground, looked around, and popped back in again.

Luke leaned his arm across the saddle. "Here's how I look at it. Len's going to die. You can cry all you want, but you can't bring him back. Before this journey's over, you'll see death many times, but if you waste your time grieving, you're a softhearted fool. You can remember the good things about Len, but what's more important is don't let a day pass without taking a look at this beautiful land you're passing through. Give thanks you still have your life. Live it and enjoy it as best you can."

Amazing a man of few words like Luke could make such a speech. He never ceased to surprise her. "You could be right."

"I know I'm right. Out of the sadness of death, we gain new strength to go on. It's like God is testing us."

Callie heaved a sigh. "It's such a cruel test."

"I know, but you will survive and be the stronger person for it. I'd like to think that I—"

She'd been listening intently and didn't want him to stop. "Go on."

He shook his head and looked toward the campground. "Time to get back."

She wished he'd kept on. He was about to reveal something about himself, something kept hidden that haunted him every day of his life. Maybe someday he'd tell her. She flicked the reins. "All right, let's get back. Poor Len."

He had died while she'd gone for her ride. They buried him in a shallow grave under a cottonwood tree, marking the spot with a simple wooden cross. The next morning, before they began the day's trek, Callie stopped by Len's grave one last time. "I'll never forget you," she whispered, and quickly turned away. She remembered Luke's wise words from yesterday. *If you waste your time grieving, you're a softhearted fool.* He was right. She had no time to grieve. Of necessity, she'd bury her memories of Len deep in a corner of her mind, to be retrieved at another time, another place. For now, she couldn't let herself dwell on Len's tragic death, or think morbid thoughts, even though the farther they went, the more graves she saw alongside the trail. Back in Tennessee, she hadn't given much thought to death and dying, but on this wagon train, they were part of her daily life. So very real.

* * * *

When Callie first met Magnus Ferguson, she had nothing but respect and admiration for the leader of the wagon train. She still did, but as the days went by, her high opinion of him sometimes faltered when she saw the ill-concealed resentment growing among his appointed captains. Magnus was too arbitrary. Didn't listen to the opinions of others. Made bad decisions, ignoring the good advice of his captains.

One day while visiting Florida, Callie had the chance to ask Luke about the growing dissension. "What are the captains so angry about?"

"Simple. Winter's coming and we're not moving fast enough."

"What do you think?"

Luke's long pause warned his answer wouldn't be all that reassuring. "Whether we're going to California or Oregon, we're in big trouble if the snow hits before we get there."

"Magnus says we have plenty of time."

Luke frowned. "I've already told you my opinion of Magnus Ferguson. You're right. He's in no hurry. The captains think differently. They've heard the horror stories about what happened to the Donner Party when they got caught in the snow."

"Are they true?"

"Yeah, they're true. The captains fear we'll suffer the same fate. That's why they're complaining our progress isn't fast enough. The more they protest, the more that pig-headed idiot turns a deaf ear."

Florida chimed in, "Luke, didn't most of the Donner Party starve to death?"

"Not all, but many did."

"And the ones that lived, didn't they…?"

"They took to cannibalism."

Callie stifled a gasp of horror. "You mean they…?"

"Ate the dead." Luke's mouth twisted wryly. "You don't want to hear the details. Let's hope Magnus comes to his senses, and soon."

Callie remembered Luke's words when, only days later, Magnus fell ill with a high fever and ordered the company to stop while he recovered. Everywhere she went, she heard complaints. Why was Magnus so special? Others had fallen just as ill and the train had kept going. After two day's rest, Magnus recovered enough they could move on, but simmering resentments continued. By the time the train reached Fort Laramie, frayed tempers exploded when Magnus ordered a four-day halt. He had good reasons. The stock needed rest. There was blacksmithing to be done. Even so, the captains objected. That night, Callie stood with Florida and listened to a heated argument between Magnus and his captains. In the end, Magnus prevailed, but just barely.

Walking back to their wagons, Florida said, "Land's sake! Magnus had better watch out or his high-and-mighty self will be tossed out on his you-know-what."

Callie hoped he wouldn't. She still admired Magnus as a leader, although there was something about him that didn't quite ring true. But no, she must be wrong. What was she thinking? She pushed her feeling of distrust aside. Magnus Ferguson was as fine a man as they came. She'd be disloyal to think otherwise. Besides, his personal interest in her continued. Any day now, she might find herself in love with him, if only she could forget about Luke.

* * * *

After resting for four days, the company continued on from Fort Laramie. Despite her truce with her family, Callie lived for the moments she could slip away to Florida's wagon where she was always greeted with open arms and treated like a welcome friend. She kept up her lessons, her reading skills increasing every day. By now she'd graduated from primers. With Florida's help, she was reading Nathanial Hawthorne's, *The Scarlet Letter*. She never realized the pleasure one could find in books until she became deeply engrossed in the problems of poor Hester Prynne and her illegitimate child. Also, her stolen moments away from her family gave her more chances to talk with Luke. Other than their ride together the day Len died, he hadn't paid her any special attention. Often, though, they talked together by the Sawyer campfire, always when others were around.

One day Florida was driving the wagon. Callie sat beside her, admiring the skillful way her friend handled the oxen. "I wish Pa would let me drive, but he says it's a man's job."

Florida chuckled. "That's rich! Your pa has some crazy notions."

"It looks like fun."

"I don't know if having to look at an oxen's behind all day is a whole lot of fun, but—" Florida's face lit with a sudden revelation. "Why didn't I think of it before? Honey, you're going to learn to drive this wagon, and I'm going to teach you."

Callie jumped at the chance. Soon she was handling the reins with ease, yelling *getup! whoa! gee!* and *haw!* as if she'd done it for years, cracking the whip smartly over the oxen's heads. After only a few days' lessons, she became a real help, spelling Florida with the driving. She wished she could offer her help to Pa but didn't dare suggest it. She already knew what he'd say.

By now, Callie was enjoying herself. No longer did she feel awkward and out of place. These were people she knew, and they liked her. The men paid more attention to her now. At the nightly campfires, she never lacked for dancing partners. Magnus Ferguson never let a night pass by that he didn't ask her to dance several times. Sometimes she caught him watching her intently. She still marveled at his interest, finding it hard to believe the esteemed leader of the wagon train could be interested in an uneducated farm girl from Tennessee. He was, though. So far, she'd been friendly and nothing more, but she knew in her heart if ever she signaled she liked him especially, he might propose.

* * * *

Late one afternoon, Callie and her stepsisters were combing the prairie looking for buffalo chips when Nellie burst out ecstatically, "I have news. You would never guess."

"Uh-oh," Lydia answered. "I'd wager I can guess."

"I'm going to have a baby." Nellie pressed her palms to her stomach. "Coy's baby. I've never been this happy in my whole life."

Oh, no. Callie couldn't smile. She tried to keep her dismay from showing. "Are you sure?"

"Positive."

"Does Ma know?"

"Not yet."

"I won't even ask if Pa knows."

Nellie laughed with giddy unconcern. "Of course he doesn't know yet. I don't plan to tell him until our plans are set."

"Have you told Coy?"

"I plan to this very day."

Lydia, too, looked doubtful. "How do you know he wants to marry you?"

"Are you daft?" Once again, the usually sullen Nellie broke into joyous laughter. "Coy adores me. He'll jump at the chance."

Apparently convinced, Lydia broke into a smile. "Nellie, that's wonderful. We'll have the wedding right here in camp. Reverend Wilkins can marry you. Afterward, we'll have a grand party to celebrate."

"How perfect! What should I wear?" Nellie's eyes sparkled with happiness. Callie had never seen her so excited.

Callie kept silent while her two gleeful stepsisters discussed Nellie's wedding plans. She wished she could join in the excitement. From the bottom of her heart, she hoped Nellie was right and Coy Barnett would jump at the chance to lead her to the altar, but a nagging uncertainty prevented her from sharing Nellie's joy.

That night, an especially buoyant group joined together around the campfire with more than one reason to celebrate. They had traveled more than twenty-five miles on an easy trail. Best of all, they'd reached Independence Rock, the most noted landmark along the way. The site was a popular stopover for the trains headed west. Tomorrow they would spend the day adding their signatures to the thousands already scratched into the sturdy granite.

At one point during the evening, Callie saw Nellie disappear with Coy Barnett, no doubt so she could tell him her news. She hoped for the best.

Please, let it be all right. Much later, Nellie returned, her face wreathed with a smile. "I told him," she whispered to Lydia and Callie. "He's so happy he's about to burst. We're going to get married."

Lydia clapped her hands with delight. "That's wonderful. When?"

"Tomorrow night, but don't say anything yet. I'm going to talk to Ma and Pa first thing tomorrow. Then Coy's coming over. He's got to talk to Pa. You know, ask for my hand."

Callie asked, "Do you think Pa will approve?"

"He'd better. If he doesn't agree, I'm counting on Coy to talk him into it. After all, I'm twenty-three. I've got a right to marry whoever I please." Nellie's newfound bravado caused her to break into a wide, happy smile. "If worse comes to worse, I'll tell him he's going to be a grandpa. That'll change his mind in a hurry." She turned accusing eyes on Callie. "You thought Coy wouldn't marry me, but you were wrong, weren't you?"

"Looks like I was." Callie was only too happy to agree.

The next morning, Nellie, brimming with excitement, asked Lydia and Callie to make themselves scarce during the first break of the day because that's when she was going to tell Ma and Pa. They readily agreed and strolled to Florida's wagon when the train stopped for the morning break.

"You girls look all excited," Florida commented when they settled themselves outside her wagon. "What's going on?"

Lydia smiled. "Nellie and Coy Barnett are getting married. She's telling Ma and Pa right now."

"Lordy me, that is exciting news." Callie caught the hesitancy in the older woman's voice. "When?"

"If Reverend Wilkins agrees, it'll be tonight. Everyone's invited to the wedding…"

While Lydia rattled on in her scatterbrained fashion, Callie and Florida exchanged guarded glances. Callie could plainly see her friend was just as wary as she was and no doubt guessed the reason for such a hasty wedding. Lydia was still chattering away when Callie caught sight of Gert Gowdy headed toward them from across the encampment. Even at a distance, Callie could tell from the woman's long, purposeful strides she was angry.

Gert arrived at the Sawyer wagon. "He's gone." She stood with clenched fists. "I want Luke to go after him."

"Go after who?" Florida asked.

"My hired hand, Coy Barnett, that's who! That little weasel ran off during the night. He's gone, no warning, no nothing! Who's gonna drive our cattle?"

Luke appeared. "How do you know he's gone for good, Gert? Maybe he—"

"Coy's gone. Took all his gear and lit out. Never even waited for his wages. Go after him, Luke. Bring him back. He can't do this."

Luke shook his head. "Sorry, Gert, but he's within his rights to leave if he wants. I can't force him to come back."

Lydia gave a little cry of realization. "Oh, no!" She slapped a hand over her mouth.

The awful truth struck Callie, too. *Coy's gone...Nellie!* She leaped to her feet. "There's something I've got to do." Not waiting for an answer, she hiked up her skirt and started running across the field toward her wagon, fast as her feet would carry her, Lydia close behind. She had to get there before Nellie had a chance to talk to Ma and Pa.

* * * *

Luke watched as Gert, still angry, stomped back across the field to her wagon. "She'll be all right once she calms down. I'll see she gets enough help. Coy won't be missed much, if at all."

Florida wrinkled her nose with disgust. "Good riddance to him. I swear, that man was as randy as a goat, chasing after half the women in this train." She looked toward the Whitakers' wagon across the way. "Oh, dear. Nellie's in such big trouble."

Luke remained silent. As always, he avoided gossip like the plague, even when talking with his sister. She was right, though. Coy and Nellie had been sneaking off to the woods for weeks. It all fit. Even Callie and Lydia rushing off like they did came as no surprise. It was obvious they were in a hurry to tell Nellie the news about Coy. What a mess. Caleb Whitaker's family lived in fear of him, and rightly so. God help any daughter of his who got herself pregnant out of wedlock. "Better say a prayer for poor Nellie."

Florida clucked with sympathy. "Those Whitakers, a strange family if ever there was one. The only one I feel sorry for is Callie. I don't envy her having to live with that bunch. She deserves better."

Luke responded with a noncommittal nod. Smart though she was, his sister had no idea what went on inside his head. A good thing, too, considering how he kept reliving the night he held Callie Whitaker in his arms and they had nearly made love. He'd wanted Callie so bad he was barely able to restrain himself. He'd done the right thing, but even now, was there ever a time when she wasn't on his mind? Just the other day he caught himself wondering where she was. It was then he'd realized how he kept track of her whereabouts every minute of the day. Crazy. He'd better get over it. He didn't want a woman in his life, not now, not ever.

He smiled at his sister. The white cap on her head, the one she always wore, was a constant reminder of that terrible day that changed his life and hers, too. The never-to-be-forgotten day carved deep into his memory.

* * * *

When Callie arrived, gasping for breath, her stepsister and stepparents stood by the wagon. It looked as though Nellie was about to speak.

"Nellie!" Callie gasped for breath, her chest heaving. "I need to talk to you right away. It's something private."

Ma and Pa regarded her as if she'd gone berserk. Nellie cast her a scathing glance. "Can't you see I'm busy right now? As you very well know."

Lydia arrived, equally breathless, and gasped, "Nellie, we need to discuss something."

Ma scowled. "What's this all about?"

"Nothing important." Callie sent Nellie the most significant look she could muster. "Whatever you were planning can wait. We need you right now, this instant."

"All right then." Nellie frowned with annoyance. "I'll come with you since you insist, but you'd better have a good explanation."

Callie and Lydia led Nellie away from the wagon, leaving Ma and Pa with puzzled expressions. By the time they reached a nearby strand of woods, Callie's mind was racing. Up to now, she'd acted on instinct, thinking only that she must stop Nellie before she talked to Ma and Pa. But now what? Her heart sank. Nellie had to hear the awful truth, and hear it right now. She turned to Lydia. "Will you tell her?"

Her stepsister's eyes widened with alarm. "Me? Oh, no, I couldn't. You tell her."

Callie should have remembered her flighty stepsister avoided disagreeable scenes as much as possible. No time to argue.

They reached a secluded spot beside a little stream. As they settled themselves on the moss-covered bank, Callie said, "There's no easy way to say this."

Nellie stared at her, baffled. "What's this all about?"

"I'll have to tell you flat-out. Coy's gone for good. Gert says he lit out and took all his gear. He's not coming back."

The blood drained from Nellie's face. "You're lying."

Her response was what Callie had expected. "Why would I tell such a horrible lie? It's the truth, I'm afraid, and I'm terribly sorry."

"He's really gone?"

"Gone. I doubt you'll ever see him again."

Nellie looked toward Lydia. "Is this true?"

Her sister returned a slow, silent nod.

"Oh, my God." Tears rolled down Nellie's cheeks. She regarded Callie, eyes wide with desperation. "What am I going to do?"

"I don't know."

"I thought he loved me. I know he loved me. How could he have run off that way?"

"I can't imagine why he would do such a terrible thing." *Because he's a no-good low-life.* Mercifully, she kept the truth to herself.

"If Pa finds out, and he will, he'll kill me." Nellie buried her face in her hands and started to sob.

Callie reached to pat her stepsister on her shoulder, a useless gesture, considering the circumstances, but what else could she do? Nellie had gotten herself in deep trouble. Callie had no solutions and couldn't see there were any. "Pa's not going to kill you." It was hard to sound convincing when she suspected he very well might.

Frowning with concern, Lydia took her sister's hands. "I'm so, so sorry, Nellie."

"I can't believe it," Nellie cried.

"But it's true, I'm afraid," Lydia replied. "That no good skunk!"

"What shall I do?" Nellie's voice shook. "When Pa finds out, if he doesn't kill me, he'll throw me out. I'll be disgraced. I'll have no place to go." Her voice rose to ever-higher levels of desperation. "I'll have to kill myself."

"You will do no such thing, you hear me?" Callie got to her feet and began to pace. "We'll think of something." Over Nellie's quivering, sobbing form, she exchanged troubled looks with Lydia. Both remembered Pa's rants over the years, his dire threats should any of his daughters so much as let a man touch them, let alone allow a man to do the unthinkable and "get herself in trouble." Callie dreaded to even think of his rage when he discovered a daughter of his was pregnant. He could indeed cause her bodily harm. Even if he didn't, Nellie was right. Most likely he'd throw her out. Where would she go? Nellie would have a hard time finding anyone who would take her in. Her snobbish, superior attitude had made her no friends among the members of the wagon train.

Nellie's sobs stopped. She looked up with a surprising trace of a smile on her lips. "I just thought of something."

Callie asked, "What?"

"He's coming back."

"What do you mean?"

Nellie wiped her eyes. "I remember now. Just the other day Coy said he wished he could find a faster way to California. This wagon train's been moving awfully slow, you know."

"So?" *Where is this leading?*

"So, isn't it obvious? Coy's gone off to search for a wagon to buy so we can go off on our own. Or maybe join a wagon train that's faster than this one."

Callie exchanged incredulous glances with Lydia over Nellie's head. "I don't think so, Nellie. I know it's a shock, but you've got to accept that he's not coming back."

"That's not so!" Nellie's eyes blazed with purpose. "He *is* coming back. I know he is."

Lydia shook her head. "Sister, I don't think—"

"I don't want to hear another word." Nellie rose to her feet, fists clenched. "Coy's coming back. Now you leave me alone." She darted away, leaving Callie and Lydia staring at each other in dismay.

"What can we do?" asked Lydia.

"There's nothing we can do, except wait until she comes to her senses."

* * * *

After one day's rest, the train headed out from Independence Rock, next stop South Pass and the Sweetwater River. Despite the generally happy mood of the campers, Callie heard grumbles. According to legend, they had needed to reach Independence Rock by July fourth if they wanted to get to their destinations before the snow fell. It was now August fourth. Although the grumbling continued, Magnus Ferguson, using his jovial persuasive skills, convinced most of the members they had plenty of time to get where they were going and therefore had nothing to worry about.

During the following days, nothing Callie or Lydia could say would change Nellie's belief Coy would return. If anything, she looked happier than she ever had before, sullen pout gone, her eyes ever alert for that inevitable moment when Coy would reappear and whisk her away to the grand life she imagined would be hers.

A week went by. The company stopped for the day near Devil's Gate on the Sweetwater River and circled the wagons not far from another, much larger, wagon train which they learned was called the Donovan Train. Callie was cleaning up after supper when Luke passed by and remarked, "Looks like we've got company."

Callie stopped to watch as three men rode over from the Donovan Train and into the center of their camp. How solemn-faced they were, as if they weren't riding over for a friendly visit but something deadly serious. She, along with many in the camp, drew closer as Luke, Magnus Ferguson, and the captains gathered around a tall, broad-shouldered man with the look of authority about him. "I'm Sam Donovan and these are two of my captains from our train."

Magnus stepped forward. He introduced Luke and his captains then offered the hospitality of the camp.

"Can't stay." Donovan and his unsmiling companions remained mounted. "We have come on a serious matter."

"Go on, Mister Donovan."

"Tomorrow morning we will have a trial. We're looking for jurors to volunteer."

"What kind of trial?"

"Murder."

Murder. A stirring ran through the crowd. Callie brought her hand to her heart. The very sound of the word alarmed her. Beside her, Nellie stiffened. "How awful," she whispered.

Magnus asked, "What kind of murder, Mister Donovan? Can you give us the details?"

"It's a sad affair, Colonel Ferguson." Donovan cast a quick glance to where Callie and the other women of the camp stood listening. "It's not one I relish discussing in front of the ladies, but the fact is, this morning one of our members was gunned down in cold blood. The man who murdered him was a member of your wagon train. In all fairness, we decided to let you know, in case you'd care to supply jurors for his trial."

Magnus frowned in puzzlement. "He's from our company?"

"Yes, sir. He joined up with us a week or so ago. A young man by the name of Coy Barnett."

Chapter 10

Members of the Ferguson wagon train were so engrossed in Donovan's shocking news, nobody but Callie heard Nellie's gasp of horror, nor saw the look of stunned disbelief that crossed her face. Callie caught her arm as she started to sag and pulled her up straight again. "Hold on, Nellie," she whispered, "we've got to hear this."

The whole camp listened with rapt attention while Sam Donovan told how Coy had appeared in their midst a little over a week ago. He seemed a nice young man and was hired immediately by Elihu Hawkins, a banker from Boston, who needed another hand to drive his wagons. Almost immediately Elihu began to find fault with his new hire. Coy's laziness and insolent attitude were not to his liking. Worse, Coy was paying far too much attention to Sarah, Elihu's sixteen-year-old daughter, who, despite her father's warnings, continued to cast sheep's eyes at the new hire whenever he was around. Hawkins warned Coy not to make free with his daughter, but the young man paid him no heed. When Hawkins found Coy and his daughter together "in intimate proximity," as Donovan delicately put it, he immediately dismissed him. Backed by his captains, Donovan ordered Coy from the camp. A short time later, Hawkins caught the young man red-handed in his wagon, about to make off with his hidden stash of gold coins. He immediately leaped toward the thief, trying to restrain him, but before he could, Coy drew a pistol and shot him in the chest. "Hawkins fell backward from the wagon. He was dead before he hit the ground." Sam Donovan shook his head with deep regret. "Hawkins was a fine man and respected by all. Left a wife and four children."

Amid murmurs of sympathy from the crowd, Luke spoke up. "So, you're holding a trial?"

"Tomorrow morning, nine o'clock. Any man wanting to volunteer as a juror is welcome to join us. We'll give Barnett a full and fair trial."

Gert Gowdy called, "What if you find him guilty?"

Donovan looked surprised, as if the question was unnecessary. "He'll be hanged. The sooner the better. We've wasted enough time on Coy Barnett."

* * * *

Callie got little sleep that night. She and Lydia spent hours trying to console Nellie, who cried her heart out until finally she fell into fitful slumber. Morning came, and with it a dreary leaden sky. Nearly every member of the Ferguson wagon train traipsed the short distance to the Donovan Train for the trial of Coy Barnett. The Whitaker family was among them.

Along the way, Pa noticed Nellie's tear-stained face and despairing manner. "Don't know why you're crying, Daughter. I always said he was no good."

Nellie gave an answering wail.

"Don't waste your sympathy. He deserves to hang. There's no call for you to be so upset."

If you only knew. Callie gave her distraught stepsister a pat on the arm.

Magnus Ferguson fell into step beside her. "It's a shame you have to see this, Miss Whitaker."

She was happy to see him and glad for his reassuring presence. "Oh, Mr. Ferguson, who are they to think they can give him a trial? What right do they have?"

Magnus shrugged. "Who else will do it? We're not in the United States any more. Beyond the Missouri River, we're on our own. From there on, the trains create their own justice. Some agree on a constitution with bylaws. That's what we have. Before we started, we drew up a constitution and created rules for every dispute we could think of, and every crime, including murder. From what I understand, the Donovan Train has a constitution similar to ours. That being the case, they have every right to hold a trial."

"Must they hang him?" Nellie asked in an anguished voice. "Aren't there other kinds of ways to punish him?"

"Of course there are. There's everything from banishment, whipping, a stakeout, or even a simple admonition."

"Then why—"

"It appears Coy has committed an abominable crime for which he must be punished accordingly." Magnus gave Nellie a grim smile. "If what I heard is correct, death is none too good for the likes of Coy Barnett. I hope he suffers while he's dangling at the end of that rope."

How harsh. Callie gazed at Magnus in surprise. She had thought he was nothing but kind and caring. Now, for the second time, she saw a side to him she'd never seen before. "But to put a young man to death, whatever the reason, seems so very cruel."

Magnus gazed back at her with a look that, though sympathetic, revealed his slight disdain. "You're a soft-hearted woman, Callie, like most women are. So of course you'd think that way. Let the men handle it, my dear."

They reached the Donovan Train. Callie said no more. She had to focus all her attention on getting Nellie through this terrible day. Later on, though, she'd remember this conversation with Magnus and why she didn't like what he'd said, didn't like it at all.

In the middle of the Donovan campground, preparations for the trial were almost complete. Two rows of six chairs were set up for the jurors. A makeshift table stood at one side, presumably for the judge. An ominously empty chair was placed directly facing the jurors' chairs, only a few feet away. Callie guessed it was for Coy. A cold knot formed in her stomach. At first she couldn't believe this was happening, but now it was becoming so very real.

A noisy crowd had gathered around. It fell silent when a stern-faced Sam Donovan appeared and spoke in a voice that rang with authority. "Let's get started. The jurors may take their places." He looked toward a tent nearby. "Bring the prisoner forward."

Twelve men, including Pa and five others from the Ferguson train, seated themselves in the jurors' chairs. All eyes focused on Coy Barnet as four burly men dragged him across the campground. Callie hardly recognized him. The cocky young man with the impudent smile was gone. Hands tied behind his back, his clothes in disarray, he trembled with fear. A blackened eye and hideously swollen cheek marred his once-handsome face.

At the sight of him, Nellie cried out, "Coy! What have they done to you?"

Coy glanced in her direction but gave no sign of recognition.

Ma gave Nellie a sharp nudge with her elbow. "Keep your mouth shut. I won't have you wailing and moaning over a murderer. If you can't keep quiet, you can go home."

Nellie stood mute as Sam Donovan, who had been appointed judge, called the trial to order.

Three men testified, all respected members of their company. They said much the same thing. They heard the gunshot, saw Elihu Hawkins fall backward from his wagon mortally wounded and saw Coy Barnett jump from the wagon, still holding a pistol. They pounced on him, foiling his futile attempt to get away.

When the last witness finished, Sam Donovan addressed Coy, who sat silent, head down, tied to the chair that faced the jury. "There's no doubt you killed Elihu Hawkins. Do you have anything to say for yourself, Mister Barnett?"

Coy seemed in a daze. He barely lifted his head, looking as if he'd like to speak but hadn't the strength. His head dropped down again. "No," he replied in a barely audible voice that held no hope.

The jury didn't bother to retire while they considered their verdict. They stayed where they were, whispering among themselves. Within five minutes they announced their decision.

Coy Barnett was guilty of murder. He would be hanged immediately.

* * * *

Callie noticed Luke didn't attend the trial. When she returned to their camp, she passed by his tent. He was sitting on a log cleaning his rifle, not the least interested in the happenings at the Donovan train. When Callie stopped to talk, he raised his head. "So, is it over?"

"It was horrible."

"Is he dead yet?"

"I suppose so." After the trial, a group of grim-faced men, one with a coil of rope in his hand, led Coy away. The ladies were instructed not to follow.

"Then it's done." With a sad shake of his head, Luke arose. His observant gaze swept over her.

She took a breath and tried to calm herself, knowing he'd be sure to notice how upset she was.

"Try not to let it bother you." His voice was surprisingly gentle. "You don't always find justice in the wilderness. Nothing you can do about it."

The horror of it all boiled up within her. "I never liked Coy. He was awful in so many ways, but even he deserved a fair trial. *Why*, Luke? That trial was a farce. What right did they have to kill him?" Remembering Magnus's callous words, she wished she hadn't asked. Luke probably felt the same.

He laid a gentle hand on her arm. "If this was a perfect world, there'd be fairness and justice for all, but it's not a perfect world. Coy's gone now. It's over. Like I said, you can cry all you want, but you can't bring him back."

"I suppose you're right."

"I know I'm right. You'd better get back to your sister. She's going to need you."

"Nellie is…very upset."

"Nellie's in trouble, isn't she?"

Luke's question caught her unaware, so much she didn't consider any sort of denial. "How did you know?"

"Just knew. Never mind how."

"She was certain Coy would come back for her. Now he's gone…" She fought to keep the hysteria from her voice. "Pa's going to kill her."

"I wouldn't be surprised."

"I can't think what to do."

His eyes brimmed with sympathy. "It's a bad situation, but knowing you, you'll think of something. I'll help if I can."

She left his campsite with a lighter step. Whether or not he could really help, Luke made her feel better, bolstered her sagging spirits. Her mood lasted until she reached her tent.

Nellie was sobbing inside. When she saw Callie, she swallowed a sob and asked, "What shall I do?"

Callie hesitated. What should she say? How strange Nellie was looking for answers, not from Lydia or Ma, but from her previously scorned stepsister. And even stranger, why was it she actually wanted to help? Looking back over the years, she couldn't think of one nice thing Nellie had ever done for her. She'd never even said a kind word, or given her much of anything other than sneers and insults. *I'd be a fool to help her. If I have any sense at all, I should be rejoicing over Nellie's well-deserved misery.*

And yet… When she looked into Nellie's tear-stained face, she wanted only to help. How could she hate someone who hadn't the sense of a goose? Whose ignorance and gullibility led her to this awful mess? Callie knew the answer. Despite everything, she'd help Nellie if she could because she was the strong one, stronger than Nellie, stronger than poor, silly Lydia. Besides, she loved her family. How could she turn her back on a family member, awful though she might be? *I won't back away. It's up to me.*

She reached to take Nellie's hand. "Stop your crying. I want you to look perfectly fine at supper tonight, like you haven't a care in the world."

"How can I when Coy is dead and my life ruined?"

"You can and you will. You're not showing yet, so you're safe, at least for a while, and that will give us time to think what to do."

* * * *

The days following Coy's death, Nellie's behavior ranged from despair, to anger with Coy, to forgiveness of Coy, along with the belief those witnesses had lied and he hadn't killed anyone. Only Callie and Lydia knew of Nellie's hysterics. She managed to hold herself together when others were around, although everyone noticed she was not, as Ma put it, "herself."

"Nellie, you look pale." For the journey, Ma had brought along a big bottle of sulphur and molasses, guaranteed to cure any ailment from thinning hair to a heart attack. She forced Nellie to take a big spoonful every day, lamenting she couldn't see any results.

Only at night when the girls were in their tent could Nellie give way to her growing terror. Often she whispered into the darkness, "What am I going to do, Callie? You promised you'd help me."

"I don't know yet." Callie racked her brain but so far could think of no way Nellie could avoid their father's wrath. The easy solutions weren't going to happen. Coy was gone for good. Nellie showed no signs of losing the baby. If she hadn't by now, she probably wouldn't. "There's still time. You don't even show yet."

"But I do." Nellie placed a hand over her stomach. "There's a bulge there. I can definitely feel it."

"Your dress and apron will hide it for a long time."

"Not 'til California they won't."

Callie had no answer.

Nellie stayed close to the wagon, hardly ever venturing out to visit other members of the train. But one evening she was gone for a while. When she came back, her eyes gleamed with excitement. "Come in the tent, Callie. I've got something to show you."

Once in the privacy of the tent, Nellie reached in her pocket and drew out a small vial. "Look! The perfect answer. I'll soon be rid of the baby." She laughed with relief. "Just think, my troubles will soon be over."

Callie remained unimpressed. "Where did you get this?"

"Gert Gowdy. We got to talking. She guessed about the baby, but she promised she'd keep quiet. She said it's perfectly safe."

Callie wished she could share Nellie's excitement, but a warning voice from within told her she could not. She pointed at the vial. "What is it?"

"Gert says it's an herb called blue cohosh. I take twenty drops in a cup of warm water every three to four hours until things start to happen. And then..." In the cramped confines of the tent, Nellie did a little jig. "My worries will be over. I'll have my life back again."

"How do you know it's safe?"

"Because Gert said so." Nellie frowned in puzzlement. "Aren't you happy for me?"

"I suppose, but..." Callie bit her lip. In all her sheltered life, she'd learned next to nothing about having babies and what prevented them. She had only the vaguest notion that certain herbs could be used to end a pregnancy. Somewhere she'd heard that some of them could be dangerous. "Of course, I'll be happy for you if it works like it's supposed to, but I'm not sure. It might be harmful."

Nellie flung her head back. "So what? I'll take that risk if I have to. Besides, Gert said—"

"I want to hear for myself what Gert says." Callie held out her hand. "Give me that vial. I'm going to talk to Gert, just to make sure."

Nellie's lower lip protruded into its familiar pout. "I don't see why..."

"Give me that vial."

"All right then." With great reluctance, Nellie handed over the small glass bottle.

"You wait here. I'll be right back." Without a backward glance, Callie left the tent and started a purposeful march across the campsite. She was halfway to Gert's wagon before she realized she'd been so concerned, she'd forgotten to be her usual humble self, had practically yelled at Nellie, took command, and told her what to do. *What's happening? Not like me at all.*

Luke came riding up. He slid from his horse and fell into step beside her. "What's going on?"

She didn't slow down. "I'm going to Gert's. I need to ask her about something she gave Nellie."

"To lose the baby?"

She nodded. "Have you ever heard of an herb called blue cohosh?"

He stopped in his tracks, took her arm, and brought her to a halt. "Is that what Gert gave her?"

"Yes. She's supposed to take twenty drops every—"

Luke muttered a curse. "I saw an Indian woman die from taking blue cohosh. It wasn't a pleasant death. The convulsions, the pain she suffered..." His eyes narrowed with disgust. "You can't let her take it. That stuff could kill the poor girl."

"She's desperate."

"Better desperate than dead."

His words hit home. "You're right. I can't let her do it."

"It's up to you. You can handle it." His smile carried a touch of irony.

"I wouldn't have said that a few weeks ago."

Any other day she would have been flattered by his remark and yearned to hear more. Not today, though. "I must talk to Gert right now."

"So go." Luke backed away. "I won't stand in your way. If you need any help—"

"I can handle the likes of Gert Gowdy." Without another word, Callie drew herself up and headed toward the Gowdys' wagon.

After grueling weeks on the trail, no woman in the train looked her best. Even so, there was no excuse for Gert Gowdy's slovenly appearance. Thin and sharp-nosed, she peered down at Callie from the wagon seat, her apron dirty, her fingernails none too clean. "You don't want Nellie to take it?" She pressed her lips together. "I'm only trying to help the poor girl."

Callie held out the vial. "It's too dangerous. Nellie doesn't want it."

Gert eyed her shrewdly. "It isn't Nellie who don't want it, it's you."

"All I know is she's not going to take it. Take it back or I'll pour it on the ground."

"Ain't you something!" Gert's hand swooped down to grab the vial. "You've got a nerve. You think you're doing her a favor? She won't thank you for what you done, especially when her Pa finds out she's got a bun in the oven and the father dead. Likely he'll skin her alive."

"I don't care about that. All I know is, what you gave her is poison and you'd better not do it again." Callie turned and walked away, leaving Gert silenced and wide-eyed. Her anger was such she had almost reached her wagon before she realized what she'd done. Never had she sounded so bossy, telling an older woman like Gert what to do. No regrets, though. Gert deserved it.

Only when she reached her wagon did the results of her actions hit her hard. What if the blue cohosh had worked perfectly? Nellie's problem would be solved. She'd be happy again, the fearsome burden lifted. She could then go on with her life. Instead, Nellie remained in deep trouble. *Thanks to me.* She almost wished she'd stayed quiet, let Nellie have her way and risk the consequences. She hadn't, and with good reason, but as a result, Nellie's fate rested squarely on her shoulders. What an awful responsibility. What was she going to do?

A few evenings later, as they were circling the wagons for the night, a lone wagon appeared. It was heading east, back to where they came from. Lately they were encountering many such wagons. Sometimes a family decided it could no longer endure the rugged life of a wagon train and just wanted to go home. Sometimes families ran out of money or there'd been a sickness or a death. This was the case of the man and his children who stopped and joined them for the night. "The name's Abraham Jonckers."

The driver was a husky man with a bushy beard who appeared to be in his mid-thirties. "I'd be obliged if you'd let us camp with you tonight." He waved at three small blond heads peeking from the wagon. "We were headed to California. I hated to turn around, but a few days ago the wife came down with mountain fever. She died." Choked up, he had to pause before going on. "Couldn't keep going. Three little children to care for. It's too much. Now all I want is to get back to New York and buy another farm. Shouldn't have left in the first place."

Bighearted Florida immediately invited the Jonckers' family to dinner. When the children arrived with hair uncombed, clothes dirty and much in need of a wash, she enlisted help from Hetty and Callie to clean them up.

Seeing his children clean, in fresh clothes with a well-cooked meal in their bellies, Jonckers expressed his gratitude. "My Greta kept them as neat as a pin. I do the best I can, but as you can see, I'm a poor substitute for their mother."

That night after supper, Callie visited Florida's campfire, as she'd begun to do most nights. Magnus Ferguson often stopped by, too. Florida always made him welcome and Callie still enjoyed his company. By now she'd almost forgotten his thoughtless remark about Coy. When she did think about it, she tried to convince herself she hadn't heard him right. Lately he'd been more attentive than ever. If only she could forget about Luke and fall in love with Magnus!

Sometimes Luke joined them around Florida's campfire. Callie loved being near him and felt more drawn to him than ever, even though the night he kissed her with such passion was a distant memory. Tonight only Florida and Callie remained after Jonckers had left to put his children to bed. They talked about what a shame it was he had lost his wife and that his three small children were without a mother. During the conversation, Florida gave Callie an especially meaningful look. "Too bad he can't find someone to help him."

Florida's words sunk in. *What if... Of course! The perfect solution.* "I just thought of something. Maybe it's crazy but—"

"It's worth a try, isn't it? He seems like a good man who would treat Nellie kindly. As for her, I suspect she'd gladly agree. Anything to escape her father."

Callie's mind flew in several directions at once. Nellie could solve her dilemma by escaping with Abraham Jonckers. She'd been helping with the cooking and now knew enough to fix meals and, of course, she could take care of the children. Would he take her in? Would Nellie want to go? If she did, how could she get away without Pa finding out? "Mister

Jonckers said he was leaving first thing in the morning. We'd have to work fast."

Florida pursed her lips. "That doesn't leave us much time. I'm not sure we can do it."

This was Nellie's only chance. "We'll make it happen. I'll go talk to Nellie right now."

Florida rose to her feet. "Wait right here while I go talk to Mister Jonckers. No sense talking to Nellie unless he agrees."

"It won't be easy, asking a man to take on a woman he hasn't even met and who's...you know."

"I'll have to tell him, but he might, being he's desperate for help."

"He will. He has to." At last, a glimmer of hope. Callie sat down to wait for Florida's return.

Moments after Florida left, Magnus stepped into the light of the campfire. "Good evening, Callie. I couldn't help overhearing."

"You know about Nellie?"

He nodded. His expression hardly changed. "Most unfortunate. Indeed, shocking."

Callie searched for the right words. It was important he understood. "Nellie's desperate. She trusted Coy when he said he'd marry her, but now...you can imagine how fearful she is. She thinks Pa will kill her when he finds out."

"He very well might."

What was wrong? She could detect not one speck of sympathy in Magnus's voice. "Her only hope is if she can leave with Mister Jonckers, do the cooking and take care of his children. He seems like a nice man."

"He's a fool if he agrees to such an idiotic scheme."

She drew in her breath, caught off guard by Magnus's disapproval. She hated to discuss such delicate matters but had no choice. "My sister is with child. Ma and Pa don't know yet, but she can't keep her secret much longer. Naturally, she's desperate."

"Nellie should tell her father. That's what an obedient daughter should do."

"Don't you see? She's too terrified to tell him."

"Nellie has sinned. She should subject herself to whatever punishment her father metes out."

"What!" Callie could hardly believe what she'd heard. "You can't mean that. You don't know Pa. He might not physically hurt her, but he might throw her out. Then what would she do?"

"Someone would doubtless take her in."

"Would you?"

He gave her an indulgent smile. "From what I've observed, Nellie never gave you so much as the time of day. So why are you concerned?"

"Because she's my family. Because she might have been selfish, but deep down she's a good person. Everyone deserves a second chance."

Magnus waved his hand in a gesture of dismissal. "Nellie has made her bed. Now she must lie in it."

She sat there blank and amazed. This was Magnus who was talking. The man she so admired, who had always seemed so kind, so understanding. "I'm sorry you feel that way. I'm only trying to help her."

His mouth quirked with disgust. "You should leave her to her fate. And for God's sake, don't involve a fine man like Abraham Jonckers."

Why was this going so wrong? She'd never dreamed Magnus was so self-righteous, so rigid in his thinking. "I can't do that. Nellie's not the easiest person to get along with, but I was just thinking…" She liked and respected Magnus and highly valued his opinion. He must understand. It was so important her words come out right. "Can't you see how well this will work out? Poor Mister Jonckers is desperate for help. Nellie needs to get away. She isn't the greatest cook in the world, or the hardest worker, but considering the circumstances…what is so wrong with him taking her in? She'll earn her keep."

Magnus's eyes narrowed with disgust. "You're making a mistake. You're too young to know what you're doing, taking far too much upon yourself. Nothing good will come of it, I guarantee."

Before she could answer, Florida returned. She was smiling. Seeing Magnus, she curbed her words. "He said yes, Callie, you know what I mean."

"He knows," Callie answered.

"Good. Maybe you can help, Magnus. I've got good news. Abraham Jonckers has agreed to hire Nellie as his cook and children's helper, sight unseen."

Callie asked, "Did you tell him?"

"About the baby? Of course. He understands Nellie is with child. He also understands her parents won't be informed she's leaving. Nellie is of age, so legally she can do as she pleases. She's not a slave, you know. He says he'll leave before dawn tomorrow and put as much distance as possible between his wagon and us. If all goes well, Caleb won't know Nellie's gone until hours later." Florida nodded her head with confidence. "When he does learn, he won't go after her." She turned toward Magnus. "I trust you'll help us."

Magnus's lip curled with scorn. "Your scheme is insane. I'm tempted to go straight to Caleb Whitaker and tell him what you're up to. However, since I want no part in this, I'll refrain. Shame on you both. Good night." He strode off, leaving his stern rebuke ringing in her ears.

Florida was the first to speak. "Well, I never! What's got into him?"

"He says Nellie's a sinner. He thinks she should confess everything to Pa and take her punishment."

Florida eyed her shrewdly. "What do you think, Callie? Should I go back to Mister Jonckers and tell him to forget about it?"

Magnus's attitude had shocked her. She drew in a slow, calming breath. "Let Colonel Ferguson decide what's right? Absolutely not. Nellie needs help and we're going to give it to her, despite what he thinks."

Florida looked relieved. "We're doing the right thing, even though there'll be hell to pay when your pa finds out. He can be mighty mean."

Callie pictured that awful moment when Pa learned Nellie was gone. "I worry Pa might go after them with his rifle and kill them both."

"I can't say for sure, but I don't think so. If I were you, when the time comes, I'd just tell him the truth, that she's pregnant and Coy is the father. In that narrow mind of his, he'll decide Nellie committed a terrible sin and isn't worth saving. I wager he won't raise a finger to find her."

"I hope you're right." Callie managed a wry smile. "Even so, I dread telling Pa."

"You must put it off as long as possible." A shadow of worry crossed Florida's face. "Will he notice if Nellie's not there first thing in the morning?"

"He's always busy with the oxen. Nellie sleeps as late as possible. I don't think he will."

"Good. The longer he doesn't know, the farther away Nellie will be."

"Wish me luck."

Florida flung her arms around Callie and gave her a hug. "You're going to need it, honey. Remember, we're your friends. We care about you and we're here to help. Now go talk to Nellie. Let's hope that foolish girl will agree."

* * * *

Beneath a grove of trees, away from the wagon, Nellie stared at her wide-eyed. "You mean you want me to go off with a strange man I've never met before?"

"It's your choice. I know it will be hard, and I don't know when we'll see each other again, but it's either that or face Pa."

Nellie brought her hand to her stomach. "I'm showing. Ma's looking at me funny already." Terror rose in her voice. "More than anything else in this world, I'm scared of Pa."

"I know. Why else would we take such a chance?"

"How will I know where to find you? Maybe I never can. Maybe I'll never see Ma and Pa and Lydia again…and you."

Had the situation not been so heart-rending, Callie would have laughed at being such an afterthought. "It's a choice you've got to make."

A long, silent moment went by. Callie waited while her stepsister struggled with her thoughts. "I'll do it!" Nellie surprised Callie with an adventurous toss of her head. "Abraham Jonckers… I saw him. He's not bad-looking. Maybe he'll fall in love with me."

"Better yet, maybe *you* will fall in love with *him*." Callie clasped her stepsister's shoulders. "I'm glad you decided this. Florida talked to Mister Jonckers, and he's already agreed to take you. I know it's hard, but it's for the best."

Nellie's face lit. "Oh, Callie, my prayers are answered if this works. Do you know how happy I'll be? Not to have to worry about Pa anymore? I'd give anything—*anything*."

"Go pack your things and write a note to Ma and Pa. This is going to work, Nellie, I know it will."

Doubts and fears kept Callie awake far into the night. What if Pa heard them leave? What if he went after Nellie with his rifle? What if Jonckers changed his mind? So many what-ifs, she hardly slept at all. The sun had not yet risen when she awakened, quickly dressed, and gently shook her stepsister. "It's time, Nellie. Shh… We must be quiet. Everything's ruined if Pa wakes."

"I'm ready." Nellie was dressed. She'd slept in her clothes. "Should we wake Lydia?"

"Let her sleep. You've already said your good-byes." Callie didn't care to repeat last night's tearful scene with her stepsisters, both of them crying, especially Lydia when she'd realized she might never see her sister again. Nellie had wept with the sorrow of knowing she must leave her family, yet when she'd talked about Pa, and what he might do, she remained steadfast in her resolve to run away.

"All right. We'll let Lydia sleep." In the near darkness, Nellie picked up her bundle of clothes. "You've got my note?"

"In my pocket. Don't worry, I'll put off giving it to them long as I can."

Callie's heart pounded as they crept from the tent. *Mustn't wake them.* All was silent. Where was Florida? She'd promised to lead them to Jonckers' wagon. It was parked somewhere on the other side of the campsite, but she didn't know exactly where. As they crept along, she began to worry they wouldn't find it until a muted command came out of the darkness. "Follow me, Callie."

Luke. Just hearing his confident voice eased her concern. "Where's Florida?"

"Sleeping. I'll handle this."

"I didn't know you knew," she whispered.

"Of course I did. You're going the wrong way. Follow me."

In silence, the three moved stealthily across the campground until they reached Jonckers's wagon.

He was already awake, hitching up the oxen. One of the animals gave a muted bellow. "Dang it, Mabel, quiet now," Abe whispered, placing a calming hand on the ox's back. In dawn's first light, he was barely visible. He looked toward her and her stepsister. "Which is Nellie?"

"I am, sir." Nellie stepped forward. "I want to thank you—"

"No need for that. You better get in the wagon before somebody sees you. There are three kids asleep in there, but you'll find a place to lie down. Get some rest if you can. We'll talk later."

It's going to be all right. Callie had worried Jonckers could be mean like Pa, or even worse, but she could tell from the way he talked he was a kindhearted man who'd treat Nellie well.

Nellie gave a muted sob. She dropped her bundle to the ground and threw her arms around Callie. "You've saved me," she whispered. "From the bottom of my heart, I thank you. I don't know what I would have done—"

"Shh, no need to thank me." Callie hugged her back then let her go. "You better get in the wagon."

"I'm afraid for you, Callie. I worry about what Pa will do when he finds out."

"You let me worry about that. I'll be fine." She hoped she was right but doubted it.

"Will we ever see each other again?"

"Of course we will. When you're settled, all you have to do is write to Pastor Carter at our old church. We'll let him know where we are, and then he can tell you." The bark of a dog broke the stillness. Soon the whole camp would be awake. "Now go. Right now. There's no time to waste."

Nellie picked up her bundle. Without another word, she gave Callie a swift hug and climbed into the wagon.

Callie and Luke watched as Jonckers hitched up the last two oxen and declared, "Guess we'd better get going." He climbed to the seat, picked up the reins, and called a muted "Gee-up!" With only the barest of squeaks, the wagon rolled from the camp and headed east, back to where they'd come from. Callie, Luke beside her, followed, silently waving to Nellie, who kept waving back from the rear of the wagon. Would she ever see Nellie again? How awful they must part this way.

At last, when they had left the campsite and followed the wagon a short distance, Luke touched her arm. "This is far enough. We'd better get back."

She stopped, waved a final good-bye. The wagon rolled out of sight.

Nellie was gone. A vast sense of loss enveloped her. "I know it's for the best, but it's hard."

"I can tell Jonckers is a good man. It had to be done. This way Nellie has a chance. Come on, I'll walk you home."

On their return to the campground, Callie felt an increasing flood of relief. No longer did she have to worry over her stepsister. Nellie was gone and she was safe. Even after the briefest of meetings with Abe Jonckers, she knew in her heart Nellie would have a good life with him. "I was worried, but I think it's going to work. Nellie's safe now. I can only hope Pa doesn't—"

"He won't." Luke stopped short. His hands gripped her shoulders. "Listen to me. Nellie will be fine. It's you I worry about. If your Pa gets out of hand, you come to me. Is that clear?"

"I suppose so… Yes, of course you're right." An alarming thought struck her. "Oh, dear God."

"What is it?"

"It just sunk in what I've done."

"You helped your sister out of a terrible mess. Nothing wrong with that, is there? You've done a good thing."

Again she was struck with how understanding Luke was and how caring. This was so new, knowing someone would actually listen to her with genuine sympathy. Her words poured out. There was no stopping them. "All my life I did what I was told. Now I've gone against Ma and Pa. When I started this journey, I never dreamed of doing such a thing. Now, here I am, totally defying them. I can hardly believe what I've done."

"I can believe it. You're not the same meek little mouse you were when you left Tennessee."

"No one calls me that anymore. All the same, I'm scared to death to face Pa. My stepmother too."

"You can handle it. Your doormat days are gone."

Doormat days. His words hit hard. "You're right. I'm not like that anymore."

His hands still rested on her shoulders. As an orange sliver of sun rose above the nearby hills, he drew her closer. "Not anymore." His voice shook. As his hands explored the hollows of her back, his dizzying masculine smell jarred her heart. Buckskin mixed with gunpowder, and a touch of the towering pine trees thrown in. "Callie," he whispered, his breath hot against her ear. She sunk into his cushioning embrace, slid her arms around his neck, and tilted her head back to gaze at him. His mouth covered hers, hard and hungry. It was a kiss that was urgent, as if a dam had burst, releasing a flood of pent-up emotion. An aching need flowed through her. She wanted nothing more than to press tighter against him than she already was. He broke off the kiss and backed away, shaking his head in disbelief. "My God, I vowed I wouldn't do this."

"Why not?"

"Because..." A wry smile tipped one corner of his mouth. "What is it about you that I find so damnably attractive?"

She stepped back, held out her faded skirt and gave him a little curtsy. "The stylish way I dress perhaps?"

His face lit. "That's it! You make me laugh. You make me think of you in the middle of the night. You..." He seemed at a loss for further words, so instead pulled her back into his arms. Her heart was thundering as he pressed her tight against him. He was trembling. "I've never met a woman like you. I've never wanted a woman like I want you." Again his mouth covered hers, his lips hard and searching. This time his tongue explored the recesses of her mouth, sending shivers of desire racing through her. At last, with a shuddering intake of breath, he raised his lips from hers and looked into her eyes. "The sun's coming up. I don't want this to end but it must." Gripping her arms, he thrust her away. "Go now. If you need help, remember, I'll be standing by."

Chapter 11

"You cooked a good breakfast." Caleb Whitaker helped himself to more bacon.

"Thanks, Pa." Compliments from her stepfather were rare. If her stomach hadn't been clenched tight with anxiety, Callie might have laughed. This would be the last of her happiness for a while, probably forever. As it was, she hadn't even tried to go back to bed. To keep her mind off what was bound to be a horrible scene, she'd thrown herself into the task of fixing breakfast, adding stewed apples and extra bacon to their usual morning fare.

Pa looked toward the tent. "Where are the girls? Time to get going."

"Go get them up, Callie," Ma said.

"Yes, Ma."

When she entered the tent, Lydia was already dressed, sitting on her bedding, twisting her dainty hands together. "Pa's going to kill us. I'm afraid to come out."

Callie sat beside her. "Don't be silly. You'll be fine. I'm taking the blame for Nellie's leaving. When Pa asks, you tell him you didn't hear her leave, you didn't know she was gone, you don't know a thing."

Lydia gazed at her with frightened eyes. "He won't believe me."

"Yes, he will. I'll tell him it was nobody's doing but mine. You knew nothing about it. Believe me, you're not the one he'll be after. It'll be me."

A shadow of sympathy stole across Lydia's face. "All you did was help her. I hate to think what he'll do to you."

Despite her anxiety, Callie managed a smile. This was the first time Lydia had said something nice to her and meant it. "You let me worry about that. Now, go have your breakfast. Act like it's just another day. If Pa asks about Nellie, tell him what's closest to the truth without giving anything away."

"Like I thought she was already up?"

"Perfect. Remember, the longer Pa doesn't know, the farther away Nellie will be, and the better chance Pa won't go after her."

The morning went by with Pa busy driving the wagon and Ma sitting beside him. Doubtless they assumed Nellie was in the wagon or walking behind, out of sight. In an attempt to calm her nerves, Callie took a short ride on Duke. That didn't work. Her stomach remained tied in knots. She ended up walking behind the wagon with Lydia and Tommy. Her anxiety grew as each hour passed, even though she kept telling herself every mile they traveled made Nellie safer.

Not until they stopped for the noon break did Ma climb down from the wagon and look around with curiosity. "Where's Nellie? I haven't seen her all morning."

Callie stepped forward. "I know you haven't, Ma." She drew a trembling breath and called to her stepfather who still sat perched on the wagon seat. "Pa, will you come down here? I have something to tell you."

Pa climbed down slowly, a frown on his face, almost as if he suspected bad news was coming. He stood in front of Callie and looped his thumbs through his suspenders. "What is it, girl?"

"Nellie's gone."

Ma frowned. "What do you mean, she's gone?"

Callie's heart pounded in her chest. "I mean she's really gone. She left because…"

She told them how Nellie had fallen in love with Coy, how he had promised to marry her, how he'd run off, joined the Donovan Train and they knew what happened there. "You see, the reason she was so upset was because…"

Callie had to pause. This was like standing at the edge of a cliff about to jump. When she did, there would be no return, not ever. "Nellie got herself with child. That's why——"

"*What?*" Ma's mouth dropped open.

Pa had listened stony-faced and unmoving. He remained so. "How long have you known this?" His voice sounded so deadly calm it was frightening.

"Just about from the beginning."

Pa's body stiffened. His face turned red. "And you didn't tell me?"

"Nellie was afraid."

"Where has she gone?"

I'm in for it now. Judging from the murderous look in her stepfather's eyes, not only had she jumped off that cliff, she was fast falling to total disaster. The best she could do now was try to save Nellie from the same fate. She pulled the note from her apron pocket and handed it to her stepfather. "This is from Nellie."

Pa snatched the note from her hand. Without taking his eyes off Callie, he handed it to Ma. "Read it."

Ma unfolded it and read aloud in an unsteady voice.

Dear Ma and Pa,
I am sorry I run off. I love you and hope you will forgive me. I will be all right. Please, please don't follow me. I hope to see you again some day.
Your loving daughter, Nellie

"Nellie wrote this?" Ma stared at the note, as if she couldn't believe what she was reading. "She never said a word to me."

Pa ignored her. He had yet to take his eyes off Callie. "Where has she gone?"

Callie's driving instinct was to flee, but she forced herself to stand her ground. "Nellie didn't want me to tell you. You see—" The rest of her words died in her throat as he took a menacing step toward her.

"I don't want excuses." Pa raised his hand. "Where has she gone?"

Nothing could strike more terror in her heart than when Pa got angry. Now he was angrier than she'd ever seen him, his face twisted with rage, his hand raised and ready to strike her. Every fiber of her being said run. By God, she would not. "I'm not going to tell you, Pa, except she's in safe hands."

His hand came down on her so fast, she didn't see it coming. She staggered back and almost fell but caught herself in time, a throbbing pain on her cheekbone near her eye. Lydia screamed and rushed to her side. "Oh, Callie, you're hurt." She looked toward Pa. "Don't you hit her again!"

So stunned she hardly knew what happened, Callie touched the throbbing spot on her face.

Ma yelled, "For God's sake, Caleb, stop it. That's enough."

"Shut your mouth, woman!" Pa's enraged gaze went back to Callie. He was going to strike her again.

Ma screamed and grabbed his arm. "Caleb, stop! The whole camp is watching."

Pa ignored her, but before he could strike another blow, Lydia grabbed his other arm. "Stop it, Pa! I'll tell you where she's gone."

He lowered his hand. His breath coming hard, he swung his gaze to Lydia. "Tell me now or I'll—"

Lydia recoiled, as if Pa's next blow would be aimed at her. "Nellie ran off with that man from New York."

"Abe Jonckers?" He looked incredulous.

Callie found her voice. "Yes, Mister Jonckers. She doesn't want you to follow. *Please* don't follow. She's not a child. She's twenty-three. She went of her own free will."

Callie was fully prepared for Pa's next blow, but before he could deliver it, Luke strode into their campsite. "What's going on?"

Pa glared back at him. "It's a family matter. Don't interfere."

Luke looked closely at Callie's face. From the way his jaw clenched, the blow must have left a mark. He turned to Pa. "You hit her again, you're a dead man." Callie couldn't miss the bridled anger that lay beneath his lethally quiet voice.

"You keep out of this!" Pa cried.

Ma cringed. "Caleb, for Lord's sake, the whole camp can hear you."

Callie looked around. Dear God! She hadn't realized the usual bustle around the campsite had ceased. Everyone in sight had stopped in their tracks, all eyes turned toward the spectacle at the Whitaker wagon.

Pa saw them, too, and uttered a furious "Damnation." Through gritted teeth he replied, "I can handle my family, Mister McGraw. Just go."

Luke cast a concerned look at Callie. "Are you all right?"

"I'm fine." She wasn't fine but wanted only to have this horribly embarrassing scene come to an end. "You can go. It'll be all right."

Luke looked back at Pa with eyes that were flat, hard, and filled with anger. "Will it be all right now, Mr. Whitaker?"

Pa made a growling sound. He let loose a sigh that was half frustration, half an admission of defeat. "You can go now, Mr. McGraw."

"You won't hit her again?"

Pa looked ready to burst with fury but gave Luke a curt shake of his head.

For a long, tension-filled moment, Luke stood silent, as if he wanted to make sure Pa understood. "All right. Callie, call if you need me." Quickly he strode away.

Pa glared after him. "Bastard!" he muttered under his breath. When Luke was out of hearing distance, Pa faced Callie again, icy rage in his eyes. "So you knew about Nellie from the beginning?"

She would not cringe with fear. She would try to explain. "Quite a while. Ever since..."

Pa listened intently while Callie described in detail Nellie's so-called romance with Coy and how he had deceived her. "Like I said, Nellie is with child. Surely you can see how desperate she was and why I wanted to help her."

Pa showed no reaction, just continued staring at her with his cold, granite eyes.

"After Coy died—and you know how horrible that was—she was afraid what you'd do when you found out. So, when Mister Jonckers arrived, and I saw he needed help, I figured he could hire Nellie to be his cook and help with his children. So that's...that's..." Her courage was failing fast under her stepfather's withering gaze. "It was my idea. Ma didn't know. Until today, Lydia didn't know either." She was in so deep now, what did a little lie matter? "I'm to blame and nobody else. Just, please, don't go after Nellie."

A long, terrible silence followed. She, Ma, and Lydia stood unmoving, as if they were frozen in time, waiting for a response from Pa. When he finally spoke, it was in a voice so cold and distant she would have preferred his anger. "I will not go after Nellie. She's dead to me. I never want to hear her name spoken again. Is that clear?"

Nellie was safe! Pa wasn't going to chase after her. On the other hand... Callie struggled with both grief and despair. Poor Nellie. What an awful thing to be cast out forever from your family.

Ma stood dazed and totally bewildered, as if she had yet to understand. "Nellie...gone forever? You can't mean it, Caleb. It's not too late. You must go after her."

He ignored her. Fastening burning eyes on Callie, he raised his arm and pointed away from their campsite. "Get out of my sight. You're no longer welcome in this family."

Ma gasped and turned pale. "You can't mean that."

"She's no daughter of mine."

"But we need her, Caleb. Who will do the cooking? Wash the clothes? Take care of Tommy?"

Despite the turmoil of the moment, Callie clearly saw how she stood with the family. Even though she called him Pa, he'd never thought of her as a daughter. As for Ma, she was only concerned she might lose her slave. That's all she ever was to her stepmother, not like a daughter at all. So far, Ma had uttered not one word of affection or concern. Her one feeble attempt to come to Callie's defense was only because the neighbors were watching. Ma had never loved her. Never would, no matter how hard she tried to please.

Pa still stared at her with his stony, hate-filled eyes. "Go, Callie. Now."
I must leave. What will I do? Where shall I go? It didn't matter. Rather
than stay another minute and beg, she'd sleep in the woods if she had to,
exist on roots and berries, probably be eaten by some wild animal, but
right now she didn't care. "I see now I was never your daughter. I'll get
my things."

"Where will you go?" Ma called.

"I don't know and I don't care, as long as it's as far away from here as
I can get."

Numb from shock, she went to the tent. She could hardly think straight
as she collected her possessions and blindly stuffed them into a canvas
bag. Lydia arrived, her face stained with tears. "Oh, Callie, this is terrible.
Please don't go. We'll wait 'til Pa calms down and then——"

"He means it. You know Pa. He's not going to change his mind."

"But to throw you out like that is so cruel. Maybe if I went to him and
told him I knew, too, so I'm as guilty as you are."

"Don't you dare. This was my idea, not yours. You don't need to be
involved."

Lydia truly looked stricken. "You lied to save me."

"You must be strong now. Ma needs you. So does Tommy. He——"
Callie choked up, thinking about the little boy who needed her so much.
"Don't let Ma be mean to him. Pa, either." She reached out and caught
Lydia's hand. "Now, will you please stop crying? Don't worry. I'll be
fine."

Lydia wiped her eyes. "I'm sorry I was ever mean to you."

Any other time Callie would have been amazed to hear such words
of regret coming from her stepsister's lips. Not today. "It doesn't matter
now. Really, it doesn't." Callie picked up the small bundle that held her
possessions. "Tell Tommy I love him. Tell him he hasn't seen the last of
me, and I——"

She choked up again and could say no more. After giving Lydia a
heartfelt hug, she slipped from the tent and walked away from the only
family she'd ever known. For a moment she stopped and surveyed the
circle of wagons around the campground. By now she knew the family in
each wagon, how many children, where they came from and where they
wanted to go. If she asked, out of kindness someone would take her in,
but how humiliating to have to beg for help. And besides, how could she
impose on these good people when, after months on the trail, their food
supplies were dwindling? Just the other day Florida had mentioned she
was running low on flour. And her with seven mouths to feed. She seemed

the best choice, though. *I'll be a burden, but where else can I go? Maybe I can earn my keep.*

She was about to walk to Florida's wagon when she heard a familiar voice. "Where are you going, Callie?"

Magnus. "To Florida's wagon, Mister Ferguson." Her voice trembled, but she couldn't control it. "Pa threw me out."

Magnus's eyes swept over her in a raking gaze. He'd been doing that a lot lately. "Come with me." His fingers touched her arm with gentle authority, giving her a small measure of comfort. Maybe she wasn't completely alone. She walked with him to his campsite where his two hired men, Hank and Seth, had built a fire and were cooking the noon meal. "Sit down, Callie. Hank, fix her a cup of coffee." Apparently Magnus had forgotten his disgust of last night. Now his gray eyes brimmed with sympathy. "So you've been banished by Mister Whitaker? Tell me what happened."

There wasn't much to tell he didn't already know. When she finished, he stroked his chin thoughtfully, taking his time to form an answer. "By far the best solution is that you come to me."

"I was thinking maybe Florida—"

"I have need of a woman. You'll be much better off with me."

Need of a woman? She didn't like the sound of that. "Thanks for your kind offer, but I already have a plan. Florida always needs help and I'm thinking if I go with her, I won't be a burden."

Magnus frowned with concern. "Have you forgotten Florida is heading for Oregon? We'll soon be reaching Fort Hall, and you know what that means. We'll be splitting off. Half the train, including myself and your family will turn southwest to California. The rest, along with Florida and Luke, will head northwest on the Oregon Trail. Is that what you want? Never to see your family again?" He paused to chuckle. "Perhaps it's for the best. I wouldn't blame you for wanting to get as far away as possible from that family of yours."

Oh, no. For the moment she'd forgotten Florida was heading to Oregon. Her whole being rebelled at such a thought. "They're my family. I don't feel that way at all."

"Of course, I can see how you feel. There's always the hope your stepfather will relent. At any rate, you've got to realize if you go to Oregon with Florida, it's doubtful you'll ever see your family again."

He was right. What would become of Tommy? How could she desert him? She could not. Even though Pa had thrown her out, she had to find a way to watch over the little boy who needed her so much. Did she want to go with Magnus? Despite the dissension among the captains, he was still their leader. Everyone still looked up to him, except Luke, of course, who thought him a fool and worse. Magnus had always been kind to her, though. His harsh words about Nellie had shocked her, but if she had any sense, she would put them out of her mind. Considering her situation was desperate, who was she to be particular? "I accept your offer, Mr. Ferguson. I promise I'll work hard to earn my keep."

Magnus offered a satisfied smile. "Splendid. I shall talk to Reverend Wilkins."

"Why do we need the Reverend?"

"To marry us, of course." He nodded his head decisively. "We must. Else, how would it look? As the leader of this train, I must set a good example. I cannot have a young, pretty woman share my wagon without benefit of matrimony. Surely you can see we must be married."

Chapter 12

After making sure Callie would be all right, Luke had left the train to scout ahead. He returned late in the afternoon in a good mood, pleased at how Nellie had escaped her father's anger and moved on, he was sure, to a better life. He wouldn't have to worry about Callie, either. She was safe. Caleb wouldn't dare raise a hand to her again. The train had stopped for the day. When he passed Florida's wagon, she beckoned him. The way she was standing, all stiff and tense, he knew something was wrong. He quickly dismounted. "What is it?"

"It's time you got back. Wait 'til you hear what happened."

"If you're talking about how Caleb lost his temper this morning, I already know. It's been taken care of."

Florida nodded her approval. "Thanks to you, he only struck her the once. Best of all, he's not going after Nellie, so she's safe, thank God."

"Glad to hear it."

"That's only the half of it." Florida proceeded to describe how Caleb told Callie to go and never return. "She's banished from her family, but she's all right."

His fine mood vanished. "Damn! I might have known Whitaker would cause more trouble. Where did she go?"

"Magnus Ferguson took her in." She placed a calming hand on his arm. "There's something else. Now, Luke, I'm well aware of your opinion of Colonel Ferguson, and I want you to stay calm."

"Just tell me."

Florida hesitated, like she knew her next words could set him off. "Magnus is concerned about appearances. According to him, they'd be living in sin unless…unless…"

"Unless what?"

"Reverend Wilkins is going to marry them."

Luke clamped his jaw. Damned if he'd let his sister see the black rage that engulfed him. "When?"

"Tonight at the campfire."

"We'll see about that." He grasped Rascal's reins and led him away.

* * * *

When word spread Magnus Ferguson was going to marry Callie Whitaker that evening, the women of the Ferguson wagon train, who weren't finding much to celebrate these days, seized upon the opportunity to brighten the daily drudgery of their lives. They built a bower of vines in the middle of the campground where the wedding would take place. They collected wildflowers from the nearby woods for a colorful bride's bouquet. Someone baked a spice cake. Others baked berry pies. Callie would wear the dress Florida gave her, the one found at the side of the road. Although not new, she'd saved it for special occasions. It was the best she had. The wedding would take place in the early evening after everyone finished supper, after the big campfire was lit. Afterward, refreshments would be served, including a couple jugs of wine that had miraculously appeared.

I'm going to marry Magnus Ferguson. Throughout the day, Callie kept running the words through her head. The more she did, the less sense they made. She should be honored and delighted that the esteemed leader of the wagon train wanted to marry her. The problem was that Magnus's calloused views on Coy and Nellie remained seated in her heart. *Nellie should tell her father. That's what an obedient daughter should do.* His lack of compassion had repelled her, yet she still admired him. Everyone did, and she should be filled with happiness at the thought of sharing his bed, bearing his children, spending the rest of her life with him. According to Magnus, their marriage made sense. He was right, of course. How could a man of such standing and integrity not be right? They must be married, because if they weren't, the whole world would scorn them because they'd be living in sin. What was wrong with her? She should feel flattered, thrilled, and excited that a man as prosperous as Magnus, and good-looking besides, was glad to marry her. *Wanted* to marry her. Try as she might, though, she couldn't persuade herself how lucky she was.

As the day wore on, she remained full of misgivings, even though she kept telling herself how grateful she should be to Magnus, for not only taking her in but making her his wife. By marrying Magnus, she could stay close to Tommy, and that meant a lot. Only an hour ago, she'd seen her little brother at a distance. He waved and she waved back, delighted he recognized her. He'd been making steady progress, not only in his reading, but lately he seemed even more alert, as if on the brink of recognizing her and the world around him. What a shame it would be if he slipped back into his lonely, isolated world, and he very well might if she wasn't here to help him.

That settled it. Tonight she'd marry Magnus Ferguson. No sense thinking about it any further. She was going to do it. Only…

She'd never forget Luke McGraw. For the rest of her life, her heart would ache for what might have been but never was.

* * * *

Late in the day, Lydia found Callie by the Ferguson wagons and cast a worried glance behind her. "I hope Pa doesn't see me talking to you. Is it true you're going to marry Magnus?"

"Yes, tonight."

Lydia sighed. "I wanted him, too, you know, but"—she shrugged and managed a small smile—"oh, well, I'm happy for you."

Callie wrinkled her nose. "I never wanted him and I don't now."

"You don't want to marry Magnus? Are you daft?"

"I don't love him." Callie attempted to explain her feelings, not easy when she hardly understood them herself. "I don't see any other way out."

Lydia nodded sadly. "I'm afraid you're right. You have no choice. Pa's not going to change his mind."

"Does he know about the wedding?"

"Yes, and he wants no part of it. I won't be there either, or Ma or Tommy. We're forbidden to get anywhere near."

How hurtful. Callie swallowed hard, willing herself not to cry. "I'll be thinking of you all and wishing you could be there."

Lydia sighed. "Why does Pa have to be so mean? I don't understand."

"That's the way life is, I guess. We cope as best we can. None of this is your fault. I don't want you to worry. Just take care of Tommy and Ma. That's all you can do."

* * * *

It was almost time for the wedding. In her best dress, her hair fixed by Hetty, Callie was by herself, washing her face at the nearby creek.

"So how's the blushing bride?" Luke stood on the bank above her in that casual stance of his, a wry smile on his face.

The sight of him caused her heart to jolt. She hastily straightened and glared back. "I'm not a blushing bride."

"But a bride." Luke's smile vanished. "Magnus Ferguson? My God, what are you thinking?"

"He's a fine man. Everyone says so."

"Don't give me that." Luke swiftly stepped down the embankment and looked her in the eye. "I can't think of anything more stupid than marrying that oaf."

"I don't have a choice, Luke. Pa threw me out. What was I supposed to do?" She shouldn't sound so defensive. "What makes you think I don't want to marry him?"

He laughed with scorn. "Go ahead, throw your life away, but you don't have to."

"I'm as good as married already. I can't back out now."

"Why not?"

"I have no place else to go."

"Florida wants you to stay with her."

"Florida's going to Oregon. I don't want to go to Oregon."

Her reasonable protest didn't faze him in the least. "We'll work it out."

"How? Can't you see I'm committed? The Reverend is ready to read the vows. They've baked pies and cakes. Everybody's expecting a wedding. I can't possibly—"

"You can damn well do anything you like."

She was about to answer when Magnus, a fierce scowl on his face, appeared on the bank above. "Callie, what are you doing?"

She felt uncomfortable, as if she was doing something wrong. "Just getting some water to wash my face..." She inclined her head toward Luke. "And talking."

Magnus shot Luke a quick, icy gaze. "Come along, Callie. You don't have time for chatting."

"Yes, Magnus."

As Callie started up the bank, Luke softly repeated his words. "It's not too late. Remember, you can damn well do anything you like."

When she reached the top, Magnus grasped her arm, more firmly than necessary. "What were you doing? It's time for the wedding. They're beginning to gather."

"Yes, Magnus."

Fighting a battle in her head, Callie accompanied her husband-to-be back to the campground. *Yes, Magnus. Yes, Ma.* The words intertwined and spun through her head. If not for this journey, she would never have realized she'd spent her whole life saying *Yes, Ma.* Always the lowly servant, humbly obeying without question. That part of her life was over. She was definitely *not* just a servant. She was her own person, ruled by no one. But would she be? Was this the end of her newfound independence?

Just now, at the creek, she realized what would happen when she married Magnus Ferguson. The bossy way he talked to her was only the beginning. He'd want her to obey him. She'd be saying *Yes, Magnus* to a man she didn't love, hastening to do his bidding until the day she died.

Where else could she go? She ought to be grateful that if she married Magnus, she'd be taken care of the rest of her life. Such a prosperous businessman was bound to become rich and successful wherever he went. She'd never want for anything.

They got back to the campground. The whole camp had gathered.

"It's time," Magnus said.

Callie looked at the crowd. Everyone was there, except for her family, of course, and Luke. Reverend Wilkins had a broad smile on his face and his Bible in hand. Gert Gowdy wore a clean dress and polished boots. There were all those faces, staring at her, waiting for the big moment when she'd say yes to the wonderful catch, Magnus Ferguson, and the Reverend would pronounce them man and wife. *Man and wife forever and ever. No, no, no!*

Callie stopped in her tracks.

Magnus frowned. "What's the matter?"

"I can't do it."

"Can't do what?"

"Marry you, Magnus." She turned to face him. "I'm sorry. This is all my fault, but I just…can't…"

His eyebrows lifted in surprise. "Are you sure? You'll be safe if you marry me. You'll have a good life. I'll give you everything you could possibly need. Use your head, girl. You're homeless and penniless. If you don't become my wife, God knows what will happen to you."

She didn't hesitate. "I'm positive. I'm terribly sorry, but I'm not going to marry you."

Magnus's face turned white. His jaw clamped shut. Only for a moment, though. The next second a pleasant smile spread over his face. "Say no more. Come with me." Gently he took her arm. Together they strolled to where the crowd was standing, everyone smiling, greeting them with a light splatter of applause. His ever-congenial self, Magnus led her to the bower of vines where they were to be married and turned around so he and Callie faced the crowd. "I have an announcement to make, everyone." Retaining his jovial smile, he announced there would be no wedding due to "circumstances." He didn't explain further. He was terribly sorry, but that didn't mean they couldn't have a pleasant evening anyway, dancing and enjoying the refreshments, which should not go to waste. He seemed not the least concerned, as if calling off the wedding was simply a minor inconvenience.

After an initial groan of disappointment, the members of the wagon train seemed not to mind the sudden change of plans. Jake took up his fiddle, Colton his banjo, and the dancing began. Far from going to waste, the refreshments went fast. Callie actually enjoyed the evening, vastly relieved Magnus understood. What a fine man he was, so understanding, so kind. He ignored her the rest of the evening and appeared to be hugely enjoying himself. She should further apologize, though, and try to explain why she changed her mind. Only at the end, when everyone was leaving, did Callie find him alone. Before she could say a word, he gave her a curt, "Don't bother."

"But I only wanted——"

"I don't want to hear it." His eyes turned hard and filled with dislike. "It was Luke, wasn't it?"

"What do you mean?"

"Luke talked you out of it." She started to reply, but he interrupted. "Luke did this. I'll make that son-of-a-bitch pay if it's the last thing I do. As for you…" His lip curled with contempt. "What a fool you are. You could have had a good life with me, but instead you chose to go with that no-good…that…that…" He stopped and seemed to calm himself. "Mark my words, you'll come crawling back some day. Maybe I'll take you back, maybe I won't. The decision will be mine, not yours, like it was today."

Magnus spun around and walked away. With a sick feeling, Callie watched after him. How foolish she'd been to reject a man so conceited and expect he'd understand. He was a proud, arrogant man and she, foolish girl, had wounded his vanity. She should have known he would never forgive her. Even worse, she had better watch out because he might do her harm.

Today she'd made an enemy, and so had Luke.

* * * *

Florida was happy to take in the outcast. Callie had been with the Sawyers a week when Luke appeared one night as she was sitting alone by the campfire. She was surprised. He'd made himself scarce since she joined Florida. Luke poured himself a cup of coffee and sat across. "Think you'll like Oregon?"

"I haven't thought much about Oregon but, yes, of course I will."

"How are you doing?"

Another surprise. For days he'd ignored her. "Doing fine, all things considered." She loved living with this big, rambunctious family. How lucky she was to be a part of it. She might be crammed into the tent with Hetty and three of the younger children, but it didn't matter. She gladly helped with the cooking, washing, and other chores. The food might be monotonous, and the portions skimpy, but she didn't care. The rift with her family hung heavy on her heart, but she tried each day to make the best of it. Aside from that, only one thing troubled her. "I'm happy, except for Magnus. He doesn't speak to me, turns his back when he sees me coming."

Luke's dark brows drew together in irritation. "You should have come to us in the first place."

"I wish I had."

His expression relaxed a little. "Let me know if he causes you any trouble."

She told him she would, and soon he was gone, as remote as ever. At least he cared enough to offer his help with Magnus. A kind heart lay beneath that rough exterior. He'd do the same for anybody. It must have been a dream that he once held her in his arms and kissed her. But no, it wasn't a dream. The burning memory of his lips caressing her mouth kept her awake many a night. She'd never forget how he'd trembled with passion when he swept her into his arms. So why was he ignoring her? There had to be an answer. Would she never know?

* * * *

Heading to Fort Hall, they crossed some of the most beautiful country they'd seen thus far. Each day they passed rushing streams and luxuriant grassy meadows. The quality of their suppers greatly improved, what with the plentiful supply of geese, ducks, and trout in clear waters. The women baked wonderful pies from the berries of all sorts that grew wild.

Nearly every day, Lydia slipped away long enough to relate the latest news of the family. The closer they got to Fort Hall, the more distressed she became. "It won't be long before we'll part. I hate to think I'll never see you again."

Callie didn't need to be reminded. If all went well, within the week, they'd arrive at Fort Hall and the train would split. More than half would take the Overland route to California. The rest would head in a northwest direction to Oregon. From what she'd heard, it was the more difficult route, but the dangers of the trail weren't what kept her from sleep at night. She dreaded leaving Tommy. What would become of him? Ma and Pa considered him an idiot. They'd never lift a finger to help him improve.

According to them, he was what he was and would never get any better. She knew Lydia loved Tommy but was too wrapped up in herself to do much good in caring for her little brother.

One day Callie asked, "Do you think Pa might relent?"

"Never." Lydia sadly shook her head. "We can't even mention your name."

So, like Nellie, even her name was banned, as if she'd never been a part of the family. The hurt cut deep, but there was nothing she could do. She tried not to think about it.

* * * *

Fort Hall was still a couple of days away when they left the flatlands and started to climb. The trail became increasingly hard to follow. They were confronted with a labyrinth of twisting, circuitous canyons where they were obliged to chop their way through aspen, cottonwood and tangled undergrowth to clear a path for the wagons. They tried to follow established trails but occasionally had to strike out on their own. They felled trees, dug tracks high up on the mountainside, dislodged boulders, coaxed oxen over ridges so steep everyone except the driver had to get out and push from behind as the oxen struggled to pull the wagons to the top. Callie did her part, pushing the heavy wagons with all her strength alongside Florida and her brood. Tempers were easily lost on days like this. "I wish I'd never left home," Florida wailed as she sweated and strained to push her wagon to the crest of a hill. "It was all Henry's fault or I wouldn't be here in the first place. How dare he up and die!"

One day the trail became so steep they had to double-team the oxen and recruit all but the smallest children to lend a hand in getting the wagons to the top. Luke drove the first of the Sawyers' two wagons. The entire family, from five-year-old Isaac on up, pushed from behind. Callie strained with all her might. Occasionally she glanced over the side of the narrow road and quickly looked away. Dear God! She couldn't bear to look at the frightening drop, at least one hundred feet straight down to where huge boulders lay at the bottom. The two outside wheels of the wagon rested only inches from the edge. What if the wagon went over the side? She'd heard of such accidents happening. People were injured, even killed. She closed her eyes, pushed, and prayed. How awful to think this long, hard journey might end on a next-to-nothing trail in the middle of nowhere. It very well could, considering the wagon hovered only inches from complete disaster.

They reached the summit. Amid sighs of relief, they joined the group of wagons waiting in a wide area not far from the top. Callie couldn't relax, though. Worry nagged at her. Such a narrow trail. Would Ma and Pa make it all right? So far it had been a miracle anyone had made it to the top. She spoke to Florida. "I'll be right back. I've got to see if my family's safe."

Callie returned to the top and stood watching as, one by one, wagons with exhausted oxen, drivers, and whole families pushed to reach the summit. At last she spied her family's two wagons, last in line. Whip in hand, Pa was driving, his face drawn with ferocious concentration. Ma slumped on the seat beside him. She must have exhausted herself with all the pushing. Andy was driving the other wagon. He climbed down and joined Lydia and Tommy behind the first wagon, pushing hard as they could. Callie looked at the wheels. Oh no! Her hand went to her throat. The rims were less than an inch from the edge and rolling closer. *Pa, watch out!*

One outside wheel slid over the edge, then the other. The wagon began to tip. For what seemed an endless moment in time, it hung suspended. Pa cracked the whip, yelling at the oxen. Callie held her breath, praying to God he could recover. The wagon tipped again, this time so far it couldn't recover. A scream tore through the air. Was it Ma? Frightened animals bellowed as the wagon, oxen, driver and Andy, caught by a wheel, plunged over the side. Seconds later, a deafening crash sounded from the bottom of the canyon.

A deathly stillness followed. Callie stood frozen, trying to comprehend what she'd just seen. Tommy's wails brought her back to reality. Thank God, he hadn't gone off the cliff, nor had Lydia, who stood pale and shaking beside him. What of Ma, Pa, and Andy? She rushed to the edge, just as Luke arrived. Together they peered at the tangled wreckage at the bottom. Something moved, one of the oxen. But what of the rest? "I must get down there." She picked up her skirt. Steep though the canyon wall was, all she could think was she had to get to her family.

Luke grabbed her from behind. "Don't. I'll take care of it."

She struggled to break away. "They could be hurt. Dead! I must get to them."

Luke tightened his grip. "You want to kill yourself? If they're still alive, I'll get them out."

The soothing calmness of his voice brought her to her senses. She stopped struggling. What had she been thinking? The cliff was way too steep for her to climb down. Luke couldn't do it either. No one could. "How can you get down there?"

"I'll find a way. You wait here. Take care of Lydia and Tommy. They're going to need you." Luke headed back down the trail, hailing all able-bodied men as he went. Waiting was torture. Callie went to Lydia and Tommy, both of them crying, and offered what comfort she could.

At last men's voices sounded in the canyon below. Thank God, they must have found a way down. Half in anticipation, half in dread, she peered over the edge at Luke and the rest examining the wreckage. Luke called up to her. "Your Pa is alive. So's your Ma."

Alive! A sob burned her throat, but she didn't let it out. "What about Andy?"

A long pause followed, so long she guessed what Luke was going to say.

"Andy's dead. Looks like he was killed instantly."

The climb down into the canyon and back was so steep and treacherous, they had to bury Andy in a shallow grave where he died. The descent and climb were so difficult most members of the company couldn't attend the brief burial service. At least Reverend Wilkins, aided by continuous prayers for help from God Almighty, managed to climb down and say a prayer over the young man's grave. For Callie, the next few hours were a blur. Andy's death hit her hard. He was a good man, maybe not the brightest, but he'd had nothing but kind words for everyone. He and Len had so wanted to get to the gold fields and make their fortune. What cruel fate that neither ever would.

One of the oxen was killed outright. The other three survived and were put to use pulling Caleb and Hester in hastily constructed stretchers up the canyon to a place where, with the help of several strong, able-bodied men, they were hauled to the top. Ma suffered a broken arm, scrapes and bruises. Pa was much worse off with several broken ribs, a broken shoulder, and a leg shattered in the fall. In severe pain, he couldn't hold back his screams whenever he was touched or moved, which, under the circumstances, happened often and couldn't be avoided. Callie wanted to cover her ears whenever his agonized screams sounded. Mean though he was, awful though he'd treated her, she still held compassion in her heart for the only father she'd ever known.

Some of the men pitched a tent for the injured Whitakers. When Callie went to visit, they were both in such shock and pain they couldn't speak.

Poor Lydia was in tears, grieving over Andy. "I was always so mean to him. If only I'd been nicer!"

Callie marveled at how her shallow stepsister had gained a new depth of feeling. Luke was right. A long journey like this might bring out the worst in some people, but in others, it brought out their best.

That night Magnus called his captains together for an emergency meeting. Callie, along with Florida and some others, drew close enough to hear their leaders discuss the fate of the Whitakers. One problem was solved immediately when several families offered to buy the Whitakers' cattle and their three extra oxen, but major decisions remained to be made. Of their two wagons, one had been completely destroyed and left lying in the canyon. Helping hands had unloaded most of the family's possessions, hauled them up the hill to be placed in the remaining wagon. Enough oxen remained to pull it, but with both Andy and Len gone, and Whitaker badly injured, the burning question was, who would drive the wagon? Who would take care of the oxen and yoke them every day?

There were no hired hands left who weren't already busy. Although many women were capable of driving a wagon, Hester was eliminated immediately. Her arm was broken, and, besides, she had never so much as touched a pair of reins. She would be totally incapable of handling a team of four stubborn oxen. So how about Lydia? The thought of that scatterbrained girl driving a wagon caused the only chuckle of the evening. That Caleb might drive was out of the question. At his slightest movement, the pain from his broken bones brought new waves of agony. His fellow travelers had heartily disliked him, but even the most hard-hearted captain softened upon hearing his cries of suffering.

"So, what shall we do?" Magnus said at last. "Whitaker can't drive and there's no one to take his place."

Reverend Wilkins spoke up. "We could wait right here until he gets better. Shouldn't be more than a week or two."

Loud boos met his suggestion. Winter was coming. They had no time to waste if they wanted to get to California before snow in the Sierra Nevadas caught them in a deadly trap. They consulted Luke who, up to now, had listened without speaking. He confirmed they were behind schedule. At this point, they shouldn't waste a day, or they could be in big trouble.

In a boisterous voice, feisty Jack Gowdy proposed the Whitakers simply be left behind. "Just make sure they got enough food. When Whitaker's ribs heal, he can make his choice, either continue on to California or turn around and go back where he come from. He could probably find another train to join…if he's lucky."

The murmur of agreement sunk Callie's heart. How could these people even think of leaving her family in the wilderness to fend for themselves? She doubted they'd survive. Besides, Ma and Pa had sold the farm and sacrificed everything for this trip. How could they go back now?

Apparently the captains of the wagon train didn't much care. After more heated discussion, they took a vote. The Whitakers were to be left behind.

Florida shook her head disapprovingly. "It's always heartless men who make these decisions. Oh, Callie, I'm so sorry."

Callie's mind raced. She was only a woman, but this was her family, and she must do something. There was no time to waste. If anyone would know, Luke would. Earlier he'd been at the meeting, then left, she guessed, in disgust. Maybe he didn't want to talk to her, but she'd ask his opinion anyway, and right now.

"Luke?"

He was alone, outside his tent, dousing his campfire.

"I need to talk to you."

He straightened and smiled at her. "Sit down. I can guess why you came."

She sat by the remains of the campfire, as did he. "What am I going to do? They're my family."

Luke raised his eyebrows. "You care? After the way your Pa treated you?" She started to reply but he raised his hand. "You don't have to explain. It's good you love your family, no matter what."

"I can't bear the thought of just leaving them here."

"Can't blame you. I doubt they'll survive the first winter storm."

"So what can I do?"

Luke slowly unfolded his long, lean body and poured himself another cup of coffee, biting his lip in deep thought. "You know how to drive a wagon."

"Thanks to Florida."

"It's not that hard, is it?"

"No, it's not, but what——" It dawned on her what he meant. "You think I could drive my family all the way to California?"

"Why not?"

"I couldn't because…" There were so many reasons she didn't know where to begin. "I'm not a man, for one thing."

His gaze swept over her, his mouth quirking in a half smile. "Glad you told me. I'd never have guessed."

She ignored his attempt at humor. "I've driven the oxen over the easiest of trails but nothing really difficult. How could I handle a trail like the one we were on today?"

"I'm not saying it would be easy."

"It would be impossible. What about the yoke?" She remembered how Pa grunted, groaned, and cursed each morning while yoking the oxen. "Those yokes are heavy. I don't think I could do it alone."

"You couldn't. You'd need help. Your ma could never do it, but how about Lydia?"

"Lydia?" The thought of silly Lydia yoking the oxen caused her to burst into laughter. "Never. She's much too delicate."

"Delicate, my eye. Your sister is a strong, healthy girl, despite what your ma says. You'd be surprised how fast she'd learn how to yoke those oxen when her only other choice is to be left in the middle of the wilderness with winter coming on."

His words made sense. Look at all she'd accomplished since she'd started this journey, things she'd never done before, or considered doing. "Even if you're right, don't forget Pa threw me out. He never wanted to hear my name again. He's so stubborn he'd never change his mind, even now."

A faint smile crossed Luke's face. "He banished you forever, but that was before he nearly killed himself going off that cliff. Now you're the strong one. What could he do to stop you?"

She the strong one? For a long moment she let his words sink in. "You're right. Pa's weak now, and helpless. He couldn't do a thing."

"So what will you do?"

She had always obeyed her parents. Only since this journey started had she dared to defy them. She dreaded flouting their wishes again, but what choice did she have? "I'll go talk to them."

He regarded her intently. "I'll help you all I can."

She couldn't stop her little laugh of irony. "That's nice, but soon we'll reach Fort Hall. It looks like I'll be going to California after all, and you to Oregon."

He stepped forward and clasped her body tightly to his. "You think I don't know that?"

His breath, warm and moist against her face, caused a lurch of excitement within her. She wound her arms around his neck and whispered, "I will miss you."

He drew her closer and buried his face in her hair. "You think I won't miss you?"

At the sound of approaching voices, they broke apart. Her heart pounded. Her weak knees could hardly hold her up. She wanted nothing more than to throw herself into his arms again, but someone was coming and that wouldn't do. "Good night, Luke."

"Goodnight, Callie."

Her heart ached as she turned on her heel and walked away.

* * * *

The Whitakers' sleeping arrangements had changed. Ma and Pa now occupied the tent while Lydia and Tommy occupied the one remaining wagon. Callie found them fast asleep when she climbed inside and shook her stepsister's shoulder. "Wake up, Lydia. I've got to talk to you."

Lydia sat up and gazed back in startled surprise. "What are you doing here? You know what Pa said."

"Forget all that. Here's what we need to do..."

By the time Callie finished, Lydia was looking at her as if she'd completely lost her mind. "You want me to drive the wagon?"

"It's easy. I'll teach you. Don't worry, you won't be driving all the time, only when I can't."

Lydia's blue eyes grew wide with horror. "And yoke the oxen?"

"It's not that hard. I'm hoping some of the men can help, but I won't lie to you, mainly it'll be up to us."

Her stepsister shook her head in utter disbelief. "I could never, never do such a thing."

"Here's what will happen if you don't..."

Callie explained how Magnus and his captains had decided to leave the Whitakers behind. "That means you'd be left to fend for yourselves with no one to help and with winter coming on. They tried to convince themselves Pa will soon be well enough to drive the wagon, but they know in their hearts he won't. All they're worried about is themselves, and who can blame them? There's no time to lose if they want to get to California before the snow starts."

"How can I lift that heavy yoke?"

"We'll do it together."

"But what if...?"

Callie continued to answer her stepsister's questions. Lydia's resistance slowly melted. She had many fears, but the fear of being left alone in the wilderness conquered all others. "You think we can do it?"

"I know we can."

"Pa won't like it."

"What Pa likes or doesn't like isn't important right now. He's in no position to argue."

"Even so, I'd hate to be the one to tell him."

"Don't worry. I'll take care of it." Callie put a reassuring smile on her face, one she didn't really feel.

Minutes later, holding a lantern, Callie stepped into the tent where Hester was sleeping and Pa lay awake on his blankets. She set the lamp down, dropped to her knees beside him and took a moment to calm herself. It wasn't every day she defied her father. He couldn't hurt her now, but even so, her heart pounded. "Pa? Can you hear me?"

He raised his head and scowled. As if the effort was too much, he dropped his head back on his pillow and rasped, "Go away."

"I can't do that. You're badly hurt. You need me and I'm not going away."

He raised his head again. "How dare you! You are not to darken my door."

"You don't have a door. You're in a tent in the middle of nowhere. You need my help. Without it, you'll never get to California, or back home, or anywhere."

He tried to rise, but the effort caused him to clasp his side and groan with pain. Cursing, he fell back on the blankets again.

She waited until his pain subsided. "You don't have to worry. We're still going to California. I'm going to drive the wagon and Lydia will help."

"You?" His voice broke with scorn. "And Lydia?" He began to laugh, but a sharp stab of pain caused him to clutch his side and lapse into silence.

She waited for an answer, but her stepfather closed his eyes and clamped his jaw. Clearly he had nothing more to say. She got off her knees. "Good night, Pa."

She slipped from the tent. Thank goodness that was over. She'd defied Pa and got her way, but it wasn't much of a triumph. Now all she had to do was drive the wagon all the way to California. Ahead lay two huge mountain ranges and a desert so treacherous they'd be lucky if they didn't lose lives trying to get across. What had she let herself in for? God in heaven, what had she done?

* * * *

Magnus agreed the company would stay one more day. None too willingly, members of the train spent their time waiting for the Whitakers to recover sufficiently to travel. Callie caught a lot of dark looks and muttered curses. She understood their impatience and could hardly blame them. Everyone knew disaster would strike if they lingered too long before the snows came. She moved back to their wagon and fell easily into her old routine of cooking and doing the chores for her family. It wasn't the same, though. To avoid conflict, she stayed away from the tent where Ma and Pa lay, letting others bring them food and do whatever they could to ease their suffering. Ma didn't even know she was back. Lydia tended to her, as well as Florida and some of the other kind-hearted women. At least Callie's work was easier now, what with Lydia helping more than she ever had before. Tommy was delighted to have her back. When he first saw her, his eyes lit. "Callie come home?"

"I've come back, Tommy. How do you like that?"

Tommy's answering smile made her doubts disappear.

Late in the afternoon, Callie and Lydia were fixing supper when Luke and the Reverend Wilkins' shy son, Colton, stopped by. In a congenial mood, Luke declared, "We've come to give you and Lydia your first lesson."

"On what?"

"We'll be leaving first thing in the morning. You need to know how to yoke the oxen."

Lydia nearly dropped the pot of coffee she'd been making. "Lord have mercy! I don't think…"

"You can do it." Luke's voice brimmed with confidence. He nodded toward his companion. "Colton's the expert. He'll show you how."

As Callie expected, tall, skinny Colton cast his eyes down and shuffled his feet. At twenty-four, with his red hair and freckles, he wasn't much to look at, especially with an unremarkable face that turned bright red whenever he received any attention, especially from a girl. It had turned red now. She hoped he hadn't heard Lydia's barely audible sniff of contempt.

Colton finally stepped forward and removed his hat. "Good afternoon, ladies. First, you got to get your oxen and tie 'em about the same distance apart as their heads go in the yoke. Here, I'll show you." He led them to where their four remaining oxen stood grazing. Rosie and Jack, Zephyr and Thor—Callie held great affection for them, despite their being dumb animals. Colton led Rosie and Jack to the front of the wagon, where he lined them up side by side. He handed the rope that held them to Lydia. "Here, hang on to the oxen. I'll get the yoke."

Callie caught the flash of panic that crossed Lydia's face. How would her pampered stepsister handle this? She always avoided the huge animals as much as possible, but now, in the presence of a young man her age, she couldn't act like a scaredy-cat, even if it was only Colton. Sure enough, Lydia, with a show of confidence, took the rope in her dainty hand and batted her eyelashes, her customary gesture whenever a man was around. "Do you think I can do this, Colton?"

"Sure you can. Hold on." Colton left briefly and returned with the yoke, oxbow, and the bolts to hold them together. The yoke, an elongated, heavy piece of wood, had two holes drilled on either end. The U-shaped oxbow was made of iron. Colton held them both up. "See these holes in the yoke? That's where each end of the oxbow goes." He placed the yoke atop Rosie's and Jack's backs. Next, he placed one of the oxbows under Rosie's neck and slid the two ends through the holes in the yoke. He fastened the ends with iron pins, then did the same with Jack. As he worked, his confidence grew and he forgot to be shy. "See? It's not that hard." He gave a confident slap to Rosie's back and stepped back with a satisfied smile.

Luke stepped to the oxen and removed the oxbow and yoke. Like Colton, he made the task look easy, as if he were lifting a bag of feathers. "Now you do it, ladies. Put it on. Take it off."

How difficult could it be? "Come on, Lydia. It doesn't look so hard." Callie stepped to where Luke held the yoke. She took one end. A reluctant-looking Lydia took the other. Luke let go. The sudden weight caused Callie to gasp. The yoke was so heavy it took every bit of her strength to hang on and not let it fall to the ground. Lydia gasped, too, and suddenly went down like a rock, landing splat on her backside, an astonished look on her face.

"Are you all right?" Luke asked.

Lydia glared up at him. "You didn't say it was heavy."

"It's only eighty pounds or so."

The amazed look that crossed Lydia's face, along with the unforgettable of sight of her sitting spread-eagled on the ground, were too much for Callie. She started laughing. Luke and Colton did the same. Soon Lydia joined in. Even she could see the humor of it all.

Callie enjoyed the brief moment of hilarity. There'd been nothing but grimness and tragedy the past two days. How nice to laugh after all the misfortune that had befallen them. The light moment didn't last long, though, coming to an abrupt end when Ma emerged from the tent. She looked terrible, pale and drawn, right arm in a sling. Her face resembled a thundercloud. Uh-oh. Since she moved back, Callie hadn't talked to her stepmother. Now the moment she dreaded had arrived.

Ma cast a furious gaze at Callie. "What are you doing here? Why are you laughing? Have you no respect for your father and me?"

"I'm here because I want to help, Ma."

"You can help by leaving us alone. Your pa doesn't want you here."

It was hard to get her next words out, but the time had come and she must. "Pa needs help whether he wants it or not. That's why I've come back, and I don't intend to leave."

Ma looked thunderstruck. She began to sputter. "You—you—dare to go against your pa?"

"Call it what you will, I'm not leaving. I'm going to drive the wagon, Ma. That means you won't get left behind. You can go to California, just like you wanted."

"You will rue the day you defied us." Ma's voice was so cold it sent a chill up Callie's spine. Was she making a terrible mistake? Maybe Ma was right and she had no business intruding upon a family that didn't want her anymore.

But no! If ever a family needed help, it was this one. Come hell or high water, she'd get the Whitakers to California, whether they liked it or not.

Chapter 13

Next day, the Ferguson Wagon train got ready to resume its journey. To Callie and Lydia's vast relief, Colton dropped by and hitched up the oxen. Ma and Pa left their tent and after a slow, painful climb, settled in the back of the wagon. Ma seemed all right, even though she maintained an angry silence. Pa never spoke. Although heavily dosed with laudanum, he still suffered great pain and groaned constantly. His journey would not be any easy one. Callie vowed to avoid jolting the wagon as much as possible.

As the wagons moved out, Callie sat on the wagon seat, reins in one hand, whip in the other, waiting to join the line. Lydia sat beside her, tightly gripping the seat, as if the wagon might overturn at any moment. "Callie, are you sure you can do this?"

No, I'm not sure. She had hardly slept last night worrying about today's drive. Had she taken on too much? How could she possibly drive a wagon to California by herself? If only she'd thought it through, but too late now. She had finally fallen asleep, telling herself she would do the best she could and never let on to the family how unsure of herself she was. She'd act confident, no matter what. Now, as they joined the line, she flicked the whip over the heads of Rosie and Jack, a showy gesture they didn't need. She glanced at her stepsister. "Don't worry. Luke and Florida taught me how to drive. It's easy as pie once you get the hang of it."

"I would never want to try."

"Never say never, Lydia." After a hearty "Getup," Callie maneuvered the oxen into the slow-moving line of wagons. *Not so bad. I do know what I'm doing.* As they rolled along, she felt at ease. She was in control. She could handle this. "See how easy? By the time we get to California, we'll both be old hands at this."

"You think?" Lydia was actually smiling. Her fingers had loosened their desperate grip on the edge of the wagon seat.

"I don't think, I know. We're going to be fine." Finally Lydia was beginning to trust her. At that moment, with the sun on her face and the reins firmly in hand, Callie's confidence rose. Yes, she could do it! She had control of her life. Nothing could go wrong. On to California!

If only...oh, Luke.

A deepening sadness dampened Callie's spirits whenever she thought about Luke. She loved everything about him—his kindness, his subtle wit, the aching desire he caused when he held her in his arms. He'd be gone soon. She would not deceive herself that their paths would cross again. She had no idea what the future held, but one thing she knew for sure— she would never love another man the way she loved Luke McGraw.

* * * *

They had lots of help. During the remaining days it took to reach Fort Hall, Colton continued to come by each morning to hitch up the oxen, a task the sisters dreaded and hadn't yet dealt with. As time went on, Lydia grew more and more happy to see him. She'd hardly noticed him before, but now he was being so helpful, in such a strong, masculine way, she seemed to be making a point to be around when he stopped by. In turn, Colton appeared to gain confidence and wasn't as bashful.

Luke came by often. Usually he simply rode by, nodded and continued on, but Callie was glad to see him each time. If she needed him, he'd be there.

Florida stopped by when she could, not only to check on Ma and Pa, but to see how the rest of the family was doing. Often she lamented the fact they soon must part. "I sure hate to leave you, but Henry was so set on getting to Oregon. I feel I've got to honor his wishes." Her eyes lit up when she talked about her dead husband's dream. "He used to say it would be like traveling to the Garden of Eden, like living in a land flowing with milk and honey. He said the clover grew all over Oregon, and when you waded through, it reached your chin."

"Do you believe that?" Callie once asked.

"It doesn't matter if I believe it or not. It's what Henry wanted for the children and me." She choked up, tears glistening in her eyes. "So, that's where we're going."

Callie grew sadder each day, knowing they soon must part. She'd sorely miss the only true friend she'd ever known. She didn't have time to mope about it, though. Her one goal was to get her family to California. Borrowing Luke's words, she mustn't be a softhearted fool.

* * * *

Fort Hall! Surrounded by high palisades, it was a major trading post and a welcome sight to weary travelers. Magnus said they'd stay for two days. This time his captains didn't protest. They needed to stock up on supplies and let the animals rest.

They camped just outside the walls. That night, a bedraggled-looking widow named Narcissa White, somewhere in her thirties, joined the group around the campfire. She and her five children had left Oregon and were headed home. Everyone, including Callie, gathered around, curious to hear her reasons for returning. When asked, Narcissa's exhausted face went grim. "Me and my children are going home to Illinois. I've had enough of Oregon. Why anybody would want to go to that God-awful place is beyond me."

Florida broke the surprised silence. "Would you mind telling us why?"

"First off, you're lucky if you get there alive. Of course, if that's where you're going, then you probably don't want to hear what I have to say."

"You go right ahead, Mrs. White." Florida seemed anxious to hear.

"First, you got to know how hard it is to get your wagons over those hills. You've heard of the Wasatch Mountains?"

"I believe they lay between Wyoming and Utah. We've got to cross them before we get there."

"That you do." The widow's whole body slumped, as if she was engulfed in a tide of weariness and despair. "It ain't so easy. There ain't any trail, not to speak of anyway. The only way to get your wagons over those mountains is to hoist them with chains, pulleys, and ropes. Twice I saw a chain break and there went the wagon, crashing down the mountainside."

"Gracious me," said Florida. "But you made it across all right?"

"That we did, but that wasn't the worst of it. Soon it got cold. It was October already and we still had a long way to go. The trail was so bad we had to leave the wagons behind. So we took what possessions we could and began to walk. We walked for days. Mind you, it's raining the whole time. When we reached the Deschutes River, we couldn't cross it by ourselves. Some Paiute Indians offered to take us across, for a price, of course, so we loaded everything onto their canoes. By then it was a cold, wet November, and there I sat, holding two of my babies while the Paiutes took us down that raging river, clear to where it emptied into the Columbia. I never was so scared in my life." Narcissa paused at the memory and grimly shook her head. "That river was the worst I ever saw. High, fast, and dangerous. If you think the river was bad, then hear what happened next. After the river, we had to wade through tremendous swamps. And me freezing with three little children cold and crying, hanging on to my skirts. It kept raining and snowing. I froze my feet so bad I couldn't wear my shoes. Had to walk on the snow and in that icy water barefooted. I was so cold and numb, I couldn't tell by feeling if I had any feet at all. And my poor children! They near gave out with cold and fatigue. We ended up having to carry them most of the way. By the time we got there, we had not one dry thread of clothing among us, not even my baby." Narcissa closed her eyes, as if to block the miserable memories. "I haven't told you half what we suffered. I'm not adequate to the task."

Florida took a long, worried look at her small children. "Do go on, Mrs. White." Her low, subdued voice shook. "So you finally arrived?"

"We finally reached Portland, but by then my husband was mighty sick with a fever. The rain and dampness had taken their toll. I found a small, leaky cabin with two families already there and got some of the men to carry my husband up through the rain and lay him inside. For the next six weeks I never undressed to lie down, what with tending to my husband, a baby that never stopped crying and my children hungry the whole time."

Callie had listened, both fascinated and horrified at the same time. "So your husband didn't recover?"

"Patrick died six weeks after we got there. He used to call Oregon the land of milk and honey. Well, the poor man never saw the sun shine. Never saw anything but rain, snow, and cold."

"That's when you decided to come back?"

"I hung on for months, but finally, what else could I do?" Narcissa heaved another weary sigh. "There I was, left a widow in a strange land, with the care of five children, with no money or friends. Of course I'm going back. I can hardly wait 'til I set my feet on the blessed soil of Illinois. As God is my witness, I shall never leave again." She cast a sympathetic gaze at Florida. "So, you're heading for Oregon?"

"Yes, I am, Mrs. White."

"Then be prepared. I assure you, it will be a hundred times worse than you can ever imagine."

The poor woman. Callie stared at Narcissa, at a loss for words.

Florida stayed silent, too, but her look of concern showed she was deeply troubled by the widow's tragic tale. Florida was never down for long, though. She brightened and gave the widow a smile. "Thanks for telling us your story. It must have been awful losing your husband and everything else."

Narcissa's eyes filled with sympathy. "You're a brave woman, Mrs. Sawyer. My prayers will be with you on that God-awful journey. I hope with all my heart you and your children survive."

* * * *

In the middle of the night, Luke awoke.

His sister was softly calling from outside his tent. "Luke, Luke? Are you awake?"

"I am now. Come in." He pushed his blankets aside, sat up, and waited for Florida to come crawling in. In the near darkness, he could barely see her in silhouette as she sat beside him. "I know why you're here."

His sister replied in a worried whisper. "Do you believe what that woman said?"

"Every word. Remember when we started this journey? I warned you then about the Oregon Trail."

"I insisted, didn't I? Florida sighed deeply. "It was Henry's dream that we move to Oregon. What would he say if I changed my mind and we went to California instead?"

"Not much. He is, after all, dead."

"Stop that!" She playfully struck at his arm. "Be serious. He may be dead, but I know he's looking down from heaven as we speak. He'd be horrified if I chose not to go to Oregon. He'd never forgive me."

Luke suppressed the impulse to further tease his sister and chose his next words carefully. "When we began this journey, I promised I'd see you safely to Oregon, or wherever you wanted to go. It was the least I could do after all you've done for me. I warned you about Oregon, how tough it would be, but you insisted. You wanted to go so you could honor Henry's memory. Thanks to that widow, you can see what you're in for."

"You think I shouldn't go?"

"Don't go by my opinion. You should do what *you* think is best for you and the children. Leave Henry out of it, whether he's looking down from heaven or not."

"You'd rather go to California, wouldn't you?"

"It makes no difference."

"Oh, yes, it does. You don't fool me for a minute. You've been worrying yourself sick over Callie and how she'll manage after we split at Fort Hall." Florida placed a gentle hand on his arm. "You have feelings for her, don't you? Don't tell me you don't."

At another time, another place, he might have denied his sister's accusation. Not now, though. Maybe the truth came more easily in the middle of the night, in the darkness, when the pretenses of the day were stripped away. "Yes, I have feelings for Callie. That's why I've tried to stay away from her. When I'm around her, I..." Why try to explain? Florida would never understand. She'd known only one man in her life, boring Henry, a good man but about as exciting as a bag of oats. She'd never understand how it was to lie awake for hours into the night, staring into the darkness, desperately aching to hold someone, *like I want to hold Callie.*

"Ah, Luke." His sister's whispered words carried a trace of melancholy. "I knew you cared for her. Why couldn't you have opened up to me?"

"What good would it do? I have lots of reasons. You know them all."

Florida expelled a long, weary sigh that spoke of an enduring sadness. "Ah, yes, that terrible day. How I wish you could get beyond it."

"So do I, but I'm not like you."

Even in the near darkness, Luke could see his sister wasn't wearing her white cap like she usually did. She raised her hand to her head to the awful scar where the Indian had scalped her. In a choked voice she asked, "You think I could ever forget?"

"No, of course not. My poor sister, neither of us will ever forget that horrible day." He wrapped an arm around her shoulders. "It was my fault. I'll never forgive myself."

"No, no, no!" She broke loose and pushed him away. "It was *not* your fault. How many times—?"

"Let's not argue." He took her hands in his. "Let's stick to the present. You have a decision to make."

"It's not easy. Even leaving Henry out of it, there are so many things to consider."

"Like what?"

"For one thing, the trail to California isn't that easy either. They say there's that awful desert to cross and then the mountains."

"You're right. It's not that easy."

"Plus, there's Magnus. I worry, Luke. The man hates you. If he hears we've changed our minds and are going to California, no telling what he might do."

"You let me worry about that." Luke waited in sympathetic silence. His sister had a huge decision to make. Not easy, trying to decide her and her children's entire future.

She gave a decisive nod. "I've decided. We're going to California, dear brother." Her voice rang with resolve. "I don't care what Henry thinks."

It was a good thing Florida couldn't see his face clearly or she'd see his joy at her decision. Now he could watch over Callie and protect her from that scum, Magnus Ferguson. "Good for you, Florida. You've made a good decision. You won't be sorry." Would he be sorry? Time would tell but, for the moment, he rejoiced he could stay close to Callie Whitaker. Aside from his obligation to his sister, that was all he cared about.

* * * *

Florida was going to California! Next morning when she heard the news, Callie wanted to do a little dance. She wasn't about to lose her dearest friend after all, and, of course, that meant Luke would be going, too. She hadn't seen the last of him after all, and for that her gratitude knew no bounds. Nothing had changed, though. These days when he spoke to her, he was polite but as remote as a stranger. Had they ever exchanged those passionate kisses? Those precious moments seemed so long ago. She had no time to dwell on it, though, what with never-ending work that kept her busy from before dawn when she arose until after dark when she fell on her bed exhausted at the end of the day. At least Ma was feeling better now. She wasn't up to doing any chores, but she didn't need any extra help. Lydia was a godsend. Callie couldn't stop marveling how her formerly flighty stepsister had changed into a capable young woman who gladly shared the heavy burden of work. Tommy, too, was doing fine. He was even talking more, almost like a normal child would, a minor miracle in Callie's eyes. And he didn't sit huddled for hours without moving, like before. He was more active now, a mixed blessing since these days he had to be watched closely. Many a child had been crushed to death or badly injured when jumping from a rolling wagon and getting caught underneath the wheels.

As for Pa, he walked with a bad limp that Callie suspected would never go away, but at least his ribs and shoulder were healing. He wasn't moaning and groaning nearly as much. He still never spoke to her, stayed in the back of the wagon most of the time, not speaking to her or acknowledging her existence, or, for that matter, anyone's existence except Ma's.

* * * *

Callie's spirits were never so high as on the bright, sunny day thirty California-bound wagons of the Ferguson party left Fort Hall and struck south. So many things were going right for her. She'd dreaded having to say good-bye forever to Luke and Florida, but now she didn't have to. How wonderful they'd be with her all the way to California and after that, who knew? She looked forward to each day's trek without fearing she wasn't capable, or, because of her inexperience, something might go wrong. She now felt completely at home holding the reins. No more doubts. She could drive the wagon as well as any man, even over the roughest trail. Colton still helped with yoking the oxen, but she could handle the job herself if she had to.

Moving through thick forests, the Ferguson train headed toward the Humboldt River, the going easy with abundant grass and water for the animals and plenty of fish and game.

One day Luke stopped by their wagon to chat. "Our only concern right now is the Indians. There's a war party of Shoshone in the neighborhood, but likely they won't bother us. There are always the Diggers, of course. They'll steal you blind if you don't watch out."

Callie had seen so many Indians along the way, they no longer struck terror in her heart. Members of the various tribes often visited the camp, sometimes to trade, sometimes to steal. "The Diggers don't seem nearly as proud or courageous as the other tribes."

"You're right. They're different. 'Diggers' is a term for what they call the underclass of Indians from the Shoshone, Bannock, and Paiute tribes. They're mostly a bunch of outcasts and criminals. Their own people threw them out, so now they exist by stealing and grubbing a living from roots and insects."

"They eat bugs?"

"You would, too, if you were hungry enough."

"I would never!"

Luke laughed. "Be careful. All Indians can be dangerous, even the Diggers."

The next day, toward the end of their noon break, Florida came hurrying to the Whitakers' campsite, her eyes full of consternation. "I can't find Luke. Rascal came back without him." She explained how her brother had taken advantage of the break to go hunting in the nearby stand of woods. "He knew we'd soon start up again. Something's wrong."

Callie could only agree. Luke would never be careless enough to let his horse get away. "Have you looked for him?"

"Everywhere close by. I waited and waited, thinking he got thrown off his horse and would soon come walking back, but he didn't."

"Then we'd better start looking." Panic welled in her throat. It never occurred to her something bad could happen to Luke. With his massive self-confidence and easygoing manner, he always seemed so untouchable, so above the weaknesses of ordinary people. But he wasn't, of course. They had better not waste a moment. He could be lying in the woods right now, badly hurt or even worse. She *must* find him, and fast.

Loud shouts signaled the train was about to get underway again. She cast an anxious glance toward Magnus's lead wagon. "Florida, you keep looking. I'll go tell Magnus we can't leave yet."

The wagons had started to move out when Callie, at a run, caught up with the first one in line. Magnus sat on the front seat, reins in hand.

"Mr. Ferguson, you've got to stop."

With a reluctant tug on the lines, Magnus halted the oxen and glared down at her. "What do you want?"

Grasping one of the front wheels, she bent over to catch her breath. Chest heaving, all she could manage to gasp was, "Luke's missing."

Magnus frowned with annoyance. "You held me up for that? Don't worry, he'll turn up."

She hadn't explained it right. "No, listen, he's got to be in trouble. He went hunting in the woods and his horse came back without him."

"Is that all?" Magnus's frown deepened. "In case you haven't noticed, it's late in the season. I'm of a mind to disagree, but my captains keep insisting every minute counts. If we don't hurry, we're going to get caught in the snow. So don't pester me with ridiculous reasons why you want to stop. Luke knows how to take care of himself. I'd wager his horse got away somehow, so he's walking back."

Jack Gowdy and Riley Gregg arrived. Magnus told them why they'd stopped.

"Magnus is right," said Jack. "We can't be stopping every time someone goes for a walk in the woods."

Riley guffawed. "Or we'd never get our butts to California!"

Callie kept arguing. Soon Orus Brown, Doc Wilson, and Reverend Wilkins joined the discussion, along with Josiah Morgan, Lilburn Boggs and just about every male member of the train. To a man, they sided with Magnus, some declaring in the most forceful manner they didn't want to wait for Luke McGraw, or anyone else who straggled behind. Even the Reverend Wilkins feared getting caught in the snow. After professing his concern over Luke's whereabouts, he, too, declared Luke would surely turn up and they should move on. Doc Wilson agreed. Callie did her best, but soon realized she was wasting her breath. What did it matter Luke was a loyal and valued member of the company? These men were so hell-bent on getting to California before the snow fell, they'd lost all reason and compassion. Magnus was the worst. He hated Luke's guts and wouldn't lift a finger to help him, but saying so would get her nowhere. Hopeless! She hid her resentment and managed a casual shrug. "All right then, gentlemen, I see I can't persuade you."

"He'll turn up. Callie." Magnus spoke indulgently, as if speaking to a child.

"I'm sure he'll show up soon, Mr. Ferguson. I'm not going to worry." She hurried off. Time for anger later. Otherwise, she'd be seething at the selfishness of Magnus and the rest of the leaders. Stupidity, too. How could they manage without Luke? Didn't they realize how much they depended on him? Right now she couldn't allow herself the time to fret about what fools they were. She must concentrate on finding Luke.

Seconds later, the train got underway again. How selfish. They couldn't wait a minute? When she got to her wagon, she found Lydia had taken up the reins and was waiting to take their place in line. "Good for you. Lydia. You go ahead if I'm not back." She saddled Duke and was about to ride to Florida's wagon when she glanced toward the dark woods where Luke had disappeared. Something ominous—she wasn't sure what—hung over them. She needed a weapon. She'd never carried one before but sensed she shouldn't go in those woods without one. She'd get one of Pa's rifles. They were in the wagon…and so was Pa.

He had yet to say a word to her. Still looked right through her as if she didn't exist. She dreaded having to face him but had no choice. She slipped off Duke and climbed into the wagon. As usual, Pa lay on his blankets staring into space. Ma sat beside him. "Pa, I've got to take one of the rifles." She opened the lid of the trunk where the guns were stored.

Ma looked horrified. "Callie! What are you doing?"

Pa turned his head and glared at her. "You will not touch my guns."

"Can't stop to talk." Callie reached in the trunk and retrieved her stepfather's Hawken rifle, along with a ramrod and small horn. "Sorry, Pa, I'll explain later." Rifle in hand, she jumped from the back of the wagon. Would she remember how to load the thing? When they started the trek, Len, of all people, had given her a shooting lesson when Pa wasn't around. She searched her memory and it all came back. First, she used the horn to measure the right amount of black powder. From the brass patch box in the rifle butt, she took a tallowed patch-cloth, carefully centered the ball on the patch, and drove it down the barrel with a smooth thrust of the rod, then tamped it down. Now the rifle was loaded. Thank God she'd remembered.

She mounted Duke and fastened the rifle so it lay across the saddle. Now if she could just remember how to shoot it!

She rode to Florida's wagon.

Her worried friend was wringing her hands in agitation. "Oh, Callie, they're moving out. We can't leave Luke behind. Should I go or should I stay?"

"You've got to keep up." Bending from her horse, Callie untied Rascal from the rear of the wagon. "There's no sense in us both staying behind. I'll find Luke and we'll catch up with you." Leading Rascal, she started away, back toward the darkness of the thick woods where Luke must be. Was he injured? Dead? Had the Indians got him? Or some wild animal? Was she crazy to do this by herself? A wave of fear took hold of her, but no way would she turn back now. She rode into the woods where Luke had disappeared. It was rough going. Soon the thickness of the trees and dense undergrowth forced her to dismount. Both reins in hand, she began to follow the rocky bed of a nearly dry stream. Going ever deeper into the forest, she started to call, "Luke, can you hear me?" Silence. Nothing but her own words echoed back. What if there were Indians around? Or wild animals? Better keep silent.

Using the creek bed as a pathway, she continued on until the growl of a nearby animal stopped her in her tracks. She stood perfectly still, listening. There went the growl again, low and menacing. She wanted to flee, but how could she when the animal might be growling at Luke, ready to attack. She wouldn't dare call out now. She'd have to gather her courage and go see what it was, quietly as she could. She tethered the horses to a branch on the far bank and unfastened the rifle from the saddle. It was heavy and awkward in her arms. She wasn't sure how to hold the thing, let alone fire it, but she'd worry about that later.

By now, the hem of her skirt was so soggy and bedraggled, nothing would be gained by holding it up. Skirt dragging, she crossed the stream and started through the dense foliage that lined the bank. The sound again! This time a low snarl. A lion? A bear? *Turn—run—get out of here.* But no, Luke might be in trouble. She got a firm grip on the rifle and pressed on.

No more than ten feet farther, she came to the edge of a small clearing and peered through the bushes. A large tree stood in the center. And underneath the tree...*Luke.* Her knees went weak at the sight of him seated on the ground, back up against the tree, a trickle of blood flowing down his arm. Her first impulse was to call his name and run to his side, but something told her not to. He held his big hunting knife in his hand. He was looking upward, his gaze fastened on some object high above his head. A snarling animal crouched on the limb of a tree. A bobcat! She knew from its gray coat, whiskered face, and black-tufted ears.

Somehow Luke knew she was there. In a voice barely above a whisper, he muttered, "For God's sake, Callie, don't speak. Get out of here."

No, she wouldn't run away. She had to save Luke, and the only way to do it was to shoot the bobcat. She raised the rifle to her shoulder. How heavy it was. She could barely hold it steady as she peered down the long barrel through the sight. A low, menacing growl from the bobcat told her it was about to strike. She wasn't sure she was holding the rifle right, or aiming it true, but no time to waste. She pressed the rifle against her shoulder, pointed it at the animal and pulled the trigger. Her ears rang from the loud explosion, and her shoulder stung from the slam of the rifle butt. Suddenly she was sitting on the ground, legs sprawled in front of her.

In another second, Luke was bending over her. "Are you all right?"

Her ears rang so badly she could hardly hear. "Fine. Did I get him?"

"The bobcat?" He grinned. "Not even close. You scared it off, though. He won't be back."

She gingerly rubbed the place on her shoulder where the rifle butt slammed. "Guess I wasn't holding it right."

"You got the job done." He groaned as he settled beside her.

She remembered the blood running down his arm. "You're hurt."

"Serves me right. I got ambushed by a Digger Indian. The sneaky devil got an arrow in my arm before I knew he was there. I could have made it back, but then the bobcat came along."

"Sorry I missed."

"The bobcat's not sorry." Admiration filled his eyes. "How brave. Not many women would have taken on a dangerous animal like you did."

I did it because I love you. She yearned to tell him but would die before the words left her lips. No doubt he'd be shocked and horrified. Instead, she directed her attention toward his wounded arm. "Do you think it'll get infected? I mean, don't Indians put poison on their arrows sometimes?"

Despite his pain, he had to smile. "Not the Diggers. They're lucky if one of their arrows hits its target. Good thing it wasn't a Shoshone, or that arrow would have found my heart."

"We've got to take care of it. Do you think you can ride Rascal back?"

"Of course. This isn't the first time I've been attacked by Indians."

"It's happened before? You've never mentioned it."

* * * *

Luke wished he could take his words back. Why had he said that? He, the man of silence, who guarded his feelings as he guarded his life. And yet...*Callie.* What was it about her that drew him so strongly he could hardly think straight in her presence? He recalled the day he first saw that bedraggled-looking creature peering at him over the red Hawthorne bush. She was so meek back then, with hardly an independent thought in her head. Now, here she was boldly shooting at bobcats, sorry she'd missed. "I find it amazing how you've changed."

"I have?"

"From Little Mouse to a woman so brave you came to my rescue by yourself." He cocked an eyebrow. "I can guess what happened. Magnus and his captains weren't too concerned I was missing. I'd wager they didn't want to spare one extra minute looking for me when they could be making a precious extra mile or two. What happened? Did you out-and-out defy our esteemed colonel? Did you even tell him?"

"Yes, I told him. He said not to pester him with ridiculous reasons why he should stop and search for you. That's when I decided to look for you myself."

He let out a big whoop of laughter. "Good for you! Thanks for finding me. I'd wager if you hadn't come along, I'd be on that bobcat's supper plate tonight."

"You're welcome. You were worth saving." She eyed him curiously. "You said you were attacked by Indians before?"

Damn! He should have known she wouldn't let it go. A long moment passed. "I don't talk about it."

"Maybe you should."

He'd never spoken of the old, painful memory. Best it lay buried forever. But was it buried? Had a day ever gone by that the events of that terrible morning hadn't gnawed on his consciousness, haunted his dreams? *Maybe you should,* she'd said. Her probing eyes looked into his. Pretty eyes, soft and brown, filled with warmth and caring. Maybe, after all this time, it wouldn't hurt to talk about it. Maybe...yes, he wanted her to know.

"We lived in Illinois, my mother, father, two sisters, a brother and I. Florida was sixteen. My sister, Emily, was fifteen and my brother, Douglas, was twelve. I was ten. My father owned a farm not far from town, a pretty place, surrounded by woods and a stream running through.

"It happened on May seventeenth, eighteen twenty-nine, a sunny Sunday morning when we were walking to church. Halfway there, my father discovered he left his Bible behind and sent me back to get it. I ran home, got the Bible, and was on my way back when there was the most God-awful shrieks and hollering you'd ever want to hear." Luke closed his eyes a moment, as if to block a horrible memory. "A bunch of Shawnees had been waiting in the woods. They ambushed my family. I ran, fast as I could. By the time I got there, Pa already lay dead, a hatchet in his skull and scalped. Then an Indian spied me. I had to run like hell to get away from him, but I did, and hid behind some bushes." He paused again and cleared his throat. "I watched from behind that bush and saw my whole family get slaughtered. They got my mother next, hacked her to death and then scalped her. Same with Douglas and Emily, tomahawked to pieces and their scalps taken. Florida escaped, thank God, but only after they'd scalped her."

"Ah, so that's why she wears that cap all the time?"

"It's an ugly wound. You wouldn't want to see it."

"Oh, Luke, how awful for you."

"Don't waste your sympathy on me. I'm the one who escaped all harm, remember?"

"But surely you don't blame yourself."

His mouth twisted into a wry smile. He remained silent.

"Why? You were only a boy of ten, much too young to——"

"I was a coward. I ran and hid instead of trying to help my family. For that I'll never forgive myself."

"What could you have done? I mean…"

* * * *

Callie didn't finish because there was no use continuing. Luke spoke with such deep conviction that a few words from her wouldn't even begin to change his mind. Her heart swelled with sympathy. "So, is that why you've lived by yourself all these years? Never married and had a family?"

"I like living alone. The only reason I'm here is because I owe my sister a lot. After our family was killed, she raised me by herself, in spite of the wounds she suffered."

She touched a hand to his cheek. "I can't even imagine how awful it must have been, seeing your family killed before your eyes."

He leaned away from her, ever so slightly. "I don't need your sympathy."

The old, timid Callie would have jerked her hand back, hurt at his rejection. Not this new Callie. She bent closer and looked deep into his eyes. "Then I won't give you any sympathy, at least not for losing your family in such a horrible way. The sympathy I have for you is because you've spent nearly your whole life feeling guilty for something that wasn't your fault."

"Really?" He clasped her wrist and pulled her hand away from where it rested on his cheek.

For a moment she thought he'd fling it back at her, but instead he turned her hand palm up and gazed upon it.

"Such a little hand. It should be serving tea, not driving a wagon halfway across the continent."

She pulled her hand back. "You're changing the subject."

"Yes, I am." A wry smile crossed his face. "Callie Whitaker, would you mind not looking into my soul?"

She caught his lightened mood. He wanted to change the subject and she'd let him, at least for now. "If you insist. I suppose you've had enough attention for one day, what with the Digger Indian and all."

He peered at her intently. She caught her breath at how desirable he was with his ruggedly handsome face and its shadow of a beard, his powerful shoulders beneath his buckskin jacket. Their light conversation came to an end, replaced by something intense passing between them. "Callie." He placed his hands on her shoulders. "How can I stay away from you?"

"Why do you want to?"

After a moment of stillness, he caught his breath. "I don't." His arms encircled her. He began to kiss her as he eased her to the ground. His fast breathing and the hoarseness of his voice told her this time he wasn't going to stop. No more quick kisses. No more *we can't do this*. There were so many things she ought to think of right now. Was this a sin? Would she end up like Nellie? His lips caressed her forehead, slid down her cheeks, and farther to where his tongue teased the hollow of her neck. A burning need pulsed through her, deepening as his hands slid slowly in a long caress along her body. Her whole being flooded with desire. Nothing in the world mattered except Luke making love to her.

His hands fumbled at her bodice. "Damn buttons."

She reached to touch his fingers. "Let me help."

All reasonable thought left her mind. Each exquisite stroke he gave her sent her to ever-higher levels of pleasure. And when at the end, she cried out, then sighed in joyous exhaustion, she could only think of how much she loved this man and how she could never let him go. He lay spent beside her. Although he'd tried to ignore her, never said he loved her, she knew in her heart he felt the same.

The harsh caw of a crow brought them back to reality. He sat up abruptly. "We better get out of here."

"Why?" she murmured, still half in a daze from their lovemaking. "Are you afraid the bobcat might return? Or the Digger?"

"Both are long gone." He stood and pulled her to her feet. "We need to go."

While she straightened her dress, buttoning the buttons, common sense returned. So many good things had just happened. At last Luke had opened up. At last he'd made love to her, but what did it mean? He wasn't a man like Coy, taking advantage of a woman for his selfish needs, yet what kind of a man was he? He hadn't asked her to marry him, not that she expected he would. He hadn't even said he loved her. More than ever, she realized what a complicated man he was, with feelings that ran so deep she could only begin to understand. Just now, for the briefest of moments, he revealed his innermost thoughts and let her look into his soul. Time would tell if he'd ever open up to her again.

* * * *

So this is what it's like to love a woman. Luke could no longer deny his gut-wrenching passion for Callie Whitaker. God knows, he'd tried to push her away, but he wanted her too much. He'd been deceiving himself. Just now, when he broke his rules and took her, he knew he'd never get his fill of that beautiful woman. Those fine resolutions he made were gone. No more living alone. He would finish his obligation to Florida, keep his distance until the end of the trail and then...

He'd long since written himself off as a man without a past, without a future. That had just changed. He loved Callie Whitaker because she taught him how to live again, and for a lot of other reasons, too. When this journey ended and he could speak his mind, he'd spend the rest of his life telling her so.

Chapter 14

Callie's joyful mood faded fast when they got back to the train. Ma glared and Pa muttered an oath under his breath when she returned the gun. Lydia complained about a terrible blister on her hand from holding the reins. Callie might have had the most thrilling moment of her life, but on the Ferguson wagon train, it was just another grueling day.

Next evening, Callie and Lydia were cleaning up after supper when a man's angry shouting came from across the campground.

"That sounds like Orus Brown," Lydia said.

Callie was surprised. Orus was a quiet man. She'd never heard him lose his temper.

More angry shouting followed. Lydia looked around the circle of wagons to where Magnus Ferguson's were parked. "Sounds like Magnus called another meeting with his captains and they're at it again."

Callie recalled a night at the campfire when Luke had talked about dissension among members of a wagon train and how it was a common, if not an inevitable, problem. "We'll be lucky if the men in this wagon train don't kill each other before we get there."

The quarreling grew louder. From around the circle, members who'd been watching began to edge toward Magnus's campsite.

Most of the time, Callie made a conscious effort to stay away from him, but curiosity got the better of her. "Come on, Lydia. Let's go see what's the matter."

They approached Magnus's wagons. All the leaders had gathered around. Lydia was right. They were indeed holding some sort of special meeting. Judging from the number of clenched fists, red faces, and loud voices, it was an angry meeting, getting angrier by the minute.

They joined the cluster of curious bystanders.

Jack Gowdy raised a clenched fist above his head. "We'd be crazy not to take the shortcut."

Shouts of agreement followed. Soon the reason for the argument came clear. Most of the captains were insisting they take the Ferris Shortcut, which would cut fifty miles off their travels. Unfortunately, it wasn't well traveled and could be treacherous, although no one knew for sure. Callie wasn't surprised the captains wanted to take it. They were hell-bent on getting to California as fast as possible, never mind the risks. Some even talked about breaking up the company, letting people go where they wanted.

Magnus stood in a bold stance on the tongue of the wagon, his face set in its usual self-confident, slightly superior expression. He gazed upon his captains, slowly shaking his head as if they were too dumb to understand, and he, the wise one, must patiently explain. "Gentlemen, I urge caution. We have plenty of time to get to California. Therefore, I urge you to stick to the planned route and not go off on some unknown, untested shortcut. I've gotten you this far, have I not? You may not agree with my decisions, but who could lead you better than I?"

Someone shouted, "Luke McGraw could!" A cheer went up, accompanied by more shouts of agreement. Callie silently shook her head. These were the men who hadn't minded leaving Luke in the woods. Now that they needed him, how their attitude had changed.

A dark look crossed Magnus's face, quickly covered by a self-assured smile. "Stick with me, men. Have a little faith and we'll get to California in good shape."

A chorus of enraged *No's!* arose from the crowd. Someone yelled, "We want Luke for our leader," followed by howls of approval.

Magnus tried to speak again but catcalls drowned him out. He was definitely not winning this battle. In fact, Callie sensed the mood of the crowd turning uglier by the minute. Where would it lead? At the moment, she wouldn't be surprised if someone produced a rope and the great leader of the wagon train was hanged high. She looked around for Luke. Surely he could help. Up to now, she hadn't seen him, but there he was, stepping up on the wagon tongue, taking his place alongside Magnus.

Luke held his hands palms down in a calming gesture. "Quiet, everyone. Listen to me."

The crowd quieted down immediately, showing respect for the speaker.

"This is no time to be breaking away. There's safety in numbers. Stick with Magnus. I appreciate the thought, but I won't be your leader."

The crowd groaned in disappointment. Someone shouted, "It's you we want, Luke!"

Luke placed a friendly hand on Magnus's shoulder. "Give the man a chance. Quarreling can pull us apart. Let's not let that happen. I say we stick with Magnus. Let's pull together, give him the help he needs, and we'll reach California before the snow falls, and all of us safe."

Jack Gowdy raised his fist again. "Not if we don't take that shortcut, we won't! I say we split up. Those who want to take the shortcut can take it. And the rest"—he threw a contemptuous glance at Magnus—"can waste a week and get caught in the snow."

Luke's gaze calmly swept the crowd. "That's not a good idea and I'll tell you why…"

He described how foolish it would be to break up the train. In his relaxed, reasonable way, he explained there was safety in numbers, and as tempting a shortcut might be, it could be full of dangers. Better to stick with the original plan.

The angry men began to calm down. Soon heads nodded in agreement. By the time he finished, the argument was over. They wouldn't be taking The Ferris Shortcut.

"You've made a good decision," Luke said at the end. "Have faith in Magnus Ferguson. He'll get you there."

A chorus of boos went up. Someone yelled, "I still say we need a new leader. Let's elect Jack Gowdy!" More cheers. The wrangling continued. Luke stuck by Magnus's side, remaining calm and reasonable, until, in time, the crowd quieted and the captains took a vote and reluctantly agreed to continue with Magnus as their leader. Callie was weak with relief. Much as she disliked the man, this was no time to change leadership and elect a man as quick-tempered and impatient as Jack Gowdy.

The crowd broke up. Magnus quickly walked away, not saying a word to anyone.

Lydia noticed. "How rude! He should be thanking Luke instead of walking off that way."

"I didn't expect he would." Callie could tell from the rigid set of Magnus's shoulders and the abrupt manner in which he stalked away, he was in no mood to thank Luke for anything. Vain man that he was, he must be livid with anger, his pride wounded because he'd been saved from complete humiliation by a man he hated. What might he do? His vanity, along with his ruthless behavior, made him capable of anything. Luke had better be careful.

Later in the evening, all the family except Callie had gone to bed when Luke came riding by.

She smiled up at him. "Congratulations. You did well tonight."

He brought Rascal to a halt. "There was a slight disagreement, but it's over now."

"Slight disagreement? I was there, but I guess you didn't see me. It sounded like the captains were ready to string him up."

Luke swung from his horse. "They easily could have." He stood close, his dark eyes intent upon her. "Of course I knew you were there."

Excitement lurched through her. She wanted to throw herself in his arms, but they stood in view of the whole camp. Anyone could be watching, and probably was. *Don't make a fool of yourself.* "Magnus was lucky you stood up for him." She was proud she kept her voice casual. "Did he ever thank you?"

"Magnus hates my guts. I won't be getting a thanks from him anytime soon."

"It's because of me, isn't it?"

"Partly." Luke reached to touch her arm then stopped. He, too, must have realized they stood in full view of prying eyes. "Magnus thinks I'm responsible for you calling off the wedding."

"You were, thank goodness. You kept me from making the biggest mistake of my life."

Luke's mouth quirked with humor. "That's not all he hates me for. Tonight I gave him another reason."

"Because now he's beholden to you?"

"It's human nature. The man he detests most in this world just saved his butt from getting tossed out. That doesn't set well with our high and mighty colonel. His vanity's badly wounded."

She fought the urge to grip his arm. "You must be careful. Magnus Ferguson is a mean, vengeful man. I wouldn't put anything past him."

"Don't trouble yourself. You let me worry about that." He stood looking at her a moment. A tender expression crossed his face. "I haven't forgotten. Good night, Callie."

Giving her a polite touch to his hat, Luke swung back on Rascal and rode away.

Don't trouble yourself? As if she could stop worrying.

Despite Magnus, Callie spent the next few days in a happy mood. They were traveling on an easy trail. Luke stopped by every day, always a little past dawn with Colton to help yoke the oxen. Supposedly he came to see how they were doing, but Callie knew otherwise. Luke's eyes always sought her out, signaling he hadn't forgotten that time in the woods. Nothing further. He had no time for casual visits, and neither did she, but even so, she often daydreamed about what might happen after they reached California. Maybe nothing, but she couldn't bring herself to believe he would simply say good-bye at the end of the trail and head back to his lonely life in the mountains.

* * * *

Colton Wilkins spent a lot of time at their campsite. His red-faced shyness had disappeared. He bantered back and forth with Lydia, who no longer made fun of him. As time went by, she dropped her flirty ways with all the men and had eyes only for Colton. "I think I'm in love with him," she whispered one night to Callie after they'd gone to bed.

"That's wonderful, but when I think of Nellie—"

Lydia's laughter cut her off. "Do you think I'd go through what Nellie did? I may not be very bright, but I assure you, we aren't going to eat supper before we say grace."

"I'm glad to hear that." Maybe Lydia wasn't so dumb after all. *And maybe smarter than me.* To Callie's great relief, she'd just discovered her reckless moments with Luke hadn't resulted in disaster. Thank God, she'd escaped Nellie's fate, but what would she do if she and Luke were alone again? She liked to think she'd be smart enough to say no, but that would be hard because she loved him with all her heart. Often she relived those wonderful moments when she was in his arms, and he made her feel such passion that her knees grew weak just thinking about it. Now Luke's visits were casual. For the best, of course. If he so much as beckoned with his little finger, she could never resist.

* * * *

Callie managed to avoid Magnus Ferguson until one afternoon when they'd stopped for a break. She came across him watering his horse at the bank of a small stream. He was alone. She tried to make a quick retreat before he spotted her but no such luck.

"Running away?" he called. "There's no need, you know."

She stopped in her tracks and turned to face him. What a strikingly handsome man he was, with his impressive height, broad smile, and wavy, blond hair. But like Ma always said, *don't judge a book by its cover*. So true. Over the past few weeks, his acts of selfishness had so repulsed her she found it impossible to return his smile. "You wish to speak to me?"

He laughed offhandedly. "My dear, there's no need to avoid me. Rest assured you have nothing to fear."

His condescending attitude caused her temper to flare, but she didn't let it show. "I'm not afraid of you, Mr. Ferguson. It's just I have nothing to say to you."

"Considering you nearly became my wife, I find that rather hard to believe."

"It's true. I've already apologized for calling off the wedding. Do you want to hear it again?"

His smile wasn't so broad now. "Aren't you the least bit sorry you called it off? Just think, if you'd married me, you wouldn't be making a slave of yourself, driving a team of oxen all day. Rather unladylike, don't you agree? And for what? You ma hardly speaks to you. Your pa threw you out and still pretends you don't exist."

"I'm managing quite well, thank you." It was getting harder to keep the contempt from her voice, but she'd try to remain pleasant. "Lydia helps a lot. Colton yokes the oxen for us every morning, and Luke—" *Uh-oh, now I've done it.*

At the bare mention of Luke's name, Magnus visibly flinched. The cords in his neck stood out. "Luke. Always Luke." He spat upon the ground. "I've seen how you look at him. What a blind fool you were to listen to him. If not for his damn interference, we'd be married now."

She raised her chin high. "Don't blame Luke. I make my own decisions."

"You're throwing your life away, all for a black-hearted devil who'll do nothing but hurt you. He's had you, hasn't he? What did he do, take you on the ground under a bush?"

"I've nothing more to say to you." She started away, wanting nothing more than to get away from Magnus's vicious words.

"Tell your lover he'd better watch out."

She stopped in her tracks and turned. "What do you mean by that?"

He replied with a laugh so hoarse and bitter it sent a chill down her spine. He said nothing more. Still chuckling, he mounted his horse and rode away.

* * * *

Along the way, the Ferguson company kept encountering the Donovan company. They seemed to be on the exact same course, kept passing each other with irritating frequency. Magnus grew increasingly annoyed when Donovan, or any other company, passed him by, blowing up dust, hogging the best campgrounds, their animals eating the best grass before his train arrived. Bad blood between the trains sometimes went beyond hot words. Rumors flew about how members of one train, annoyed for various reasons by another, went so far as to set a grass fire that, because the wind was right, caused great devastation to the offending train. Speculation ran high among the members of the Ferguson train. What was Donovan planning? Could such a disaster happen to them?

One night when Callie visited Florida, her friend was bursting with the latest rumor. "Have you heard? Magnus wants to set a fire and burn out the Donovan company."

Callie could hardly believe it. "Where did you hear such a thing?"

"Oh, it's true all right. Luke found out. Magnus called a secret meeting with some of his captains, the ones who still have him on a pedestal, and that's not many. He suggested they wait 'til the wind's blowing right, then set a fire to burn out the Donovan train."

"Are you sure? What a horrible thing to do."

Luke appeared. "It's horrible, all right, but don't worry. No one went along with our great leader's scheme. Even his most loyal captains told him to forget it."

"Thank goodness," Florida said.

Callie had her doubts. The trouble with Magnus wasn't over and wouldn't be until the last moment of their journey when at last she could get completely away from that horrible man.

* * * *

They traveled for several days, making good time each day, until finally, when they reached the Humboldt River, they halted for a much-needed day off. The men greased wheels, mended harnesses and tended to their animals. The women hauled huge piles of laundry to the riverbank and spent most of the day beating dirty clothes with pumice stones and hanging each piece to dry on nearby bushes. Despite the drudgery, Callie looked forward to these wash days when the women could get together. Lighthearted chatter made the day pass quickly. Not only that, as the weeks went by, the women grew more friendly and began to seek her advice. Bake a pie? Ask Callie. Handle an unruly child? Ask Callie.

"You're certainly getting popular," Lydia said one day with a bit of envy in her voice. "When they need help, they come to you."

Callie was far too busy to dwell on her newfound esteem, yet she couldn't help remembering back to the beginning of the trek when everyone called her Little Mouse and looked past her like she wasn't there.

Today Callie caught a constant undertone of grumbling beneath the light banter. Gert Gowdy protested the loudest, "Jack still thinks we should get rid of that skunk, Magnus Ferguson. He don't care what Luke says." Murmurs of agreement followed.

Mary Gregg, Riley's wife, chimed in, "Magnus cares for no one but himself. I won't forget how he put us days behind that time he got sick. If we get caught in the snow, it'll be his fault."

"Luke had better watch out," said Orus Brown's wife. "I saw Magnus look at him with murder in his eyes."

Callie listened with growing alarm. *Murder in his eyes.* Yes, Magnus would be capable of murder. Such crimes happened often on the trail. Sometimes, like with Coy, the criminal was caught and brought to justice, but law and order didn't always come first in the wilderness. People were always in a rush, some to get to the gold fields, others to finish their journey before the first snow. Crimes went unsolved. Criminals went unpunished. The emigrants traveling west had far more important things on their mind.

* * * *

That night, Luke awoke abruptly from a sound sleep. Was that a noise? Maybe it was just the wind blowing. He raised his head and listened. There was the noise again and it wasn't the wind. Men's muted voices. Indians? He didn't think so. He pulled on his boots, grabbed his knife, and slipped from the tent. In the bright moonlight, three figures came into view for a quick moment before they disappeared into the heavy growth of trees that bordered the campsite. Instantly he recognized Magnus Ferguson and his two hired hands, Hank and Seth. Those scoundrels! The Donovan train passed them today, stirring up clouds of dust, making life even more miserable for the Ferguson train. Later in the day, Magnus sped up the train and gleefully passed the Donovan company while they were taking a break. Magnus wanted to stay ahead and would go to any length to do so. Luke had a good guess what he and his hired hands planned to do.

With silent footsteps, he followed the three as they made their way through the woods, following the same trail they'd traveled that day, back toward the Donovan wagon train. When they came to a series of bluffs overlooking the Humboldt River, they left the woods and followed the trail along the edge. They stopped when they came to an open meadow covered with high, thick grass that was beginning to dry in the late summer heat.

The grass would burn well. The brisk wind coming from the northwest would carry the fire straight toward the Donovan camp.

The three men separated and began to move about the meadow. Luke caught a whiff of kerosene. A sudden flare of light revealed Magnus lighting a torch. No time to lose. Luke stepped forward. Dammit, he should have brought his gun instead of his knife. "Not a good idea,

Ferguson. You start a fire and you'll live to regret it." In the darkness, he could barely make out Magnus stopping in surprise. *Should have brought the gun.*

"Stay out of my business, Luke. Now I've got to kill you."

Every fiber in Luke's body tingled with alarm. Magnus meant what he said. No mistake. Why the *hell* hadn't he brought his gun? "Put that torch out, Colonel, then we'll talk. You're not a cold-blooded murderer."

"That's where you're wrong." With a curse, Magnus hurled the torch high in the air where it sailed in a fiery arc, scattering a blazing path of embers over the meadow. Before the torch reached the ground, he drew out his pistol, took aim, and fired. Luke went down fast, ears ringing from the sound of the shot. Smoke filled his nostrils. An excruciating pain ripped through his chest.

Callie...Callie...

So this is what it's like to die.

* * * *

They buried Luke in a pretty spot by a fern-lined stream. The short service ended with a prayer from Reverend Wilkins. Every member of the wagon train attended. Now, despite their shock and grief, they hurried back to their wagons. Nothing, not even the death of a man as admired as Luke McGraw, could cause them to delay their journey. Only Callie and Florida remained at the hastily dug grave.

He's dead. Callie couldn't bring herself to believe the man she loved was gone. "I still don't understand. Why was he chasing after Indians in the middle of the night?"

Florida wiped away her tears. "We'll never know. Magnus thinks he must have heard Indians in our camp, probably robbing us blind. They left and he started to follow. When he saw them set the field on fire, he tried to stop them. That's when they shot him——"

"And left him to die in the fire." Callie struggled to erase the gruesome image that filled her mind.

"Thank God everyone in the Donovan party escaped the blaze." Florida gazed upon the mound of earth and the plain wooden cross at the head, marked simply *Luke McGraw.* "You know I don't like Magnus, but at least he and his hired men tried to help. Dug the grave, made the marker and all. Thank God, they buried him before we could see the body. Magnus said"——Florida swallowed a sob——"there wasn't much left after the fire."

Callie placed a comforting hand on her friend's shoulder. "I don't think I could have borne to see him...like that." She refrained from voicing her opinion concerning Magnus. If Florida chose to think he'd been helpful, then fine, but Callie was filled with dark suspicion. His account of how he and his hired men tried to go to Luke's rescue didn't ring true. Although she wasn't sure how, Magnus and his men had something to do with the fire and Luke's death. She wouldn't be surprised if they set the fire, not the Indians as they had claimed.

Why dwell on it? She'd be a fool to think she'd ever learn the truth. Other than herself, not one single person questioned Magnus's story. No one could spare the time for anything that might delay their progress. How completely frustrating to know there was nothing she could do. Life would go on as before. Magnus would get away with whatever evil deeds he'd committed. Who was there to stop him? Poor Florida. How could she survive now? "Will you continue on, Florida? Or will you go back home?"

"Of course I shall carry on." Florida raised her chin. "I've got Hetty to help. I wouldn't dream of turning back."

Thank heaven she still had Florida, but how could she live without Luke? She had so depended on his strength, his caring ways. Now she'd never know the joy of being in his arms again. Her secret, middle-of-the-night thoughts of her and Luke together would remain only fantasies, fulfilled once, and never again. A flash of wild grief ripped through her. She wanted to throw herself on his grave, press her cheek against the cold earth that covered him and stay there forever. But, of course, she'd do no such thing. Tommy needed her, and Lydia and Ma, and even Pa, though he still refused to speak to her. She must be strong. She *would* be strong. That meek, obedient servant girl bore little resemblance to the woman she was today.

Callie raised her eyes to the sky then lowered her gaze to the distant snow-capped mountains. "I'll never come this way again, but I'll never forget Luke. He'll always be in my heart."

Florida took her arm. "It's time."

"Yes, it's time. We still have a long way to go."

Chapter 15

Troubles mounted as the Ferguson wagon train continued to follow the Humboldt River. Each day seemed worse than the one before. Sweltering hot days turned into freezing cold nights, extremes in temperature that brought misery to both humans and animals. Food supplies were running low and game grew scarce, forcing them to exist on a monotonous diet of mostly hard tack and dried beef. The Digger Indians caused the most suffering. Not that they ever attacked, but nearly every night they sneaked into camp and stole food, weapons, pots, pans, and whatever else they could get their hands on. Worst of all, they were adept at stealing animals.

"Land's sake!" Florida lamented to Callie one day when losses were especially bad. "If I don't tether my horses right next to my wagon, those pesky Indians will get them for sure."

The dreaded desert lay ahead. Callie heard nothing but horror stories about the forty barren miles they soon must cross. These days she coped because she had to, grateful for the never-ending toil and deprivation that took her mind off Luke's tragedy. Occasionally something good happened, like the day she was driving the wagon with Tommy beside her, silent as always. Often she tried to interest him in driving the team. Most little boys begged to get their hands on the reins, but up to now, her little brother hadn't shown the slightest interest.

Suddenly he held out his hand. "Let me drive."

She managed to conceal her astonishment. "All right, Tommy." Like she'd done it dozens of times, she casually handed him the lines.

He gave them a smart snap. "Gee haw!" No hesitation. He urged the oxen on as if he'd been doing it all his life.

Ma was walking alongside the wagon. When she saw Tommy take the reins, she gasped, "I can't believe it!"

Callie put her finger to her lips. "Shh. Act like it's nothing unusual."

"But it's wonderful to see him like this, thanks to you, Callie."

"Thanks, Ma." For the first time in ages, Ma said something nice. Callie could scarcely believe it.

Ma continued, giving Callie a smile and a nod of approval. "I've noticed how Tommy has been improving lately, and now this. You never gave up. I thought he would never improve, but I guess I was wrong and you were right."

"This is just the beginning. I know he's going to get better every day." Callie hid her relief that after all these weeks, Ma was speaking to her again. *Now if only Pa would, too.* But no. Pa wasn't one to forgive and forget. She'd be crazy if she thought he ever would. His leg had mended, although he still had a bad limp. He could walk if he wanted, but mostly he chose to lie in the back of the wagon, sullen and silent. She had little time to think about her future, but she knew one thing for sure. Pa didn't want her. When they reached their new home in California, Pa would be in charge again, and she'd have to move on. She had no idea where she'd go, but it didn't matter. Other than getting her family safely to California, nothing mattered now that Luke was gone.

* * * *

They finally reached the Humboldt Sink, a marshy area that marked the start of the forty-mile stretch of desert. The night before their hazardous journey was to begin, Magnus called everyone together for some dismal warnings. There would be no water for the next forty miles. No game to hunt. No wood for fires, so no hot food. No grass for the animals. Magnus looked in her direction. "Think you can make it, Miss Callie? Will you need extra help?"

She smiled to hide her annoyance. "We'll be fine, Mr. Ferguson. No need to worry about us." Like he cared. Ever since Luke had died, Magnus treated her with thinly veiled contempt, like he knew she'd fail, wanted her to fail.

Magnus had been right. Crossing the forty miles of desert was a nightmare experience for everyone, worse than she'd ever imagined. Sometimes she didn't know how she could keep going. At some spots they found themselves knee-deep in alkaline dust. In others, the hot sun beat down over surfaces that were torture—razor-sharp ridges of coral-like rock that cut through their shoes, causing stabbing pains and bloody feet. The animals suffered greatly. One by one, those on horseback dismounted and walked in an effort to save their exhausted horses. Callie noted with disgust that Magnus was the last to do so. Selfish to the end. How she despised the man. A fear always lurked in the back of her mind that he meant to harm her, just as he must have harmed Luke. She didn't have much time to think about it, though, what with trying to keep her despairing family from giving up. Like many in the train, Ma, Lydia, and Tommy were, at times, so bone-weary and discouraged, they wanted to turn back. Pa said nothing, of course. He just lay silent in back of the wagon, an extra burden for the poor oxen to haul.

"I can't go on," Lydia cried when they were halfway through. "I'm thirsty, I'm hungry, and my feet hurt. Just leave me here to die."

Ma joined in. "That makes two of us. I don't think I can go another step."

More than once, Callie pointed toward the jagged silhouette of the Sierra Nevada Mountains that lay to the west and seemed forever out of reach. "See those mountains? We're going to reach them before you know it. We *will* keep going. We are *not* going to give up."

The oxen were exhausted. Everyone had to lighten their loads, adding to a trail already strewn with everything imaginable, left by the poor souls who crossed before them. Stoves, furniture, mattresses, clothes, and heartbreaking choices like family mementos and pictures had to be left behind.

Even stalwart Florida grew discouraged. Forced to dump her precious box of books, she fought back tears. "I planned to open a school with these books, but my oxen are about done in. It about kills me, but I've got to leave my books behind."

The Whitakers, too, were forced to discard precious possessions. Her face pale and drawn from fatigue, Ma carefully laid the family silver and set of china on the barren sand. "I can't believe I'm doing this." In a rare moment of disloyalty, she threw a bitter glance toward the back of the wagon where her husband lay. "Caleb could walk if he wanted. Too bad I can't dump him instead." She bit her lip and said no more, leaving Callie and Lydia to exchange surprised glances.

For another day, they trudged on until, late in the afternoon, the animals sniffed the air and bellowed.

"They smell water," someone yelled. "Unhitch the oxen. Let 'em go!"

Weak with relief, Callie watched every animal in the train join in the stampede. The humans followed not far behind. She never felt anything so wonderful in her life as that moment when she, along with everyone in the company, arrived at the banks of the Truckee River and plunged in. "We made it!" She joyfully splashed around in the cool, crystal clear water.

"We're practically there." Lydia dipped her whole self in the stream.

Callie didn't think so. They still had a long way to go, but she wasn't going to spoil the moment.

Magnus and the captains decided they'd stay two days in order to recover from their exhausting trek through the desert. That night, they camped at a beautiful spot by the river, surrounded by a thick forest of pine and fir trees, the snow-capped Sierras towering above. For the first time in weeks, the members gathered around a bonfire. Most were too tired to dance, but they all rejoiced their journey was almost over. Only a few mountains to cross and they'd be in the land of gold.

The next morning, Callie, Lydia, and Ma washed bedding, clothes, themselves, and everything in sight in the gloriously sparkling clear waters of the Truckee River. Only one thing marred the cheerful mood that prevailed among the campers. The leaders were bickering. The cause was the same as before, a disagreement over what route they should take. Magnus's complacent attitude had changed. Now anxious to reach their goal before the snow fell, he favored a less-traveled tributary of the Truckee River called the Little Truckee. From what little they'd heard, this route would take them through deep valleys and over steep cliffs but would get them there the fastest. Now it was the captains, led by Jack Gowdy, who wanted to stick with the main trail, a longer route but easier and considered much safer.

The bickering continued. By the second night, they still hadn't reached a decision. Callie and Lydia were returning from the campfire when Callie felt something soft and cold brush her face. She held out her hand. "Look, a snowflake."

Lydia's face lit. "Snow! What fun. In the morning we'll build a snowman."

Callie didn't share her stepsister's enthusiasm, especially the next morning when she awoke to find several inches of snow on the ground and much colder weather. Any plans to build a snowman were forgotten when Florida stopped by their wagon with her news. "Magnus is out and Jack Gowdy is in. They decided late last night. I've never heard such cussing and arguing."

Callie could scarcely believe it. "You mean Magnus isn't leading the train anymore?"

"Praise the Lord, they threw him out. The leaders were mad about a lot of things, but mostly about the shortcut." Florida broke into a broad grin. "Thank goodness, we'll be taking the safer route. I wasn't looking forward to hauling our wagons up and down steep cliffs with ropes and winches."

"That makes two of us." What a relief! Callie hadn't realized how much she'd detested following the leadership of a vengeful man who meant to do her harm. Maybe she wouldn't have to see him again. "Will Magnus come with us now, or will he take the shortcut anyway?"

"Who knows? I don't care if he comes with us or not. All I care about is we're going the safer way." Florida poked the toe of her boot into the snow. "Guess we'd better hurry, though. Wouldn't it be awful to get stuck in the snow and have to spend the winter here?"

Callie couldn't even imagine how terrible that might be.

* * * *

The oxen were hitched and the wagon packed. Callie sat on the seat, reins in hand. They were about to take their place in what would now be called the Gowdy wagon train when Magnus Ferguson rode up. He appeared tired and haggard, as if he hadn't slept for days. "Good morning, Callie. I've come to speak to your pa."

"We are about to leave, Mr. Ferguson." What could he possibly have to say?

He gave her a hard, cold-eyed smile. "My business is with the head of this family, not you."

She was so taken aback, she was speechless. Before she could think of an answer, Pa stuck his head through the canvas flaps. "If you wish to speak to me, Colonel, I'll be right there."

Slowly and painfully, Pa climbed down from the wagon. He and Magnus walked a distance through the pine trees until they were out of earshot. Callie couldn't imagine what Magnus wanted and neither could Ma or Lydia. The wagons began to move out. With growing impatience, they watched Pa talk with Magnus in what appeared to be a lively discussion, until finally Magnus walked away and Pa limped back to the wagon, a slight grin on his face. It looked like a smile of triumph, but what could he possibly feel victorious about?

Ma addressed him. "Hurry up, Caleb, they're moving out."

"We're not going with Jack Gowdy."

After a moment of stunned silence, Callie was the first to speak. "What do you mean?"

"Magnus will be following the Little Truckee. We're going with him. Two other families have stayed loyal. Everyone else has lost their minds." Pa gave Callie a look full of scorn and hatred. "You took advantage, girl. For too long I've let you run things around here. Not anymore. From now on, this family will do as I say."

Ma stepped forward. "Caleb, that's not true. Callie has gone out of her way to help us. If it hadn't been for her—"

"I won't hear another word. I've let you women bully me around long enough. If it hadn't been for Magnus just now... Thank God he made me see how you've all taken advantage of my accident. No more. Those days are over. I'm back in charge. Callie, get your things. You're not welcome here. Go with that skunk, Jack Gowdy. Maybe Florida will take you in."

Ma placed her hand on his forearm. "But, Caleb—"

"Shut your mouth, woman." He shook her hand off and looked toward Callie, who still sat on the wagon seat, reins in hand. "Get down from there. I'm driving."

Up to that moment, Callie had merely stared, tongue-tied, at her raving stepfather, too astounded to utter a word. But now reason and logic were returning. "Wait a minute, Pa. Are you saying you can manage this wagon and the oxen by yourself?"

"That's what I'm saying."

Over the past weeks, she'd observed Pa crawling with agonizing slowness in and out of the back of the wagon, grunting with pain each time. "You can hardly get yourself in and out of the back of the wagon, so how on earth are you going to climb way up here to the seat, let alone take the reins and drive all day?"

Pa glowered at her. "That's not your business. Get down from there."

She flung aside the reins and climbed down. Standing in several inches of snow, she faced him and glowered back. "I'm not leaving until I see you climb up there."

Pa threw her a look of disgust, gripped the side of the wagon, placed his foot on the hub of the wheel and painfully hauled himself up. She waited for him to step farther up to the footboard then onto the seat. Twice he tried to climb from the hub to the footboard, but he hadn't the strength. It was almost pitiful to watch. He tried a third time and failed. Muttering curses, he slowly climbed down. After he paused to catch his breath, he gave her a withering stare. "It doesn't matter. One of Magnus's men will help me drive. I don't want you here." He looked toward the last wagon of the Gowdy train, now disappearing into the trees. "Better hurry or you'll get left in the middle of nowhere."

Had she allowed herself to dwell on Pa's cruel words, she would have been deeply hurt, but she couldn't afford the luxury of wallowing in wounded feelings. All she knew was, her family needed her, whether Pa thought so or not. She considered the possibility of climbing back into the driver's seat and joining Gowdy's wagon train whether Pa liked it or not, but no, that wouldn't work. Men were the leaders, women the followers. No man on the Gowdy train would favor her, a mere woman, over her stepfather, no matter how disliked he was. So there was only one answer. She tilted her head back and looked him square in the eye. "I can't leave you, Pa. You need me to help. You can't do it by yourself."

Magnus appeared. "What's going on here?"

When Pa said he needed a man to drive the wagon, Magnus shook his head. "You've got to let her stay, Caleb. I don't have a man to spare."

Thank you, Magnus. Although she loathed that he took her side, she needed all the help she could get to convince her stubborn stepfather. "So it's settled, Pa. I'm coming with you. Later, when we get to California, I'll go my own way, but I can't do it now. I hope you understand. I hope—"

"Suit yourself." Pa fairly spit the words out. He turned his back and limped away.

"So, my dear, you're coming with me." Magnus raised an eyebrow in amused contempt. "You've made the right decision. We'll get to California long before Gowdy and those other idiots. And meanwhile…" A slow, calculating smile spread over his face. "I'd like to think you and I could be friends again."

She could think of a dozen scathing replies but couldn't bring herself to use one. Maybe she'd used up the last of her boldness with Pa, at least for the moment. "All I want is to get my family and me to California, Mr. Ferguson."

"So you shall." He laughed and tipped his hat. "Mark my words, we'll be great friends before we get there."

After he walked away, Lydia, who'd heard everything, stared at her with speechless wonder. "I can't believe the way you stood up to Pa."

"I can't believe it either."

"Oh, this is awful." An anguished expression settled on Lydia's face.

"What's wrong?"

"It's Colton. He's going one way, and I'm going another. I'll never see him again." Lydia gazed after the last wagon of the Gowdy train as it rolled out of sight. "Colton's the only man in the world I will ever love. He probably doesn't even know we've stayed behind."

Callie gave her a hug. "Don't worry. We'll find him again when we get to California." She never thought she'd feel any sympathy for her stepsister, but nothing was the same anymore. Lydia wasn't the scatterbrained, shallow girl she used to be. *I've changed a lot, and so has she, and all for the better.*

Snow began to fall again. Ahead, Magnus's wagons started moving.

Taking a shortcut like this was crazy. How could Magnus think they would not come to grief? If Luke were here, he'd know what to do. *He's not. He's gone. He's dead.* Whether she liked it or not, she must do this by herself. *The horses.* Despite the rough going, so far they'd survived. How long would they last in the cold and heavy snow? She couldn't bear the thought she might lose Duke, Pearl, and her beloved Jaide. "Lydia, climb up and take the reins. I'm taking the horses to Florida. Go ahead, I'll catch up."

Lydia climbed to the wagon seat and took the reins, a frown on her face. "Are you sure you should, Callie? Pa will be furious when he finds Duke missing."

"I don't care what Pa says. What can he do to me he hasn't done already?"

Riding Duke bareback, leading Pearl and Jaide, she quickly caught up with the Gowdy train. Florida was more than happy to take the horses. "I wish you were coming with us, Callie. I'll leave word where we're going when we get to Sutter Fort. When you get there, you can follow." She gave Callie a tearful hug. "I won't rest until I know you're all right."

Losing Luke was bad enough, not this wonderful friend, too. Callie vowed that somehow, someway, she'd find Florida and her family when she got to California. With a heavy heart, she stood watching until the last of the Gowdy train disappeared from view. No time to waste or she really would get left behind. She turned and started to jog, anxious to get back to her family. If ever they were going to need her, it was now.

Chapter 16

Josiah Morgan and Lilburn Boggs and their families had also chosen to follow Magnus, so at least they weren't entirely alone. Callie didn't think much of Josiah, a meek sort of fellow who idolized Magnus and agreed with everything he said. His wife, Margaret, was the strong, outspoken one in the family. Callie admired the competent way she managed her weak-spined husband and three small children. She was obviously the one in charge.

Callie didn't know Lilburn and his shy wife, Hannah, very well, except they had a baby and a two-year-old, and Lilburn, an ambitious young man, was eager to make his fortune in the gold fields. Maybe that was why he chose to stay with Magnus, so he could get there a little faster.

By the end of the first day, the five wagons, all that was left of the Ferguson wagon train, had made good progress over fairly easy terrain. The snow had stopped, but the low-hanging clouds promised not for long. That night they camped in a broad meadow beside an old log cabin, probably built by a trapper. Callie felt a pang of sorrow when she saw it. Luke must have lived in such a cabin. He was never far from her mind.

When Callie and Lydia went looking for wood, Lydia gazed at the high, snow-swathed peaks looming above them. "How will we ever get across?"

"Don't worry. We'll make it." Callie spoke with a conviction she didn't feel. It was clear they were in a desperate race against time, but why upset her stepsister before she had to?

When they got back, Pa was waiting with fire in his eyes. "Where's Duke? Where are Pearl and Jaide?"

Since morning, Callie had been waiting for her stepfather to notice his horses were missing. He'd spent the day in the wagon but was bound to come out sooner or later. She dreaded the moment when he did, but now it was here, she was surprised at how her heartbeat remained normal and she could reply in a fearless voice. "They're with Florida."

She told him how she'd worried the horses wouldn't survive on such a harsh and dangerous trek and Florida agreed to take them in. "She'll leave word at Sutter Fort. Don't worry. We'll get our horses back when we get to California."

Pa gave her a frigid stare. He opened his mouth to speak but shut it again. With a resigned shake of his head, he hobbled away. She was sad, yet pleased at the same time. She no longer feared her stepfather. His strength was gone. The terrible injuries he'd suffered made him a stoop-shouldered, feeble old man. He'd never be the same. Considering the awful way he'd treated her, she should be glad to see him get what he deserved, but somehow she wasn't. Why couldn't he forgive her? Even now, she longed for his smile, or even an approving nod. It wasn't likely. Pa would go to his grave unrelenting and unforgiving, and that hurt, but nothing she could do.

Before they set out the next morning, Magnus, who by now had regained his confidence, gathered his followers together. He struck a pose and, with a grand sweep of his arm, pointed to the peaks above them. "My friends, beyond those last few mountains lies the golden land. A little hard work and we'll be there in no time."

Josiah Morgan stepped forward. "Are you sure, Colonel? We've hauled the wagons up some pretty steep hills, but those mountains look like the worst ever."

Magnus appeared annoyed anyone could even ask such a question. "I know whereof I speak. You must trust me."

"I hope he's right." Ma muttered, "or we'll starve to death."

No wonder Ma was worried. They'd used up the last of their coffee and bacon. They were nearly out of flour, nearly out of everything. Everyone in the train was running low on food supplies, so the danger of starving to death was very real. Callie wished she could give her stepmother a positive answer but couldn't. She, too, was worried sick they might run completely out of food.

They began the day's trek under a slate gray sky that threatened snow at any moment. The temperature had dropped considerably. The hand-me-down wool coat Callie had brought from home wasn't enough. She wrapped herself in a blanket but still shivered as she drove the wagon. Because the oxen were so weak now, only Pa stayed in the back. Ma, Lydia, and Tommy, dressed in their warmest clothes, walked alongside. They spent the morning traveling upward through a thick forest, over ever-steeper slopes, sometimes having to push the wagons from behind. As they traveled ever higher, they encountered deep snowdrifts in which both humans and animals floundered. It started to snow, lightly at first, then heavier as the hours ticked by.

They struggled on. Magnus shouted his reassurance. They had only to get over that top peak and their troubles would be over. The growth of trees grew thinner as they approached the tree line. Gusts of wind nearly blew them over. It was harder to breathe in the higher altitude, and at times, Callie had to gasp for breath. They were barely moving when they came to a slope so steep it appeared impossible they could get their wagons to the top. Except for Magnus, they all wanted to turn back. He refused to listen. "We'll get the wagons to the top one at a time. We can do it! We'll be headed down the other side in no time."

They reluctantly agreed to keep going. By now Callie was so cold she couldn't feel her fingers or toes. Her family suffered, too. She especially worried about Tommy. Such a frail little boy, not an extra ounce of fat on him. So far he seemed fine, but he wouldn't last long without enough food in this horrible, cold weather.

With the exception of the Gregg family's three small children and the Brown's baby and two-year-old, everyone, even Tommy, joined in the all-out effort to push the first wagon to the top. Pa also climbed down to give what meager assistance he could. Teams were doubled up. Humans and beasts struggled together. They blocked wheels with stones dug from beneath the snow. They heaved and strained at ropes. For hours they struggled, but in vain. As the day went by, the snow fell harder and the drifts grew deeper, making progress nearly impossible.

One by one, the oxen floundered. Clearly this was the end. The exhausted animals could not go on.

"We can't do it," Magnus finally announced in a grudging voice. "Take what you need from the wagons. We'll leave the animals here and walk back down to that cabin we saw in the meadow. It'll be warmer there. Less snow."

"What about the oxen?" Callie asked.

Magnus shrugged with indifference. "Shoot 'em. They're done for."

Rosie and Jack. Zephyr and Thor. They might be just dumb animals, but over the months they'd been her faithful friends who'd worked so hard and suffered so much. Now, as their reward, she must put them to death. With a bitter swell of pain beyond tears, she got Pa's rifle from the wagon. "Ma, Lydia, take Tommy so he won't see."

After they moved away, she loaded the rifle four times, and four times she placed the barrel to an ox's head and pulled the trigger. It had to be done. How much more could she endure? She clenched her jaw to kill the sob in her throat, knowing she'd go on because she had to, but 'til the day she died, she'd never forget this terrible day and the terrible thing she had to do to those poor animals.

Bone weary and nearly frozen, Callie gathered her family together. Lydia and Tommy were crying. Ma looked so exhausted she was beyond crying and could barely stand. Pa collapsed and lay helpless in the snow. Drawing on what seemed the last of her strength, Callie had to shout at her family above the whistling wind. "We'll take what we can from the wagon. Be sure to get all the food."

"What about Pa?" her stepmother called.

Pa. Oh, God. Callie knelt beside her exhausted stepfather who was making no effort to get up. "Do you think you can walk?"

Pa gazed at her with dull, resigned eyes. "Leave me here."

"I'll do no such thing." What could she do? Her stepfather couldn't walk by himself. "I'm not going to leave you here. I'll get help."

She got up and slogged through the snow to where Magnus and his hired men were unloading their wagons. "I need help, Mr. Ferguson."

Stony-faced, Magnus listened while Callie told him Pa was in bad shape and could no longer walk. He would have to be carried down the mountain. When she finished, Magnus shook his head. "I'll be needing both Hank and Seth to haul what we need down the mountain." He turned away, calling over his shoulder, "Maybe Josiah can help, or Lilburn. Ask them."

Magnus's unconcern left her watching after him with disgust. Hard to believe he hated her so much he wouldn't help her family, but obviously he did. His one suggestion was useless. Josiah Morgan had a wife and children to look after. Lilburn Boggs the same. No one could help. If Pa was to be saved, she and her family must do it. She waded through the snow back to her family, gathered them around, and had to shout to be heard over the howling wind. "Ma and Tommy, you carry as much as you can. Lydia and I will do the same, but it won't be much because were going to help Pa down the mountain."

"But I can't," Lydia cried in protest. "I'm freezing cold and starving. I don't think I can walk another step, and you want me to carry Pa?"

"Do you want to leave your father here? We can do this, Lydia. Pa can walk a little. We'll support him between us. It'll be easy." Not for a minute did she believe what she was saying, but it was like her brain was numb from the cold just like the rest of her, and all she could focus on was that no matter what, she wouldn't leave her stepfather lying in the snow to die.

She kept arguing until Lydia finally agreed. They managed to get Pa to his feet. Huddled together, they and the other dejected members of Magnus's wagon train started back down the mountain. She was right. Pa was able to walk some, supported by Lydia and her as they floundered through giant snowdrifts. At least they were headed downhill, so the going was easier, and the size of the snowdrifts lessened as they made their way down. She'd been right about the Morgan and Boggs families. They could barely manage carrying the smallest children in their arms, making the older children walk through snowdrifts where they almost sank from sight.

Callie tried to ignore how miserably tired and cold she was. Now her only goal was to get her family and herself to that old trapper's cabin in the meadow. When she first laid eyes on it, she thought how awful it must have been to live in such a rough, primitive place. Now she could hardly wait to get out of this unbearable cold and snow and find shelter inside its rough-hewn walls.

They were almost at the cabin when Pa collapsed. Try as they might, they couldn't get him to his feet again. "What shall we do?" Lydia cried.

"We'll carry him." Callie expected Lydia to protest, but she didn't. Amazing how her delicate stepsister had found enough grit to try to save her father, but obviously she had. Between the two of them, they carried Pa the last few hundred feet to the trapper's cabin and collapsed inside. What a relief to get out of the storm! And what blessed warmth. Magnus and his men had arrived first and lit a fire in the hole in the ground that passed for a fireplace. They gathered around, savoring its warmth while they thawed their frostbitten fingers and toes.

Divided into two crude rooms, the cabin offered the barest of shelters. The wind came whistling in through chinks in the rough log walls. Snowflakes found their way through a porous ceiling constructed of poles covered with pine boughs. Callie hardly noticed. Pa had barely moved since they had carried him in and laid him by the fire. His eyes were closed, his breathing labored. She knelt by his side and clutched his hand. "Pa, are you all right?"

Ma knelt beside her and took a long look at her husband. "He's not all right. He's dying."

Callie felt such a heaviness in her chest, she could hardly speak. "He can't be dying, Ma. Surely—"

"He's dying." Ma's voice turned bitter. "I warned him not to go on this crazy journey. This is all his fault."

Callie had only to look at Pa's deadly white face and hear him struggle for every breath to know Ma was right. Even now his eyes seemed sunken into his head. He might never open them again, but when she squeezed his hand and quietly called, "Pa," his eyelids fluttered open. For a brief moment, he showed no sign of recognition, but then he focused on her face. "Callie," he murmured.

"Yes, Pa?

"I'm...dying." He could hardly get the words out.

"No! You're going to get well."

He shook his head ever so slightly. "Take care of Ma." He spoke in a voice so low she had to bend close to hear him. "I was wrong... You're a good girl, Callie." Pa shut his eyes. The effort to talk was too much.

She kept hold of his hand. His breathing slowed and in a few minutes stopped altogether.

For a long time, Callie knelt over her stepfather's body. She couldn't weep for the man who'd been so harsh and cruel to her all her life. Yet, in the end, when he said she'd been a good girl, a terrible hurt lifted from her heart. She'd done her best for him. If not for her, Ma and Lydia would have left him to die in the cold and snow, so at least she had the satisfaction of knowing she did everything she could to save him. In the process, she had discovered something about herself. She'd never be a mindless follower again. From now on, she'd lead. If this family was to survive, and she wasn't sure they would, their deliverance was up to her.

Chapter 17

The brutal storm wouldn't let up. For three days, ten adults and six children huddled in miserable discomfort around a barely adequate fire that left the corners of the cabin freezing cold. Their food supply dwindled to practically nothing. The children wailed constantly from cold and hunger. The cries of the Boggs' baby slowly faded until they ceased altogether, replaced by the weeping of his grieving mother.

They couldn't bury Pa or the baby but instead had to lay them in the snow behind the cabin. The storm was so fierce no one could venture more than a few feet away until finally, on the fifth day, the snow stopped and the sun returned. Some of the men started out with their rifles, hoping to find some game to shoot. They returned empty-handed. All the game had apparently moved to lower elevations, leaving only helpless humans to cope with the ravages of a heavy winter snow.

In desperation, Magnus sent Hank and Seth back to the site where they'd abandoned the wagons to salvage what they could. They didn't find much but managed to uncover one of the oxen. The rest were buried too deep. Everyone rejoiced when the men returned with all the meat they could carry, plus pieces of ox hide that would help keep them warm. The meat didn't last long, partly, Callie suspected, because Magnus hid some of it for himself and his men.

The break in the weather didn't last. One storm after another kept the wretched band of survivors huddled in the cabin with no thought of even trying to cross the peaks again. By now, an air of desperation and despair hung over them. Day after day, they huddled around the small, inadequate fire, miserably cold, their food nearly gone. Callie feared for her family. Ma had hardly spoken since Pa died. She seemed not to care if she lived. Lydia stayed strong, but her thin body and pale, drawn face held little resemblance to the pretty, rosy-cheeked girl who'd started the trek. Callie worried the most about Tommy. Like the other children, he was among the weakest and most vulnerable. He didn't talk now. He just lay in his blankets, staring up with eyes that looked huge in his small, emaciated face.

On the eighth day, the snowfall let up long enough for the stronger ones to leave the cabin and slog through deep snowdrifts in a desperate search for food. Acorns and pine nuts were all Callie could find. Maybe if she ground them up, they wouldn't be so bad. Back at the cabin, she did just that and put a small taste of the mixture in her mouth. *Awk! Awful.* She couldn't get it down, had to spit it out. Better to starve to death. The next day they had nothing to eat. All they could do was chew on strips of bark to try and stop the hunger pangs. Lydia began to weep. "I don't think I can go on much longer."

Callie couldn't comfort her. What encouragement could she give? The cold, gnawing hunger would soon mean the end of all of them, and there was nothing she could do.

Throughout the ordeal, Magnus and his men were of little help and pretty much kept to themselves. Callie couldn't prove it but suspected a secret cache of food, including the oxen meat, prevented them from looking as gaunt as the rest. Others suspected it too, and feelings ran high against him.

On the tenth day, a break in the weather brought new hope. Magnus declared he and his men would attempt to cross over the mountain. To cope with the deep snow, they'd make snowshoes. If the weather held, they were sure to get across.

"What about us?" Josiah Morgan sat huddled with his family.

"We'll send help soon as we can."

"Like hell you will." Josiah struggled to his feet. "Our wives and children are starving. They're not going to last much longer. I'm coming with you, Magnus, just to make sure you send help back right away." His voice was filled with contempt.

Lilburn Boggs stood up. "Josiah is right. I'm coming, too."

Magnus shrugged. "You'll need snowshoes. Otherwise, you'll slow us down, and I won't have that."

Callie made a quick decision and got to her feet. "I'm coming with you."

Magnus regarded her with scorn. "This is a man's job. You'll only hold us up."

"You let me worry about that."

"Suit yourself, but if you lag behind, don't expect us to wait for you."

"I'll be fine, Colonel Ferguson."

Shirley Kennedy

She bent to speak to her family, huddled on the crude dirt floor, covered with blankets. The blank expression on Ma's face these past few days hadn't changed. Callie doubted she even knew or cared what was going on.

Lydia gazed at her, dull despair in her eyes. She had been pretty once. Now, what a heart-wrenching sight she was with her sunken eyes and hollow cheeks. With an effort, she asked, "How could you even think of going out in all that snow? Maybe the sun's out now, but it won't last. You'd better stay here. At least we can all die together."

Callie firmly shook her head. "Do you think I'd trust Magnus Ferguson for one moment? I'm going to get us some help. I won't sit here and watch my family starve."

Lydia gave no further arguments. Instead, she reached out and weakly clasped Callie's hand. "I pray to God you make it, dear sister. Please, please hurry."

* * * *

Along with the men, Callie fashioned herself a pair of crude snowshoes out of strips of ox hide and split oxbows found in the cabin. Bundled in blankets and all the warm clothes they had, they set out on a cloudless day, bright sunshine causing sparkles on the snow. Their food supply consisted of a glue-like paste boiled from ox hides, powdered bones, twigs, and barks from trees. The five men trudged uphill in a single line. Callie brought up the rear. No doubt Magnus thought she'd soon falter and fall behind, but during the day, she kept up just fine. Not easy, considering her gnawing pangs of hunger. Everyone was hungry. Only sheer desperation kept them climbing.

By nightfall, they reached the abandoned wagons and spent the night huddled in the only one not completely buried in the snow. Callie could hardly choke down the paste made from ox hides, but she forced herself. She must eat or she'd die.

They had all begun to look like scarecrows, but surprisingly, it was Magnus, with his great wide shoulders and muscular build, who seemed to age overnight. His once-handsome face had thinned to a near skeleton-like appearance. He walked with an old man's shuffle, all stooped over. His eyes held a wild look, as if he might lose his sanity at any moment. Wrapped in his blankets, he kept staring at her. "I see you've kept up thus far."

She raised her chin in defiance. "As well as you, Magnus. Just like I intend to do tomorrow."

Lilburn Boggs spoke up. "Tomorrow! If all goes like it should, we'll reach the top and be well on our way down the other side."

Dear God, she hoped so. Her strength was waning. By pushing herself to the limit, she could hang on maybe one more day. Tomorrow they must cross the summit. If they didn't... She pulled her blankets closer around her. She couldn't think about it. Instead, she concentrated on Luke, how much she loved him, how he must be looking down from heaven, keeping her and her family safe. He wouldn't let them come to harm. Everything was going to be all right.

After a night of fitful sleep, Callie awoke to a howling wind. Her worst fear was realized when she peered outside. Another storm. Snow falling heavily again.

No sense going back now. What would be the use?

The despairing band of travelers had no choice but to keep going. Moving at a snail's pace, they started out, fighting their way up the steep incline through ten-foot snowdrifts. Everyone had frozen feet. Magnus and Seth were beginning to suffer from snow blindness. Josiah Morgan started hallucinating, claiming he saw a sunny, flower-filled meadow ahead. The storm raged on. By early afternoon they couldn't continue. Without a fire, they were done for, but with the snow drifting up to fifteen feet, they couldn't find any wood. The best they could do was spread blankets on the snow, tent them over with other blankets and crowd together underneath. By now, they could offer no words of encouragement to one another. A sense of impending doom hung over them. In their desperation, Magnus's own men turned against him. "You fool," cried Seth. "You said we'd make better time on this stinking shortcut. Look where it got us."

"We should never have listened to you," Hank bitterly echoed.

Callie kept quiet but heartily agreed. Time and again, she'd had to quell her anger over Luke's death and her suspicion Magnus was responsible. She'd never forget the shabby way he'd treated her. Now this latest, his arrogant insistence they take this shortcut was about to be the death of them. No use saying so. Magnus was failing. With each passing hour, his condition seemed to deteriorate. Suffering from frozen feet and severe snow blindness, he sat shivering in his blankets. If he heard his men berating him, he gave no sign, but instead gazed into space, as if he hardly knew where he was. As the hours passed, he began to babble words that made no sense. "Swim the cattle... It's time for dinner... I see California!" His men yelled at him to shut up, but he didn't seem to hear.

In the middle of the night, Magnus got to his feet. "Got to yoke the oxen!" Before anyone could stop him, he stumbled from the makeshift tent and disappeared into the raging storm.

"He's a goner." Seth made no effort to go after him.

Neither did Hank. "Guess we'll find what's left of him in the morning."

Callie remained silent as did Josiah and Lilburn. They hadn't the strength to care.

The storm ceased at about noon the next day. The lack of food and water for over twenty-four hours had taken its toll. Josiah was too weak to travel. Lilburn refused to go on, moaning, "Just leave me here to die."

Both Hank and Seth were strong young men but frostbitten, exhausted, and starving. They, too, had lost the will to go on. Callie felt the same. How easy it would be to simply lie down in the snow and drift into the sleep that would last forever.

No, no, no. My family is waiting. I will not give up.

She threw aside her blankets and got to her feet. Drawing upon the last of her strength, she addressed Hank and Seth, who sat huddled before her, fearful and drained of their willpower. "God hasn't brought us this far to let us perish now." She pointed toward the top of the peak. "It's not that far. We can make it. I know we can."

Perhaps the shame of being lectured by a woman made the two hired hands gather their strength. The three put on their snowshoes and started climbing again. At least the snow had stopped and the skies cleared so they could see to the top of the peak. Just having it in sight gave Callie the strength to go on. It wouldn't be much longer. Then they could start downhill to warmth, food, and help for her family. She kept having to battle faintness from hunger and a fatigue so great she could hardly put one foot ahead of the other, but it didn't matter. Yes, she was going to make it!

They hadn't gone far when they came across Magnus Ferguson's body half buried in the snow. They paused for only a moment to take a look.

Only Seth spoke. "God have mercy on him." His was the only prayer said over the former leader of the wagon train. Callie couldn't have cared less, and neither could Hank and Seth.

They plodded on and had almost reached the top when the temperature dropped. It started to snow again, the flakes driven sideways by a cutting wind. Callie could hardly see but fought on, her weary body protesting every painful step. She soon lost sight of Hank and Seth in the raging blizzard.

She couldn't see the top now...but if she kept going up, she was sure to find it. Not there yet...so tired...how nice if she could lie down a minute...but, no, she couldn't, because if she did, she'd never get up again...but so very tired...

What would it hurt to lay her weary body on the snow and take a rest? A very short rest...

She fought on, but when her knees buckled and she fell, she knew she'd never get up again. It was over. *Ma...Lydia...Tommy...now I'll see you in heaven. Luke, how I loved you. Luke...*

Sleep, blessed sleep. It was all that mattered.

Chapter 18

"Wake up! Wake up!"

Callie forced her eyelids open. What was that voice? It sounded like Luke's, but it couldn't be because he was dead. And yet...

Where was she? It must be heaven because Luke's face loomed above her. "Callie, you're all right. I've got to get you warm."

"Am I dead?"

"No."

Maybe this wasn't heaven. It seemed like she was in a tent, covered with blankets. Outside the storm raged. Someone was rubbing her hands, then her feet, then back to her hands again.

She had to gather all her strength just to speak. "Luke? Is that you?"

"It's me." He was rubbing her hands and didn't let up.

"But you're dead."

"Does it look like I'm dead?"

"But how——?"

"I'll explain later. Right now you've got to concentrate on getting warm."

Was Luke not dead? Was she still alive? She was definitely in a tent. There were other people in the tent besides Luke. He was bending over her. Yes, it was definitely Luke McGraw, and he had a deeply concerned look in his eye as he tried to bring back warmth to her frostbitten hands and feet.

A man she didn't know brought her a cup of steaming hot coffee and asked, "How is she?"

"She'll be all right."

"Lucky we found her when we did. She wouldn't have lasted much longer."

Her mind cleared when she sat up to drink the coffee. She was alive and Luke was alive. She wasn't in heaven after all. The hot liquid tasted wonderful, even more so when it slid in a warm path down her throat. After she'd had a few swallows, she looked at Luke, who still knelt by her side. "Why aren't you dead? How did you find me?"

"It's a long story. I'm not dead because Magnus didn't kill me, although he meant to when he shot me point blank in the chest. He saw me go down, so, of course, he and his men figured I was dead, and there'd be no trace of me after the fire burnt out the field."

"But how did you—?"

"When they ran for their lives to escape the fire, I crawled to the cliff and threw myself off. Landed in the Humboldt River, which was, thank God, deep enough I didn't break my neck. I drifted downstream until a couple of Shoshones found me and dragged me out. Took care of me until I got on my feet again." He gave her a wry smile. "So that's the story of why I'm not dead."

"I cried over your grave."

"What a sly devil he was. That grave was empty."

She'd been right. Magnus killed Luke, or tried to. She still couldn't quite believe Luke was alive, but she was trying. "How did it happen that you found me?"

"When I was well enough, I got a horse from the Shoshones and set out to find you. I crossed the desert in a day. From the Truckee, I followed Jack Gowdy and his train across the Sierras, caught up with them at Johnson's Ranch, which is well on the way to Sutter's Fort." He broke into a smile. "Florida was happy to see me."

"I should think! She must have been overjoyed."

Luke turned serious again. "But you weren't there. That's when I learned Magnus had chosen to take some crazy shortcut and took you and your family with him. You hadn't shown up yet, so we knew something was wrong. I organized this rescue party, six men with plenty of provisions. We got back to the Truckee. Then we followed Magnus's shortcut and got to the old trapper's cabin—"

"You found them?" Callie's heart leapt with excitement. "Please tell me how they are."

"I guess you already know about your pa, but Lydia, Tommy, and your stepmother are fine. Weak from hunger, of course, and cold, but they're going to be fine."

"It's such wonderful news I can hardly believe it."

"It's true, all right. They told me you'd gone off with Magnus and were worried sick and didn't think you'd survive."

"I almost didn't."

"I know." A strange look came over his face. He seemed to be fighting to control his feelings. "I told you once that when the train got where it was going, I'd head back to the wilderness and live the rest of my life alone." He took her hand. "I can't do that."

"Why not?"

"Because I love you, and we should be together." His eyes grew hauntingly dark with some unnamed emotion. "I can't imagine life without you."

No, this was one miracle too many. She couldn't believe so many good things were happening at once. Her appearance! When was the last time she combed her hair? She reached up to touch it. What a tangled mess. "I must look awful."

For a moment he stared at her, then burst out laughing. "You think I care what you look like?" He wrapped his arms around her and held her tight against him, like he never wanted to let her go. "Callie Whitaker, you are the most amazing woman I've ever met. You're smart and you're loyal. You're as brave as any man. To me, you're beautiful and always will be."

The last of her confusion disappeared. "Oh, Luke, I fell in love with you from the first moment I saw you at the creek."

"We'll have a lifetime to talk about it, won't we?"

There were others in the tent, but she didn't care when he crushed his lips to hers and gave her a kiss full of love and promises. She melted against him and gripped his broad, sheltering shoulders. Now she knew for sure the old Callie was gone. The new Callie looked forward to a wonderful life with the man she loved.

Epilogue

Angel's Camp, California, 1860

For at least the thousandth time, Callie McGraw went to the front window of McGraw's Trading Post and Outfitters. She peered down the main street and sighed. "Not yet."

Lydia walked to the window and gave an impatient sigh of her own. "Three months since they left New York. It's got to be soon."

At that moment, Callie saw a covered wagon rolling up the street. A man and a woman sat in front. Several children peered out from the back. "It's them!"

She ran outside to the wooden sidewalk, Lydia close behind. They shouted and waved as the wagon drew up and stopped in front of the store. Nellie Jonckers jumped from the seat and threw herself into her sisters' arms. "All those years! At last we're together again."

"Nine years, to be exact." In a more dignified manner, Abraham Jonckers climbed down and stood beside his wife.

Callie's mind flew back to that never-to-be-forgotten day when she had helped Nellie escape Pa's wrath. She'd always wondered if she'd done the right thing, but now knew for certain she had. Nellie's eyes sparkled with happiness as she cast an adoring look at her husband. She looked slimmer now, despite the three babies she'd borne.

When the children climbed down, six altogether, Callie knew immediately which was Coy's son, not only from his looks but from his age. He looked like a happy child, just like the rest. She knew from Nellie's letters the boy believed he was Abraham's child. He'd never know his real father was a murderer and hanged in disgrace.

After the first heady moments of their meeting, Callie put her arm around Nellie's shoulders. "Come inside. I have so much to show you and

Shirley Kennedy

so much to tell you. Luke's on a packing trip, but he'll be home in time for supper."

The McGraw family lived in a spacious two-story house on a hill overlooking the bustling mining town high in the Sierras. That night, supper was a joyous affair. The younger children sat at a table of their own: Nellie's three youngest, Lydia's four, including the twins, and Callie's two lively boys who so resembled their father. All day Callie had gone around in a glow. How wonderful they were all together again. Lydia and her husband, Colton, lived close by. He worked with Luke in the store and as a guide for the pack trains, two ventures that provided a comfortable living for both families. Now Nellie and Abe had trekked clear across the country and planned to buy a farm in the valley below. Florida, too, lived in the valley. Not long after she had arrived, she fell in love with a prosperous farmer. She and "the love of her life," as she called him, lived not far from Sutter's Fort.

Tommy sat across from her at the table. What a fine young man he'd become. He would always be on the quiet side, but at sixteen had proven his worth helping in the store and on pack trips with Luke. Often young ladies who came in the store went out of their way to flirt with him. He didn't seem to mind.

Not all her memories were happy ones. She'd always remember her stepparents with a pang of sadness. Ma was never the same after Pa died. Her mind seemed to fade until she spent her days sitting in a rocking chair, staring into space. One night, only a year after they were rescued, she went to bed and never woke up. "It's for the best," everyone had said.

Sometimes in the middle of the night, when she couldn't sleep, she stared into the darkness, her mind drifting back to her unforgettable journey. Ma and Pa...Andy...Coy...cocky Len, dying from his own carelessness. She remembered the faithful oxen—Rosie and Jack, Zephyr and Thor—and that awful day she had to shoot those poor, trusting animals. Until the day she died, the memory would haunt her, but, like Luke had once told her, if she wasted her time grieving, she'd be a softhearted fool. She should give thanks she still had a life and enjoy it as best she could.

Luke sat beside her. Underneath the table, she slipped her hand into his. The warm glance he sent back showed how much he, too, was enjoying the evening. Never since they'd been married had he given any sign he missed his lonely life in the mountains.

Luke must have guessed what she was thinking. He leaned to give her a quick kiss on her cheek. "Love you."

The quick smile she returned said it all. To think there'd been a time when she thought she'd always be a servant. No longer, thanks to Luke and those months she spent on the wagon train that totally changed her life. Now she couldn't be happier, with a husband she adored, a comfortable home, two bright, healthy children and a warm, loving family, all of them close by.

And nobody ever, ever ordered her around.

Meet the Author

Shirley Kennedy was born and raised in Fresno, California. She lived in Canada for many years where she skied at Banff nearly every winter weekend and rode the trails of the Rocky Mountains on her horse, Heathcliff. She's a graduate of the University of Calgary, Alberta, Canada with a B.S. in Computer Science.

She worked several years as a computer programmer/analyst, but because her true passion was always writing, she finally decided to devote herself to becoming a published author and quit her day job—something they say never to do! But she never looked back and since that rash decision has published novels with Ballantine, Signet, and several smaller presses. She writes in several different genres including Regency romance, western romance, and contemporary fiction. She is currently working on another western romance.

Shirley lives in Las Vegas, Nevada, with her older daughter and two feline editorial assistants, Brutus and Sparky. She's an active member of the Romance Writers of America, Las Vegas chapter.

Acknowledgements

My thanks go to Jackie Rowland Murray, president of the Oatman Historical Society, for her help in the research of all things western. Also, my special thanks go to the late Andy Kohut, artist and gun expert, who told me what I needed to know about how to load and fire a rifle in 1851.